THE MAPLE
AND THE BLUE

Jox McNabb Thrillers
Book Three

Patrick Larsimont

SAPERE
BOOKS

THE MAPLE
AND THE BLUE

Published by Sapere Books.

24 Trafalgar Road, Ilkley, LS29 8HH

saperebooks.com

ISBN: 978-0-85495-047-8

For The Few of my generation that left us too soon
- Susan Johnstone (née Neale), my beloved sister-in-law
and for Hamish Newlands, Willie Robertson, Johnny Bullough and
Julius Denny.
All brothers of my youth.
Also, to Teddy the Border Terrier, my companion of seventeen years.
Per Ardua Ad Astra.

PROLOGUE

London, 1990

Winter and spring seemed to be wrestling for control of the day at Roehampton Vale Crematorium in suburban South London. A brisk wind blew through the budding trees and shook the pale snowdrops bursting through the muddy green lawns. The heavens above were clear and blue, though, a fitting fighter pilot's sky for the funeral of Squadron Leader David 'Pritch' Pritchard.

The conveyer belt nature of funerals at crematoria are always rather distasteful, but here it was an unfortunate function of the facility's location, servicing a good proportion of South London. The previous ceremony had over-run, since saying goodbye to the matriarch of a large Cockney family had proven hard for her many children and innumerable grandchildren. Lettered floral tributes to 'MUM' and 'NAN' fluttered on the display lawn, swamping the rather more muted wreaths that were there for Pritchard.

His affair was a discreet, sombre occasion, made colourful by the uniforms, banners and flags of those present. Representatives of the Royal British Legion, the Chelsea Pensioners and the Queen's Royal Air Force Colour Squadron all added to the pomp of the ceremony. Present too were officials from the Ministry of Defence, the French and Belgian embassies, as well as both the incoming and outgoing commanding officers of No. 111 Squadron, currently based at RAF Leuchars in Fife, Scotland.

Melanie McNabb — the granddaughter of Jox McNabb, David Pritchard's deceased best friend — was listed as Pritchard's sole family. Jox and Pritchard had served together in No. 111 Squadron during the second world war, forging a lifelong bond. Earlier that morning, Melanie had collected Nancy Wake, Pritchard's particular friend, from the impressive Royal Star & Garter Home on Richmond Hill, the stateliest of care homes for the nation's heroes in their twilight years.

Like Pritchard, Nancy was a decorated war veteran, in her case from her time as a Special Operations Executive agent during the second world war. Codenamed the 'White Mouse' by the Germans, she had been considered the deadliest SOE agent in the whole of occupied France. Melanie sometimes found it hard to equate this little old lady to the scourge of the Gestapo and the saviour of countless downed airmen. Only Nancy's steely look and her iron grip on Melanie's arm gave any indication of the inner strength and resolve within her tiny, frail frame.

Walking together towards the chapel, they were followed by a ragged gaggle of Royal Star & Garter residents, those deemed sprightly enough to cope with the next few hours in the cold. Included amongst them were several veterans in state-of-the-art wheelchairs, whose quiet whirring was suddenly drowned out by the pulsing throb of helicopter rotors overhead.

Melanie and Nancy looked at each other quizzically. They'd been told there would be a flypast tribute, but no one had said anything about helicopters.

A large helicopter appeared through the denuded branches of the surrounding beech trees, then hovered as the pilot tried to find a suitable landing spot. It was only because Melanie was a bit of an aircraft geek that she recognised the chopper model. It was an interest her 'Grandpa Bang-Bang' had encouraged, indirectly leading to her job as a military historian and curator with the Imperial War Museum. Of course, being the granddaughter of Group Captain Jeremy A. E. McNabb GC, DSO, MC, DFC & Bar, in other words the legendary fighter ace Jox McNabb, had also helped.

This was a Sikorsky VH-60N White Hawk, a variant of the UH-60 Black Hawk, the workhorse of the US military. The livery was unusual, with the top part of the aircraft including the twin turbines on either side of the rotor stem painted white and emblazoned with the Stars and Stripes. The lower two thirds were a sort of non-military green, with a horizontal white strip and UNITED STATES OF AMERICA in large letters on the rear of the fuselage.

Buffeted by the powerful downdraft as it landed, the Royal Star & Garter pensioners reacted either with exhilaration and the reminiscent thrill of their youth, or by being bodily bundled aside by the force. Frailer ones might well have fallen, if not for their carers holding onto them for dear life. Whether Melanie was holding Nancy, or vice versa was unclear, but there was no doubting the venom in the White Mouse's voice when she exclaimed, 'Who the devil is that?'

The White Hawk touched down surprisingly gently on shock-absorbing tyres. Its turbines slowed and the rotor cadence dropped. A side door opened, and steps unfolded automatically.

Two white-capped US marines in dress blues took up positions on either side of the door. Melanie realised their hats must surely be strapped down, or else they'd be lost in the downdraft. Both were senior NCOs, immaculate in dark blue, with a white belt and a red stripe down their trouser legs.

They came stiffly to attention as a bulky, white-haired man disembarked. He wore a dark civilian suit paired oddly with what looked like cowboy boots, but he gave a crisp military salute and by the way he carried himself, it was evident he'd been a soldier for a long time. What was most striking about him was a black cloth patch over his left eye. The pale, piercing blue partner to the hidden eye surveyed the grounds with unexpected intensity.

Following him off the chopper were several more suited men and a woman carrying a briefcase. They all wore dark sunglasses and tell-tale curly wires in their ears, characteristic of the US Secret Service.

Melanie knew that this wasn't the president or vice president of the United States, but it was certainly someone important. The man was surrounded by his phalanx of bodyguards as he crossed the crematorium lawn, waving at the stunned pensioners like any good politician would. He smiled widely and nodded a florid-faced head towards Nancy and Melanie, before entering the chapel. His security detail took positions in the rearmost pews, keeping all others away by looking rather intimidating in dark glasses worn indoors.

Pritchard's casket was carried from the hearse by three RAF Regiment Gunners at the front and two No. 111 Squadron wing commanders and a foreign military officer to the rear. The foreign uniform was unfamiliar to Melanie, consisting of a dark blue tunic jacket with golden buttons over grey trousers, a white shirt and black tie. His lapels bore gold badges on either side with decorations on the left breast, and a name badge and flag on the right. Before removing his headgear to carry the casket, he'd worn a large green beret, which contrasted markedly with the peaked caps of the airmen. It was a voluminous affair, like a Basque beret with a gold badge of a wild boar's head. He wore the three stars of a captain.

Sitting beside Melanie, Nancy noticed her eyeing up the foreign pall bearer, leant over and whispered, 'He's quite a dish, isn't he?'

Caught red-handed, Melanie blushed like a schoolgirl.

The ceremony was short, with Melanie feeling the lump in her throat as the bugler played 'The Last Post' and the flagbearers dipped their banners in mute homage to Pritchard. Standing beside her, Nancy was stoic and unmoved, despite her closeness to and obvious affection for Melanie's honorary uncle.

Afterwards, the pair stood in lieu of blood relations as the jets roared overhead, then went on to greet the line of well-wishers. Absent amongst them was the American politician, who sent over the woman in his entourage instead. She spoke to Melanie.

'Ma'am, Mr Darren Beans, the US Secretary of Defence has asked me to pass on his deepest condolences at the passing of a true hero and an esteemed comrade of old. He looks forward to meeting you at the reception being held on Richmond Hill.' The woman turned on her heel and hurried back to the helicopter, where turbines were already whining.

Bemused, Nancy and Melanie greeted the twin COs of RAF Leuchars, who were equally mystified but very impressed that the US Secretary of State would wish to attend the funeral of one of their Treble One predecessors. Both were fulsome in their praise of Squadron Leader Pritchard, and very keen to pass on the deep respect and affection with which he was remembered by the squadron, both past and present.

As they moved on, next in the queue was the unknown foreign officer. His pale, almost yellow eyes alighted on Nancy first, and he greeted her with an easy smile. He paid his respects in French, the accent sounding a little unusual to

Melanie. Catching sight of the red, yellow and black on his name badge, she assumed he must be Belgian. His name badge said 'DE GHELLINCK,' which seemed familiar to Melanie for some reason.

He shook Nancy's hand, then turned to Melanie, holding her gaze. '*Mes condoléances*, Mademoiselle McNabb. Your uncle was a very great man. My parents, *Chevalier* Olivier de Ghellinck and *Comtesse* Marguerite de Ghellinck have asked me to offer our family's sincerest sympathies. They both knew Monsieur Pritchard very well.'

The dashing young officer moved on. Melanie followed his retreating figure with her gaze, as Nancy giggled. 'That, my dear, is what in France they call *le coup de foudre*. Love at first sight. Consider yourself well and truly struck.'

'Don't be silly,' said Melanie, blushing. 'How do you know him? Why did he call you Andrée?'

'Slow down, my darling,' said Nancy, clearly enjoying herself despite the sombre nature of the day. 'In the resistance, my codename was Andrée. In the francophone world, I'm better known by that name. The escape line I helped set up began in Belgium, created by a lovely chap called Albert-Marie Guérisse, a Belgian officer and a bit of a hero to their military. That's probably how he knows me.' She looked over to where the officer was now chatting with the two wing commanders. 'He is a captain in the Chasseurs Ardennais, an elite unit of the Belgian Defence Force. That's why he's wearing that extraordinary beret with the boar's head. They were originally created as light infantry to fight in the forests of the Ardennes but are now something akin to the commandos or special forces.'

'Yes, but who is he?'

'I've absolutely no idea,' said Nancy. 'He knew me by reputation, but you by name. What did his name badge say?'

'De Ghellinck. Somehow it is familiar to me. He said his parents knew Uncle Pritch, which means he probably knew my grandpa as well.'

Nancy smiled mischievously. 'Well, hopefully he'll be at the reception and you can ask him then.'

'What makes you think he'll be coming?'

'Oh, he'll come,' said Nancy. 'Trust me on that one, darling. The *coup de foudre* works both ways. Gosh, how very exciting all this is! My Pritchy darling will no doubt be enjoying the shenanigans from up there. I certainly am. Come on now, let's get this dull affair wrapped up and get you dolled up for your next meeting with the *bel homme*, not to mention the bigshot Yank.'

But Melanie was distracted. 'I just remembered that my grandpa met his fiancée, Alice, at a funeral. Isn't that an odd coincidence?'

Nancy gave a knowing smile. 'Well, they do say that history repeats itself.'

CHAPTER ONE

Spring, 1942

The searing heat from the burning engine extinguished in an instant, when the tumbling colossus hit the cold waters of Algeciras Bay, within sight of Gibraltar's safe harbour. On a clear African dawn, the slab-sided Sunderland seaplane finally lost its fight with gravity. It was barely hanging together after the shredding canon fire from the Ju 88 night fighter that had attacked it from the darkness of the Mediterranean skies. Foaming white water surged through the jagged perforations in the passenger cabin, sluicing away blood that streaked the slats of the wooden floor.

Among the passengers was Flight Lieutenant Jox McNabb. He had boarded from the quayside of RAF Kalafrana in Malta, where he had been stationed with No. 249 Squadron for the last few months. Now, he was on his way to rejoin his old squadron, the Treble Ones, who had been having difficulties of late.

It was Jox who had first noticed the Ju 88 preparing to attack the seaplane, and he had given the crew enough warning to strike back before they had begun to plummet towards the water.

Jox watched briny spume pour into the cabin through fist-sized holes from the raider's cannon shells. Fabric and kapok from life belts had been frantically stuffed into the whistling holes but did little to stem the roaring flow. Jox had been braced for the impact but still had the wind knocked from him. Gasping for breath, the cold engulfing water was a shock as he tugged desperately at the toggle of his Mae West life jacket. It inflated in one quick action, the hiss of escaping gas merging with the sound of rushing seawater.

Swiftly submerged and reeling from shock, Jox kicked with his feet in what he hoped was the right direction. He couldn't hold his breath for long and had to get out of the flooded cabin.

As the aircraft dropped to the depths, it groaned and creaked. Instinctively, Jox reached for the porcelain doll's arm in his tunic pocket, his lucky talisman since the beginning of the war. Beside it he felt a handcrafted switchblade, a parting gift from his Maltese girlfriend Julianna's family. He pictured her face and realised her photos in his other pocket were surely ruined.

He pressed the button on the knife's hilt and felt it buck in his grip as his thrashing legs connected with something soft. Floating debris had started to clog up the water-filled cabin.

Jox began hacking a hole in the surprisingly flimsy escape panel beside one of the aircraft's portholes. His eyes were stinging from the saltwater as he stabbed the plywood with the desperation of a drowning man. The deep blue of the Mediterranean was calling to him through the jagged hole.

For a panicked moment his Mae West got stuck as he passed through, but then he popped out like the proverbial champagne cork. Rising through the water, he glimpsed someone else escaping through the same hole in the wreckage of the enormous seaplane.

Jox breached the surface with the mightiest of gasps, to the sight of the bluest of skies and brightest of sunrises. A white rescue launch was already making its way towards the bobbing heads, held up in the water thanks to the yellow collars of their inflated Mae Wests. The pneumatic grasp of the voluptuous starlet had never been more welcome. An exhausted Jox closed his eyes, luxuriating in her embrace and enjoying the warming rays of sunshine on his face. It was like the glow of life itself, snatched triumphantly from the clawing grip of death.

Jox opened his eyes to frantic splashing. It was Petty Officer Jack Tinker, one of the Short Sunderland's gunners, pale-faced and panicking.

'Calm down, Tinker!' roared Jox. 'You're all right man, calm down.'

The sailor reacted immediately to the voice of authority. 'Yes, sir,' he replied, hyperventilating like a blown horse after a race.

'You'll be all right, mate,' said Jox, more soothingly.

Straining to catch his breath, Tinker replied, 'Not that many made it out, sir. I've counted seven heads. Me and Phil the rear gunner, you and the big medic that was helping the wounded before we crashed, then Mark, Tom and Luke from the cockpit. The skipper's copped it. That makes you the most senior aboard, sir.' He gave Jox an embarrassed smile, the bullet-proof optimism of youth already shining through. 'Well, not exactly aboard, but you know what I mean. What are your orders, sir?'

The previous evening, when leaving RAF Kalafrana, they'd had a nine-man Fleet Air Arm crew and a dozen or so passengers. Barely a handful made it out.

'Orders? I'm certainly not senior to the major. Where the devil is he? He was right beside me,' replied Jox. He spun around in the water, but couldn't see the man anywhere. 'I think we ought to hold tight, Tinker,' he went on. 'Gather up the stragglers and see if anyone's hurt. Help me pull them together.' As the bow wave from the petty officer's thrashing lapped over him, he added angrily, 'And for God's sake, will you keep still! I've swallowed more than enough seawater. Look, there's a launch making its way out to us. Keep calm and carry on — we should be out of the drink in no time at all.'

True to his prediction, they were soon wrapped up in rough Navy blankets with a tot of fiery rum inside them to stave off the worst of the brisk sea breeze. Sitting there soaked on the varnished bench beside Jox was Tinker, rather calmer now but gaunt and blue-lipped. His reddish hair was plastered down over his forehead.

His teeth chattered. '"Take some time off," they said. "Head over to Gibraltar and take some leave. You've done more than enough, Tink. You've been in Malta for eighteen months and your nerves are shot." Now look at me.'

Jox clapped him on the shoulder. The Royal Navy NCO had certainly been through the mill and deserved a break from operations. Jox was also heading home, though, frankly, he'd have preferred to stay in Malta, despite the heat, appalling lack of food and the almost daily enemy attacks. Julianna was there, so that's where he wanted to be.

But Jox's former unit, No. 111 Squadron, was in bad shape and needed his help to get back on its feet. They'd lost their commanding officer, George 'Wee Brotch' Brotchie in a flying accident, involving several of the squadron's pilots. Jox had been told that many more had been lost in operations over the continent, and with senior pilots rotating onto new assignments, the unit was currently rudderless. Jox was being tasked with putting the fire back into the boys' bellies and getting the squadron firing on all cylinders again.

He had no idea how he would do that. *Hell*, he thought, *I'm only twenty-one, what do I know?* On top of that, he would have to contend with a new CO, who would doubtless have ideas of his own. It seemed unlikely that he would much appreciate

Jox's interference. Still, it was Badger Robertson, the squadron's stalwart adjutant, who wanted him back, and he had used his undoubted influence within the RAF to get him reassigned to his home squadron. So, needs must and whatever the outcome, the next few months were likely to be challenging.

CHAPTER TWO

A few days later, having arrived back in England, Jox McNabb marched up to the bored sentry at the gates of RAF Debden. He returned the snowdrop's smart salute.

The red and white striped barrier was lifted to let him through, and a RAF police corporal accompanied him to the guardhouse. He asked Jox to wait while he telephoned the officer of the watch to announce the flight lieutenant's arrival.

'He'd like to speak with you, sir,' said the corporal, passing the phone to Jox.

'Welcome back to RAF Debden, sir,' said the voice on the line. 'I believe you were stationed here during the first summer of the war. It's a great honour to have you back, sir. I'm really look forward to meeting you in the mess.'

Jox was unused to being addressed quite so formally and for that matter effusively. Things had certainly changed at Debden since the chaos of the Battle of Britain. Coming straight from the even greater shambles of Malta, everything here seemed rather stiff and excessively formal.

Jox peered through the grimy windows of the guardhouse at the view of winding taxiways that framed Debden's crossed runways. In the middle distance, there were a few shabby brick buildings, with a few taller, more impressive ones with sandstone columns, which served as official HQ buildings. Unusually for a fighting aerodrome, several large trees were growing alongside the roads, separated by mown lawns but also larger expanses of longer grass on either side of the runways. Beyond the perimeter fence, he spotted woodlands, grazing stock and fields of winter barley.

The corporal returned to his post at the South Gate, after giving Jox a second crisp regulation salute. He'd expected nothing less from a military policeman, always sticklers for the rules. He hadn't been back at his barrier for very long, when up it went again to let through an anthracite-coloured Hillman Minx staff car. It parked in a reserved spot where a little placard announced that the space was reserved for the CO of No. 111 Squadron. Intrigued, Jox peered out the glass of the sentry office at what he realised must be his new boss.

'Hello, here's the old man now,' said the WAAF typist from behind him. Jox watched a tall, slim man with film star good looks extricate long limbs from the cramped car. He had dark hair and such high cheekbones that he looked a little gaunt. He reached back into the vehicle, pulled out an old rag and began wiping squashed insects from his windscreen. He took his time, stopping every now and again to admire his progress. Once satisfied, he punched the rag into shape and promptly placed it upon his head. It was in fact his service cap, and a rather greasy, tatty-looking one at that. He wore it perched on the back of his head with a fringe of hair visible at the front, like some farmer or cowboy out of a western flick. The CO then looked about, shrugged and walked off with his hands in his pockets, whistling.

What an odd thing to do, thought Jox. The CO was clearly fastidious, but obviously didn't take himself too seriously — unlike his predecessor. Brotchie had always been a bit of a martinet. Jox wondered why the powers thought this new CO wasn't getting a good grip on the squadron. The next few months would certainly be interesting.

In the distance, in the long grass by the taxiways, Jox spotted several airmen playing with a small dog. From the chevrons on their arms and the wings on their chests, they were clearly sergeant pilots, but none of their faces were familiar. The dog, however, certainly was and quite unmistakable.

Wee Georgie had grown into a full-sized Border Terrier, but that meant he was only the size of a fox. Telling the leading aircraftwoman in the office that he was stepping out for a smoke, Jox walked up to the airmen. When he was about fifty yards away, he gave a low whistle. Wee Georgie reacted as if he'd been stung by a bee. He looked about frantically, sniffing the air. Jox whistled again and Georgie bounded towards him, surprising the gaggle of sergeants and launching himself into Jox's arms. Jox caught his dog after almost twelve months apart and felt a sharp catch in his throat. Georgie hadn't forgotten his daddy, but Jox wondered if he was missing his mummy too. The dog had been a present from his fiancée, Alice Milne, who had been killed in an air raid. Her death was the reason Jox had volunteered for his dangerous posting in Malta: he had been desperate to put the life they had planned together behind him.

A scrappy-looking, four-door Standard Flying Eight came screeching around the corner, skidding to a squeaking halt. Tumbling from the back were a gaggle of familiar faces, all beaming at him. The sight of David 'Pritch' Pritchard, Morgan 'Mogs' Chalmers and Badger Robertson made Jox's heart leap. Georgie was licking his face and wriggling in his arms as the men welcomed their old friend back to the fold with embraces, handshakes and resounding thumps on the back. It was a wonderful homecoming, and Jox felt happy to be back with the only real family he'd ever had.

Jox had already had a full briefing on the new CO from Badger, the Treble Ones' hoary old adjutant. They'd been corresponding ever since he'd been assigned back to the squadron and since his return from Malta. Badger was a superannuated squadron leader, in his words 'a relic from the last war,' but he was the one that kept the squadron's wheels turning.

Jox and the new CO, Peter Reginald Whalley Wickham came face to face for the first time the following morning, once the CO had been briefed by Badger. When the door to his office swung open, Wickham came bustling out with his hand outstretched.

'Welcome back to the Treble Ones, McNabb. I've been told so much about you. Please come in,' he said warmly. 'Badger, will you give us a moment? I'll come and fetch you once McNabb and I have had a bit of a chat. The three of us can then grab a pie and a pint down at The Plough in the village. I'll drive and it'll be my shout.'

Once settled behind his desk, Wickham eyed Jox. 'So, Jox, can I call you Jox? Have you been sent to check up on me?'

'Not as far as I'm aware,' he replied uncertainly. 'I've just been asked to support you in re-building the squadron after the difficult loss of Squadron Leader Brotchie. Wing Commander Thompson and Squadron Leader Robertson both felt that perhaps I might be useful to you.'

'So, the old guard don't want me to muck things up with their precious squadron?'

'I don't know about any "old guard", sir. I'm rather younger than you. I joined the service in '39, whilst I understand you entered Cranwell in '37.'

'Ah yes, but you're the squadron's favourite son, the decorated Battle of Britain hero. I'm just a clapped-out old Africa hand that no-one's ever heard of. You don't see any of those ribbons on my tunic, now, do you?'

'Well, none other than your squadron leader rings, and they're the only ones that count to me. Otherwise, I think ribbons are rather overrated,' replied Jox. 'In any case, I know you've seen more than your share of action.'

Wickham nodded and fell silent for a moment. 'How many kills do you have?' he asked. 'I've got nine destroyed and more damaged.'

Jox hated to see war reduced to a blunt contest. He carefully considered his reply before speaking. 'I'm not a fan of kill counts, as I don't find them terribly helpful, but let's say I've frightened more than my fair share of the enemy.'

'My questions stands,' said the CO testily.

'All right, then. Officially I've been credited with fifteen kills, but let's not forget I've just come from Malta, where there's no shortage of targets. One of the Canadian sergeants in my flight, a chap called George Beurling, made ace in four days, so it's all rather relative.'

Wickham continued to stare, then unexpectedly smiled. 'Good, we understand one another and won't get in each other's way. You see, my goal is to get rid of the word "Acting" in front of my Squadron Leader rank, and I assume yours is to have the opportunity to make that step up. I can completely understand that, and no doubt you deserve it as much as I do. Now look, I know that Pritch and Mogs are good pals of yours, and they've been doing a sterling job in trying conditions. I don't really want to bounce either of them out of their flight leader positions. As it is, I've already got two other flight lieutenants waiting in the wings, just needing to get a bit more combat experience, so I propose you rejoin the squadron as a supernumerary flight lieutenant with a roving role. Effectively, you'll be my second in command. Look, if Badger vouches for you, that's good enough for me.'

'That's good enough for me too, sir,' said Jox.

'Less of that "sir" business, Jox. Please call me Pete. Right, just a spot of admin before we'll get Badger to join us. He's out there pacing about like an expectant father, poor chap.'

'Oh, I wouldn't worry too much about Badger. He's tough as old boots and has seen more war than the two of us put together.'

'That's quite true,' replied Wickham. 'Now then, in spite of having served "out of sight and out of mind" in the Med, it appears I'm now to be awarded the DFC when Their Majesties visit Debden in July.'

'That's great news. Congratulations.'

'No, I'm not being terribly clear. You're to be decorated too,' said Wickham. 'I think it may be some sort of typing pool error, but the official letter here says you've been awarded the Military Cross for actions in Malta.'

'Ah yes, I'd quite forgotten about that. I'm afraid that's all part of the fanfare to celebrate Malta being awarded the George Cross. A number of awards were to be distributed across the three services and I got selected, perhaps something to do with already having the George Cross myself.'

'I see, but why the MC? Surely that's usually a pongo award.'

'Quite right, but the action involved bringing down enemy aircraft with a Bofors AA gun on the ground. I wasn't alone, of course, but it turns out we did rather well.'

'How many did you get?' asked the incredulous CO.

'I think it was two Italian bombers and a twin-engine fighter.'

'What! Are you telling me you've got three more kills on top of the fifteen you've already told me about?' exclaimed Wickham. 'Christ, I don't stand a chance. Badger! Get in here quick and save me from this golden boy. I'm convinced he's going to make me look bad. Come on, man, I need a drink. Nothing else is going to cheer me up.'

CHAPTER THREE

It was a rather long evening that started far too early, but at least it would soon be over and Jox could finally get to bed.

He still didn't know where that might be. He hoped his luggage had made its way to a room somewhere in the mess. Badger had assured him that everything was taken care of, but since he was asleep in a leather armchair in front of him, he wasn't much help.

Jox scanned the room with blurry eyes and was glad that he'd decided to pace himself through a mainly liquid lunch and the drinking session that had followed. The new CO had a fondness for alcohol but seemed to know his limit, and had left hours ago, leaving Jox and his old pals to reminisce. Only a few diehards remained, including Pritchard, whose hollow legs were legendary, and Chalmers, who was a gentle, jolly drunk.

Early on, Badger had explained that most of the squadron were available for the impromptu gathering since it had been released from readiness. Their aircraft were going through final inspections after being replaced with up-gunned Spitfire Mark Vs. Debden's other two squadrons, the wisecracking Americans of No. 17 'Eagle' Squadron and the solid, dependable No. 65 'East India' Squadron were on standby, and so the Treble Ones were officially at liberty.

The aircrew were looking forward to receiving their replacement aircraft, furnished with new bulbous blown cockpit hoods for more headroom and better all-round visibility. The new aircraft had clipped elliptical wings to allow for an increased roll rate, achievable at a lower airspeed and also at lower altitudes. Recently, when facing agile Focke-Wulf

190s with powerful engines, the squadron's ageing Spits hadn't been cutting the mustard. The new B-types were equipped with a 20mm Hispano cannon in each wing, installed within the innermost machine gun bays near the wheel wells. Here the wings bulged to accommodate 60-round drum magazines for the cannons, plus two outer pairs of .303 guns, just like in the previous variant. The additional stopping power of the cannons wasn't universally appreciated, with some pilots finding the recoil too brutal. Some also disliked the heavier handling and found the reduced stock of onboard ammunition challenging.

In contrast, Jox welcomed the extra fire power, recalling all too well the mauling his flight had received from the FW 190s of JG 26, over Cap Gris Nez. It had cost the life of the charismatic Aussie pilot Rupert 'Roo' Jones, and another Treble One, young Basil 'Bubbles' Broughton had ended up with a fist-sized hole in his shoulder. Jox himself had managed to twist the airframe of his plane so badly that it had ultimately led to his spectacular prang into The Thames and his subsequent long sojourn at Babbacombe Hospital in Devon. All that seemed so long ago, but it had only happened a year before.

Jox was pleased to catch up with so many familiar faces at the pub. Broughton was back from injury, now with four kills to his name, and was more mature and comfortable with his peers than when he'd first joined the squadron. Jox had chatted with Shane 'Kanga' Reeves, the sole surviving Aussie; Olivier de Ghellinck, or 'Ghillie', the aristocratic Belgian pilot; and Axel Fisken, the tough Norwegian aviator. Fisken wore spectacles — unusual for a pilot. Both of the latter had missing fingers, which made them an odd matching pair. Finally, Mike Longstaffe, the old 'China-hand', was quiet and considered, much like before, always a bit of a loner and still haunted by the Japanese atrocities he'd witnessed in the Far East.

There were several faces missing, but not all of them were deceased. Many of the more experienced men had been promoted into new roles, to add veteran backbone to depleted and newly created squadrons across the RAF. Pete Simpson, previously B flight leader, was now in command of his own squadron, with Miroslav Mansfeld, Otmar Kucera and Tom Wallace all flight leaders in other new squadrons.

There were unfamiliar faces too, both in the pub and the mess. Most noticeable were the foreign pilots in the corner, speaking in heavily accented English. From the patches on their shoulders, Jox identified them as Czech pilots. A thoughtful-looking flight lieutenant, a good deal older than Jox, came over to introduce himself as Frantisek Vancl. He led Green Section, manned entirely by Czech pilots. He introduced them as Flying Officer Jiri Hartman, Pilot Officer Otakar Hruby and Flight Sergeant Karel Zouhar. Vancl explained they were all experienced pilots and in Czechoslovakia, a landlocked country where 'the air is our ocean', aviators were highly regarded.

The men all got respectfully to their feet, each bowing his head when introduced. They'd all heard of Jox McNabb, as their Czech predecessors in the squadron, Miroslav Mansfeld and Otmar Kucera, had often spoken of him in glowing terms. These newest Treble Ones were keen to express their esteem and Jox was a bit embarrassed, soon finding refuge at the bar with the CO, the adjutant and his old pals Pritchard and Chalmers, who were now both flight leaders.

'You've got quite the fan club,' said Badger with a grin. 'Don't let it go to your head.' Chalmers and Pritchard happily joined in with the ribbing, but Pete Wickham looked thunderous and left soon afterwards.

Once he'd left, Pritchard leant over the bar. 'So, do tell us, Jox, what do you make of the new CO?'

Jox was suddenly conscious that all eyes were on him. 'Bit early to tell,' he replied. 'I've only just met the man. Seems all right, maybe a bit on edge. He struck me as rather a competitive fellow, and maybe a little insecure.' The others exchanged glances. Jox found this behaviour amongst old friends quite disconcerting.

'Anything else?' asked Badger casually.

'Well, maybe he's a little war-weary,' added Jox. 'He's seen a lot of action.'

Always the hothead, Chalmers couldn't contain himself. 'War-weary? Come off it, Jox. The man's completely potty! He's got us doing all kinds of crazy things. The other day, he insisted that we all wear pyjamas because we were going on dawn patrol. Last week, he had the men returning from a weekend leave line up so he could sniff them. In his words, he wanted to smell "the stink of their tarts' perfume." The chap who came back smelling the strongest got an extra day's leave as a reward. You think I'm joking, but I'm bloody not. Tell him, Badger — we've got ourselves a lunatic CO and he's going to get us all killed.'

Badger took his time refilling the bowl of his pipe. The wise adjutant finally spoke in a measured voice. 'Yes, Jox, it does appear we have a bit of a problem.'

The next morning, Jox was down for breakfast earlier than most. He found Pete Wickham sitting alone at one of the long wooden tables, looking remarkably fresh considering the skinful he'd had the previous evening.

Rather than the expected toast and scrambled eggs, he had a large white pudding bowl in front of him, with something green and unidentifiable in it.

'Mushy marrowfat peas. There's nothing quite like it for a hangover,' Pete said in response to Jox's dubious expression. 'My old father swore by them when on safari in the bush. They set him up for the day, he used to say. Mind you, they didn't help him spot that bull elephant, so perhaps they're not all they're cracked up to be.' He waved a silver spoon at Jox. 'By my reckoning, the carbohydrate absorbs the alcohol; the sugars provide depleted energy and there are plenty of other vitamins to sort out the rest. I usually like some fresh garden peas sprinkled on top, but it's the wrong time of year. Can't have everything. Come, sit with me.'

Jox took a chair opposite Wickham and ordered some tea, an egg and toast soldiers.

The CO let him order before speaking again. 'So, how did you enjoy yesterday? Feel like you've got your feet back under the table?'

'There are a bewildering number of new faces, but I'll get there. It'll take a short while to remember all the names.'

'Yes, but at least you know half of them. I've been away from Blighty for so long there are very few people I recognise.'

'I know what you mean,' replied Jox. 'I had that same problem when I got to Malta, joining the Gold Coasters of No, 249 Squadron for the first time. Soon enough, though, I found a few old pals scattered about the island, from one training course or another. The RAF's still quite a small family. You must have chaps from Cranwell dotted all about the service.'

'Yes, I suppose so,' replied Wickham. 'I do know Brian Kingcome, the wing commander over at Kenley. He was in the year above me at Cranwell but got pushed back when he had a prang in his car. Made rather a mess of his face, as I recall. When I got back from Greece, I joined his squadron for a bit, leading A flight of No. 72 Squadron. We got sucked into that fiasco of the Channel Dash. Come to think of it, Brian has invited me to a party in a couple of weeks. It's at the house of some society sisters he met during the Battle of Britain. They're known as the Belles of Biggin Hill, apparently — real beauties, I'm told. It promises to be quite a riotous soirée. Tell you what, why not come with me? I could certainly do with a wingman.'

'Sure, why not? Mind you, I could do with some recovery time after last night.'

'Ah yes,' he replied. 'Stick with me. I'll teach you how to lace up your drinking boots. In my book, it's a key social skill for a leader of men.' Wickham winked.

They finished their breakfast as the room began to fill with their bleary-eyed squadron mates. Chalmers looked particularly grim, whispering a hoarse good morning before finding a quiet corner to nurse a cup of strong coffee.

'Come on, Jox, let's leave these chaps to their breakfasts,' said the CO. 'Not terribly keen on talking shop in the mess, so why don't you walk to the squadron office with me? I can brief you on what's planned over the next few days. Badger will surely be in the office, so he can update us on aircraft readiness numbers after yesterday's inspections. We'll also get Ridgway, our squadron "spy", to update us on the general picture, what Ops have in mind and any planned targets. All set? Good show.'

Badger was indeed in the office, as was the squadron's intelligence officer, a tall, blond Mancunian, Flying Officer Tim Ridgway. He exuded quiet confidence and was obviously keen to impress the CO, who didn't appear all that interested in what he had to say. What Wickham really wanted to know was how many aircraft were available for forthcoming operations. He made quick introductions, and Ridgway reminded Jox that they'd spoken on the telephone when he'd arrived the previous day.

'Right, so if I've got things straight,' said the CO, 'we have today and tomorrow to get used to our new kites, then a Circus Operation is planned for Sunday, escorting bombers to Longuenesse Aerodrome at St Omer, deep in France, and then the next day we are due to hit St Omer-Wizernes airfield.'

'That's about the size of it, sir,' replied Ridgway. 'Circus 142 will fly east towards Boulogne, doglegging around the city to avoid flak, then head across the dune country and coastal grasslands of the Opale nature reserve to St Omer-Longuenesse. It should be fairly straightforward to recognise, due north of the racetrack at Hippodrome des Bruyères with its distinctive oval shape.'

'What can we expect at Longuenesse?' asked Wickham. 'What kind of trouble is lurking thereabouts?'

'It's quite a famous aerodrome. Some call it the spiritual home of the Royal Flying Corps,' gushed an excited Ridgway. 'During the last war it was a major British airfield, the largest on the Western Front, with operational squadrons, support units and the RFC HQ in the nearby chateau.'

The CO looked across to Badger, the RFC veteran. 'Ever been, Badger?'

'Yes, rather too often,' he replied. 'Usually, if I was in trouble or otherwise picking up replacement bodies or aircraft. We needed a lot of them at the rate we went through things.'

'I understand Squadron Leader Bader was shot down near there in '41,' added Ridgway. 'He's been a prisoner of the Germans ever since.'

'Thanks for the history lesson, Ridgway, but what I meant was what sort of trouble can we expect in terms of enemy forces?'

'Quite, sir. The airfield is one of the Luftwaffe's first-class airfields, with a concrete runway, several hangars and dispersal areas, blast shelters and flak positions. It's the operational HQ for the St. Omer group of fighter airfields. There's a large fuel dump buried on the northern boundary and ammo stores in the northwest corner. Their two main hangars are camouflaged, and the station HQ is in the chateau, with barracks dispersed in the woods outside the northern boundary. We believe there are five heavy and eighteen light flak positions encircling the airfield to the west, north and east, out to a radius of four kilometres.'

'How on earth do we have so much detail?' asked Jox.

'Well, sir, it *was* a British facility for a long time and the local French resistance are very good at keeping us updated on any changes and developments.'

'Gosh, I wonder if they're watching us as closely as we're watching them,' said Jox.

'Yes sir,' replied the IO. 'I rather suspect they are.'

'Well, that's a cheerful thought,' said Wickham. 'Can we expect much in the air?'

'Mainly Bf 109s and 110s from our old friends from JG 26. Fighters from I./JG 26 and fighter bombers from 10.(Jabo)/JG 26.'

'How about FW 190s?' asked Wickham.

'Yes, there may well be some of them too. If not from Longuenesse, from nearby.'

'So, you don't know everything,' said the CO.

'Well, they do try to keep their newest technology under wraps, sir. I think it's safe to assume that you may well run into some Shrikes.'

'Shrikes?'

'That's what the Germans call them: *Würger* — "butcher birds." Comes from their habit of catching insects and small vertebrates, then impaling them on thorns and even the spikes of barbed-wire fences, before eating them. I suppose that's what they intend for us.'

'Another cheery thought,' said Badger, sucking on the stem of his empty pipe.

'I've been up against the FW 190s before,' said Jox. 'We got quite a mauling. I really don't fancy a rematch.'

'Yes, but to be fair, you were a bit off colour back then, what with Alice and everything...' said Badger, his voice trailing off as he caught the pain in Jox's eyes. 'But you're in far better shape now.'

'Be that as it may, I'm expecting a tough few days,' said Wickham. 'Just the thing to get back in the saddle, but it won't be easy, even with superior numbers. How many aircraft are we expecting for the mission, Ridgway?'

'About thirty bombers — enough to force the enemy's defensive fighters to react. Our fighters will be in force too, with two whole wings: RAF Hornchurch, callsign LUMBA, and RAF Debden, callsign GARTER, plus a few extra odds and sods. In total there'll be about seven or eight squadrons, so all told in the region of seventy fighters. Should make for quite a ding-dong. I'm told Group Captain Harry Broadhurst will be joining the mission from the Hornchurch sector.'

The officers exchanged glances. 'Broady' Broadhurst was a former squadron leader of the Treble Ones and a legend in the service. He had famously opened the squadron's war tally by shooting down a Heinkel 111 as long ago as the 29th of November 1939. Now, having reached the lofty heights of the Senior Air Staff Officer of 11 Group, he commanded the Hornchurch sector. The fact that he was choosing to get involved indicated the importance that was being attached to the mission amongst the RAF's higher echelons.

Broadhurst was no 'paper warrior' and had at least ten kills to his credit. He could certainly hold his own and was known to have a fondness for his erstwhile squadron, keeping a critical eye on its performance and that of its senior officers. If Pete Wickham felt any pressure before, it had certainly been ratcheted up with Broadhurst now nosing about.

CHAPTER FOUR

Spring sunshine was heating the metal wings of the massed Spitfires from RAF Debden Wing parked along the airfield's long tarmacked runways. The night's condensation evaporated off in curling wisps of steam, making the aircraft look as if they were combusting. Jox hoped that wasn't a premonition of what the day might bring.

Twelve of No. 111 Squadron's newly refitted Supermarine Spitfire Mark Vbs were parked in two lines of six, facing away from the southernmost of the three hangars along the western edge of Debden's taxiway. Their noses were pointed towards the inverted T of the airfield's crossed runways, the principal one running east to west.

The aircraft were identified by their squadron prefix JU, written in large white letters on grey and green fuselages. The various iterations of Jox's previous mounts had all been named 'Marguerite', and whenever possible carried the letters JU-X. Today, however, as a newly returned usurper to the squadron, he'd been allocated JU-M, which was close enough to Jox McNabb.

Jox's lucky charm was the battered and cracked porcelain doll's arm that he had tucked inside the pocket of his woollen Irvin jacket, which he'd borrowed from Chalmers. The arm came from a doll that had once belonged to a little French refugee named Marguerite, whom he'd briefly met during Blitzkrieg, the Lightning War that had rolled over the Low Countries and France in May 1940. That was even before he'd done his part to become one of The Few, stopping the raiders over England's southern skies. In France, he'd lost sight of the little girl in the chaos of a Stuka attack and feared the worst. Afterwards, all he'd been able to find was the broken arm of her doll, and ever since, it had gone everywhere with him. He fought the war in her memory. There were others, of course, not least his lost fiancée, Alice, but it was little Marguerite who was the first. All of his aircraft had been named after her. He'd scrawled her name on the side of his latest Spit with a piece of chalk. That would have to do for now, but in due course he'd get it painted on properly.

After months in sweltering Malta, he was feeling the chill of the brisk spring air and was grateful for Chalmers' jacket. Perhaps he still had a touch of 'Malta Dog', the gastric complaint that had carpeted so many personnel serving on that blasted island. His thoughts strayed to Julianna, the young Maltese woman who had given him a second chance at love. He'd been forced to leave just as their romance had started to get serious, and in her, he'd found a new reason to fight for the future.

Jox completed his inspection of the aircraft, then had a quick chat with the duty rigger, fitter and plumber as they carried out final checks and strapped him into his parachute harness. This vital engineering crew ensured that the Spit was battle-ready, so it was always a good idea for a pilot to keep them onside and chat through the aircraft's foibles.

Recognising his dark hair, Jox was delighted to see they were led by Flight Sergeant Black, nicknamed 'Blackie', whom he'd known as a corporal during the first summer of the war. He was the senior man now, with stripes and a crown on the arms of his navy-coloured overalls. Black's hand was stained with oil, as one might expect for an air mechanic, but he shook Jox's hand enthusiastically. It was reassuring to hear Black's

Irish brogue, and Jox knew that he was in good, if somewhat greasy hands.

Before climbing aboard, Jox checked he had his Maltese switchblade in his pocket, along with his escape map printed on silk, some French currency in an oilskin-covered packet and a little hand compass. He climbed up into the cockpit, using the foothold in the side of the aircraft, a feature he certainly appreciated, not being the tallest of men. As ever, the cockpit was a snug fit, feeling familiar and comforting. The smell was a peculiar cocktail of high-grade aviation fuel, fine mineral oil and the lacquer that had been used to cover the aircraft fabric. The ground crew confirmed the engine was perfect, the guns had been checked and oiled, and the R/T had been tested.

Settling into his seat, Jox tucked a water-damaged snap of Julianna behind a dial rim on his dashboard, glancing at his scarred hands before pulling on his flight gloves. The scars hadn't been earnt in combat but were from the burns he'd suffered when he'd tried to save George Milne, Alice's brother, at Montrose when they were both still training in treacherous winds. Pulling him from his burning plane had been an instinctive action that had earned him the George Cross, but it had cost him a friend.

Jox shook his head to chase away the melancholy thoughts. He tightened the strap of his leather helmet, pressed the rudder pedals with his feet and turned to check the ailerons responded when he moved the stick. His eyes swept across the broad plain of the airfield to where the Spitfires of No. 65 (East India) Squadron and No. 71 (Eagle) Squadron were parked outside their respective domed hangars. They bore the letters YT and XR respectively.

At the briefing earlier that morning, Pete Wickham had introduced Jox to his opposite numbers, the squadron leaders that led the other Debden fighters. Squadron Leader Desmond McMullen was a burly proposition from Reigate with the striped DFC ribbon won over Dunkirk and two subsequent bars from sorties over Europe. Squadron Leader Chesley 'Pete' Peterson was a tall, blond American with a pale face. He was just twenty-one, the same age as Jox and had recently been given command of Eagle Squadron, making him the youngest squadron commander in the RAF. He certainly wasn't inexperienced, though, with forty-two missions under his belt plus the DFC awarded in October 1941. He was smoking a pipe similar to Badger's, rather incongruous with his youthful face, and he came across as a quietly spoken country boy.

The sleek fighters took off in pairs from Debden, taking a while for all three squadrons to get airborne. The early risers circled the lush green pastures, fields and woodlands beyond the airfield perimeter like a flock of wood pigeons gathering the courage to raid a farmer's crop. They ranged as far north as Saffron Walden as their numbers grew. The weather conditions were fine with some dispersed cloud, and visibility was clear and promising.

Once joined by a pair of Spitfires with 'Broady' and 'The Dook' painted on their fuselage, the formation was complete and began heading west a little after eleven o'clock. These late joiners were Group Captain Harry Broadhurst Senior Air Staff Officer of No. 11 Group and Wing Commander Myles Duke-Woolley, CO of the Debden Wing, known to the American 'Eagles' of No. 71 Squadron simply as 'The Dook', callsign GARTER Leader.

Peter Wickham led the Treble Ones in four staggered finger-four formations, Jox on his portside shoulder acting as his wingman. Once they'd climbed above some scattered cloud, the massed fighters rose into glorious sunshine and the wide blue sky. The formation rendezvoused with the Short Stirling Mk.1 bombers which they would be escorting to the target. Over the dark waters of the Channel, bright sunlight reflected from the domed canopy and sleek metal fuselage of Wickham's aircraft, JU-W. He waved a gauntleted hand at Jox then unclipped his oxygen mask to flash a smile and give the thumbs-up. They were on their way, and the excitement on the CO's face was clear to see.

In early 1941, the RAF had gone on the offensive once it was clear that bomber raids by the Luftwaffe were petering out. Fighter Command's new approach was to develop a schedule of regular 'Circus' sorties. These combined a small force of bombers with a powerful escort of several fighter squadrons. The intention was to lure enemy fighters up to take on the raiders and to then destroy a large proportion of the Luftwaffe's day fighter capability. The RAF fighter escorts' secondary role was to protect the bombers, who were there to act as bait to trigger interceptions.

The Treble Ones had the comfort of knowing their aircraft had recently been up-gunned. However, having seen the carnage the FW 190 could inflict, Jox was unsure whether they had what was needed to counter the threat.

In any event, the day's operation, Circus 142, proved to be an anti-climax. After the long slog over landscape that looked remarkably like Kent, the formation had reached Longuenesse Aerodrome without incident. On the ground, there were no aircraft visible, but the four-engine Short Stirling Mk.1 bombers had still delivered their payloads, resulting in some spectacular explosions. These were satisfying to behold, but probably of limited efficacity.

Embarking on the return leg over land and sea, Jox's neck was beginning to ache as he searched the open sky behind him, convinced they would be bounced at any moment. Others, equally nervous, milled about, cutting dangerously through each other's wakes. Ranged below the Treble Ones, the less experienced American squadron seemed particularly skittish, and Jox noticed several near-misses and erratic movements. He heard the reedy voice of their leader on the R/T. 'Say, fellas, keep it together,' said Peterson. 'You're making me look bad in front of the Limeys.' A few unidentified guffaws came over the airwaves.

'Don't worry, EAGLE leader,' said Wickham. 'We're as keen to get at them as you are. My boys are frustrated too. We'll have another crack tomorrow. WAGON leader out.'

'Roger that. Thanks, buddy, I appreciate it,' replied Peterson, then remembering procedure, he added, 'Roger that, WAGON leader. EAGLE leader out.'

'GARTER leader here, maintain R/T discipline please, gentlemen,' said the refined accent of Duke-Woolley, the Debden Wing's CO. 'We can chat once we've pancaked, but up here there may be ears on us. GARTER leader out.'

Jox considered the exchange. He wasn't the least bit sorry the mission was a virgin one for the assembled fighters. For him, any time you brought every one home had to be counted as a victory. Wickham didn't have anything to prove and neither did he. How strange, he thought, that the CO should be so intent on finding trouble. There was little doubt it would come looking for him.

At the Ops debrief, once they were all safely back at Debden, Broadhurst and Duke-Woolley reiterated that the mission had been a success. Aerial photographs confirmed that Longuenesse would be out of action for some time. They advised that tomorrow's mission would be a daytime raid with less bombers but an even heavier fighter escort, targeting the aerodrome at St Omer-Wizernes, not far from Longuenesse. It would be a larger affair than today, with Debden's thirty-six Spitfires taking off a little before eleven to meet with a half squadron of Hurricane IIB 'Hurribombers' from No. 174 Squadron, providing a fighter-bomber capability, with additional close escort from the Hornchurch Wing of Spitfire VBs of No. 122 (Bombay) Squadron and No. 313 (Czechoslovak) Squadron. Debden would be providing the high escort cover and Group Captain Harry Broadhurst would once again be in company.

In the meantime, Duke-Woolley and Broadhurst had secured several cases of beer. 'Enough,' said Broadhurst, 'to have a laugh and celebrate a good day's out, but not enough to give you a sore head tomorrow. We have work in the morning and pre-flight briefings are at eight o'clock — no excuses, gentlemen.'

Unfortunately, Group Captain Harry Broadhurst hadn't accounted for the determination of No. 71 Squadron's Americans to make a bigger deal of the modest get-together than he'd envisaged. Arriving at the designated 'party' hut — No. 111 Squadron's dispersal, as it happened — they came laden with all sorts of fare unseen for months by the war-weary English airmen more used to warm beer, beige food and wartime rationing. In spite of being part of the RAF, Eagle Squadron had close connections with the American Ambassador, John Winant, a big fan of the Prime Minister's. Winant never let his 'flyboys' want for anything and ensured that wealthy American industrialists kept them well-financed and supplied with hard-to-come-by luxury goods.

Consequently, the Yanks arrived laden with boxes of long white buns and tins of slippery sausages, which they combined to make something called 'hotdogs.' They also brought cases of pilsner beer with German-sounding names like Schlitz, Pabst and Budweiser. They came in olive-coloured tins, which the RAF airmen initially viewed with some suspicion, but Jox found he rather liked them. His switchblade was in much demand to punch holes into the cans.

Never ones to be outdone by the Americans, the Czech contingent amongst the Treble Ones and East India squadron brought their own interpretation of lager beer, which was even better. They also served fearsomely strong Czech Bozkov rum, which soon had the revellers singing at the tops of their voices. The Czechs in particular had something to celebrate, having learnt that several more squadrons wholly manned by their countrymen were being planned and they would soon be leaving to join them.

Jox was introduced to a trio of American flight lieutenants, all in RAF uniforms and wings, but with the Eagle patch on the left shoulder. Oscar Coen was from North Dakota and had been raised on a dairy farm in Wisconsin. He was squat, heavy-browed and immediately likeable. He'd already had quite a war, after joining the RCAF in 1940. On a mission over occupied France, he'd flown too close to an ammunition train he'd been strafing, and the resulting explosions had brought him down. With the help of the French Underground, he'd avoided capture then made a long 'home run' across Southern France and Spain to reach Gibraltar and a flight home. He was now Peterson's best friend and second in command of No. 71 (Eagle) Squadron.

Don Blakeslee was tall and well-built and had a bristly, blue-tinged chin. He was from Ohio and had joined No. 401 (RCAF) Squadron in May 1941. He was a good friend of Jox's Canuk pal, Maurice 'Moose' Grant.

Completing the trio was Darren Beans the Third from Louisiana, nicknamed 'Bayou', who was broad and fleshy with fair hair, a ruddy face and pale blue eyes. He was wearing tall leather boots with a stitched pattern and sloped heels. Beans caught Jox staring at his remarkable footwear and drawled, 'Hell, son, it's a party ain't it? I can't come to no party without having my drinking boots on.'

'What a load of bull,' said Coen. 'Your daddy's the state governor and you lettered at Louisiana State, so don't you play the country boy. Truth is you never wear anything else — just don't get caught by The Dook. He don't like us looking or behaving too much like "colonials", as he puts it. Now, don't you mind old Bayou, Jox. He's loud and obnoxious, but he don't mean no harm.'

'Why d'you call him Bayou?' asked Jox. 'Is he from the swamps?'

Coen and Blakeslee both grinned. 'You'll see,' said Coen.

Darren Beans was now stomping his feet on the hut's floorboards, clapping his hands and yelling, 'Woohoo! Born on the bayou! Born on the bayou!' to a tune that was discernible only to himself. His friends shook their heads in disbelief and looked a little embarrassed.

'Are those cowboy boots?' asked Jox.

'Yessir, I reckon they probably are,' replied Blakeslee. 'I'm not sure why a Baton Rouge swamp gator like Darren would favour them, but there you have it. Since you Limeys think we're all cowpokes, I'm guessing he's just living up to the image.'

It was Jox's turn to feel embarrassed. He had no idea where Wisconsin, Ohio or Louisiana were, so perhaps Blakeslee was right. What was undeniable, though, was that these fine fellows had come an awful long way to serve as their comrades in arms.

CHAPTER FIVE

There were more than a few sore heads the following morning, and several revellers were pale and in need of a restorative whiff of oxygen from their cockpits.

It was consequently a rather ragged procession that left from Debden, heading for the agreed rendezvous with the Hornchurch Wing and No. 174's Hurribombers. The total number of aircraft for today's Circus came to sixty-six. Setting a course for the forest of Clairmarais, they'd been well briefed on where to find the camouflaged fighter airfield. Aerial reconnaissance photographs had been circulated, indicating a concrete landing strip with painted taxiways turning off into the edge of a woodland, where parking stands for fighter aircraft were hidden under tall trees. This was a secondary dispersal airfield for I/JG 26, and it was believed Bf 109s were hidden under camouflaged domed concrete shelters, as well as some of the deadly Butcher Birds, FW 190s. Two maintenance hangars were highlighted on the grainy black and white prints, in addition to a trio of flak towers, some timber barrack huts, a firing range and a control tower draped with camouflage netting and foliage.

Jox was flying as the CO's wingman again, with de Ghellinck and Axel Fisken as Red three and four. Alongside the remaining three sections of No. 111 Squadron, they were scything through drifting cloud at Angels 17, providing top cover for the Hurricane fighter-bombers and the Hornchurch Wing. Five miles north of St Omer, dark flecks appeared in the sky. As the Treble Ones dove to investigate, they gradually materialised into the sinister cross shapes of eight Focke-Wulf

190s with an escort of six Bf 109s. A pair of 109s rose towards them, selecting the CO as their intended victim. It was Jox's job to defend his tail, so he manoeuvred behind Wickham's Spit and managed to get brief bursts on each plane as they dove past at a range of about three hundred yards. A sixty-degree deflection shot fired on the beam would later be confirmed by his gun camera, the tracer rounds lazily arching ahead of each before suddenly coming together in a rapid stitching burst. The first aircraft staggered then began falling at a steepening angle. There was a bright streak of flame beneath the cockpit, which then became a whitish plume of smoke. Identified by his fuselage lettering, JU-W, Wickham's aircraft cut abruptly across Jox's flight path, close enough to make him cry out into his damp oxygen mask. He jerked his controls to avoid a collision by the smallest of margins. *That idiot's going to get me killed*, thought Jox, struggling to regain control of his bouncing Spit as it reared through the CO's prop wash.

Unaware or uncaring, Wickham was blasting merrily at the first Bf 109 that Jox had already winged. There were some devastating canon strikes on the stricken bird as it fell away, dislodging some plating and spinning debris. Wickham turned his attention to the second enemy aircraft that was attempting to get out of range. Jox followed dutifully but noticed a plate-sized hole in the CO's portside wing. *He really shouldn't be pulling aerobatics with a wing that damaged*, thought Jox. *This man's proving to be a bloody menace.* Wickham finally dropped away as his intended victim made good his escape, forcing Jox to once again adjust his trajectory to avoid contact.

The hazy sky was now filled with pale stripes. So recently the scene of violent combat, it was now devoid of friends or foes, save for the pair of them. Far below, a single white parachute floated on the thermals, carrying a hapless airman onto the jagged boughs of the vast green forest. The colour of the silk identified him as an RAF pilot heading for a hard collision, but perhaps that was still a better outcome than the alternative.

Jox and Wickham were amongst the first back at Debden. The CO seemed to be in a hurry to get back, and Jox, the dutiful wingman, kept up with him. Perhaps Wickham's damaged wing was more serious than he'd initially treated it, but he gave no indication of that on the R/T. Considering the damage, Wickham made a good, if slightly wobbly landing under Jox's watchful eye. Once the CO had landed, Jox bumped down onto the concrete runway, his ears attuned to the familiar sounds of the landing routine: the throaty purr of the Merlin engine, the whirr of the undercarriage dropping then the clunk into position, the change in the pitch of the engine as it fought the greater wind resistance, and finally the squeak then rumble of the Spit's tyres on the concrete runway. He parked up in his allocated stand and sat as the aircraft cooled and ticked. He watched other aircraft come down after him, listening to the whistling of their gunports.

The day's 'butcher's bill' for Circus No. 142 proved to be a costly one for both belligerents. Altogether, the six RAF squadrons claimed nine fighters destroyed, one probable and eight damaged, with four pilots killed and one taken prisoner — likely the chap Jox had seen brolly hop onto the French forest. Three Hurricane fighter-bombers were also lost, with two killed and one returning safe, his aircraft a write-off. It was later confirmed that Debden had lost Sergeant Oswald Lindsay Clubb of No. 111 Squadron, Pilot Officer Frederick Speed and Pilot Officer Tom Gordon Grantham from No. 65 (East India) Squadron, and Flying Officer John Flynn from No. 71 (Eagle) Squadron. The Bf 109 that had been hit by both Jox and Wickham was claimed as damaged and was shared between them, since both sets of onboard cine film showed hits from either pilot. Jox had his own view on who had done the downing and who the mopping up.

Debden was a sombre place that evening. Trying to cheer things up, a group of Treble Ones visited the local pub, the Plough, a short stroll away from the airfield. Pritchard, Fisken, de Ghellinck and Mike Longstaffe were amongst them. Strolling down the sunken lane with his hands in his pockets, Longstaffe looked more morose than usual. Jox approached him. 'Cheer up, Mike. It might never happen.'

'Oh, hello there, Jox,' he replied in his vaguely West Country accent. He was originally from Reading in Berkshire, but Jox knew he was well travelled. 'That's the problem: it already has,' he added mysteriously.

'What do you mean?'

'Long story,' replied Longstaffe, peering at him with sad-looking blue eyes. 'You sure you want to hear this, especially after the day we've just had?'

'I'm not going anywhere, chum. Come on, get it off your chest,' said Jox.

Longstaffe took a deep breath. 'Well, you know I spent some years in China? I had a really marvellous time while it lasted. Life in the expat community of Shanghai was a riot, with parties all the time and anything you might possibly want at your fingertips.'

Jox couldn't imagine Longstaffe as much of a party animal. He'd always struck him as a sombre, sensible type.

'Everything changed when the Japanese soldiers arrived,' Longstaffe went on. 'I saw some terrible things. You wouldn't believe the horrors inflicted on the local population once the International Settlement was evacuated. We felt so utterly useless.' Longstaffe sighed. 'I had some investments that I didn't want to give up, but I soon realised it was just too dangerous to stay. There was a young woman involved too — Scottish, like you, Jox. She was a nurse called Carolyn; I knew her as Kari. I tried to convince her to leave with me, but she refused to abandon her patients. I left feeling desperately guilty, and I decided to make my way back to England to join up. I already had a private pilot's licence, so the RAF seemed a sensible choice.' He gave a sad smile. 'I can't tell you how relieved I was when I heard that she'd escaped China, and made her way to Taiwan and then on to Singapore. The squadron were training up in Scotland when I got a letter saying she was safe. The relief was immense.' He pushed a meaty hand through his hair. 'In her letter, she explained she'd had quite a tough time of it but was now settled in Singapore, working as a sister at the Alexandra Barracks Hospital, one of the largest and most advanced outside of Great Britain.'

'There you are,' said Jox. 'She's safe and sound, then.'

Longstaffe's hooded eyes narrowed, and Jox feared he'd put his foot in it. 'You've not been keeping up with the news from the Far East, have you?' he said pointedly. 'Singapore fell to the Japanese in the middle of February. The papers are saying it's the worst British surrender in history. Over eighty thousand British, Indian, Australian and local troops have become prisoners of war. There have been countless reports of massacres and atrocities, and don't forget, I know what the Japanese soldiers are capable of. I saw it in China and I'm desperately worried about Kari. I wasn't there to protect her.' He paused, carefully considering what he said next. 'I guess you of all people must know how I feel, losing Alice the way you did. I'm sorry, I never did get the chance to pass on my condolences. I was fond of Alice, such a lovely girl.'

Jox nodded grimly. 'Well, your Kari sounds like quite a tough lady, much like my Alice. Take comfort in knowing that she's not alone. If as many went into the bag as you say, there is strength in numbers, even as prisoners.' Jox sighed. 'In life, we need to hope for the best, Mike. Focus on where we can make an impact. You've got an important job to do, and you can't let events thousands of miles away distract you from your task. You're not doing yourself or Kari any favours by putting yourself at greater risk. It may sound like a platitude, but you've got to keep plugging on. I'm quite sure she's doing the same.'

Mike nodded. He didn't look entirely convinced, but at least they seemed to be agreeing when they reached the pub door. As they entered, it was clear that all the other resident squadrons at Debden had had the same idea. Jox recognised several faces in the dark recesses of the pub, including several of the Americans he'd met the previous evening. Oscar Coen waved a frothy pewter tankard in his direction.

Causing a commotion at the bar were several of Debden's Czech airmen, including Frantisek Vancl, leader of green section. Tim Ridgway, the squadron's 'spy' was with them, and they all appeared to be making a fuss of a handsome young Sergeant Pilot with vivid burn scars around his left eye and down the side of his cheek and neck. The red puckering of the skin had pulled his mouth into a lopsided half smile, and Jox could see where the young pilot's hairline, nose and mouth had been protected by his helmet and oxygen mask, and where they had not. Ridgway beckoned Jox over.

Jox turned to Longstaffe. 'Join us — they seem to be in a jolly mood. Might raise your spirits.'

'No, I'm all right, Jox,' he replied. 'You go. Thanks for the chat.'

Ridgway called over again. 'Hello there, Jox. Thanks for getting your after-flight report in so quickly. You're a lot more efficient than these boisterous fellows. Can I introduce you to my good friend, Ladislav Zadrobílek? He's just back from the sick bay.'

The sergeant clicked his heels and bowed his head. Jox shook his hand, noticing they both had similar scarring. The sergeant's scars were raw and looked angrier, and he winced at the handshake.

'Oh, I'm so sorry,' said Jox. 'I feel your pain, having been there myself, but I don't suppose that helps much.'

'Laddie, this is Jox McNabb,' said Ridgway. 'You will have heard of him; he's one of the squadron's old-timers. He's been away for a bit but is back with us now.'

'Nice to meet you, Laddie, and to have you back with the squadron,' said Jox. 'Wait a minute, are you the Laddie that had the accident when Squadron Leader Brotchie…'

The sergeant nodded and bit his lip as Ridgway looked embarrassed.

Jox realised he'd put his foot in it. 'No, that wasn't meant as a reproach. I just recognised the name from when Badger wrote to me about the accident. I was in Malta at the time.'

'Yes, Doc Ridgway and Adjutant Robertson were very kind to me when I was in hospital,' said Zadrobílek.

'Please let me buy you a drink and you can tell me what happened, if you don't mind talking about it, that is,' said Jox. Zadrobílek looked reluctant but agreed. Jox bought a round for the group and settled on a bar stool. An audience had gathered around them, as everyone wanted to hear the tale.

'It was a fine day, and we were practising formations, evolutions and rapid reaction scrambles,' said Zadrobílek. 'I was leader of the rear section, taking off last for a particular manoeuvre. Squadron Leader Brotchie normally led the first section, but this time he was in the one directly in front of me. The first section got airborne, followed by number two, and then I got my section moving. I was ready for take-off and waited for my fellows to form up on either side of me on the runway. I checked everyone was in position and looked for the thumbs-up from each one. My number two could see down the runway better than me; because of the Spit's long nose, I couldn't see what was directly in front of me. I assumed that since he was moving everything was clear, so I began to accelerate. As my tail rose and I could now see ahead, I was horrified to see the previous section had stopped at the end of the runway. All I could try to do was clear them by passing directly overhead, so I applied full power. Maybe it was stupid. The rest of my section saw the obstruction and turned off onto the grass on either side. I tried to lift my Spit off the ground, but there just wasn't enough space to clear what was ahead. I hit it with a terrible crash and was immediately surrounded by fire.' He dropped his head with emotion.

'The two fuelled-up Spitfires were entangled and burning. Mine was vertically above the other one. Thankfully, I had my seat straps properly fastened, or I would have been thrown clear of the cockpit and no doubt badly injured. I loosened the straps, slid back the canopy and jumped through the flames, rolling away to escape the inferno. My clothes were alight, but the ground crew quickly extinguished the flames. My face and neck didn't escape, and my hands were burnt too. Squadron Leader Brotchie was trapped and burned to death. It was a terrible sight. I still see him in awful slow motion.' Zadrobílek fell silent, overcome by the memory. He then shook himself and took a swig of his pint. 'After the crash, I was rushed to the sick bay for first aid. I was in pain, but I can remember

Flight Sergeant Karel Zouhar helping to carry my stretcher into the ambulance.' He looked over and Karel raised his glass. 'I went to hospital in Cambridge and was treated for my burns. They said my helmet saved my forehead, ears and hair, but it had burnt and shrunk onto my head so tight they had to cut it off. The mask protected my face — most of it. I know I am lucky; it could have been worse. After, they smeared me in yellow ointment, but I still didn't know how badly burned I was. I asked the Canadian chap next to me for a mirror. At first, he refused, but later he lent me one. It was very nasty to see the burns. After the crash, the swelling shut my eyes and I was worried I was blind. It was three days before I could see light again. It was a terrifying and very painful three days.' He rubbed the back of his hand across his eyes. 'They transferred me to a burns hospital, where they gave me many saltwater baths, then always more yellow ointment and fresh bandages. Saltwater helps with the healing, they said, but it stung like hell. I was feeling very sorry for myself but came to realise that many other burns cases were much worse than mine. I was being selfish and ungrateful.'

Jox thought of his time at Babbacombe Hospital in Torquay, where he'd been sent to recover from wounds, both physical and mental, during the London Blitz. He knew of the ravages of fire, blandly referred to as 'airmen's burns', a term that didn't begin to describe the horrors that he and undoubtedly Zadrobílek had seen.

'I was in hospital for six weeks, and the doctors say I am recovered now,' said Zadrobílek with a shrug. 'My grafts still itch and sting, but I am alive.' He looked at Jox, who raised a hand in apology for the firm handshake earlier. Zadrobílek smiled and shook his head. 'I am happy to be back with you boys, but my heart is heavy for Squadron Leader Brotchie. He was a good CO, always correct and kind to me and my Czech comrades. Please, raise your glasses to his memory. *Na zdravi.*' His audience all stood and raised their drinks.

Brotchie's favourite expression suddenly came to Jox. He stood, raised his pint mug and in a voice that carried across the noisy pub said, 'Bang-bang, you're dead. Head for the showers.'

His squadron mates burst out laughing. Among the newbies and old hands, whether they had known him or not, Brotchie had certainly not been forgotten.

CHAPTER SIX

About a week later, Jox was out walking Georgie along Debden's taxiways. The little dog had become rather confused, torn between Jox, who he clearly still remembered, and Pritchard, who'd become his surrogate father over the last year.

Jox was mulling over what to do about it, when a corporal he didn't recognise came running after him. He was being summoned to the squadron office. The note from Badger simply read, *Hurry and get to my office. I've got a surprise for you.* Jox handed Georgie's lead to the surprised corporal with instructions to get him back to the squadron dispersal, where he knew there would be no shortage of airmen to keep him entertained.

Jox knocked on the frosted glass of Badger's door. The squadron adjutant called out, 'Come in, it's open.' Jox entered and found a beaming Pritchard, arms crossed and barely containing himself. Badger was seated behind his desk, nonchalantly packing his pipe, the signature white stripe in his hair carefully combed. He was calm as usual, but with a twinkle in his eye that Jox hadn't seen since his return to the Treble Ones.

Sitting opposite Badger, with his back to the door, was a small, tired-looking man with a weathered face. Jox acknowledged him but didn't know who he was. The man glared at him, and Jox wondered if he'd done something wrong. There was something familiar about the man's pale-eyed stare. It triggered something deep within Jox, an odd combination of trepidation, growing recognition and an overriding wave of affection. How was this possible? It just couldn't be — Cam Glasgow couldn't be back in Blighty. That was when the penny dropped and Jox realised this gaunt version of his friend and mentor wasn't Cam. It could only be his older twin, also his one-time mentor and friend, Anthony Glasgow.

'B-bloody hell, Ant,' stuttered Jox. 'How the hell…?'

Anthony struggled to get to his feet, his spare frame swamped in an outsize warrant officer's uniform. He had a walking cane in each hand and was balancing on what were evidently very sore feet shod in strictly non-regulation tartan slippers. 'That's Mister Glasgow to you, laddie!' he roared, before falling into Jox's embrace. After several thumps on each other's backs, they stepped apart but still held on, each with shining eyes. There was no doubting the emotion behind this reunion.

'By God, you're sight for sore eyes,' said Jox. 'Cam's going to be over the moon when he hears you're back safe and sound. You haven't changed a bit.'

'You're a lousy liar, laddie,' said the elder of the indominable Glasgow twins. 'I've lost over two stone for a start, and there wasn't exactly that much lard in there in the first place.' His Dundonian accent was music to Jox's ears, for he knew how much he owed to Anthony Glasgow. If anyone had kept him alive during the first desperate months of the war, it was this man here before him.

'Anthony, for goodness' sake, sit back down before you fall over,' said Badger. 'You listen to me now, *Mister* Glasgow. I don't want any of that infamous Glasgow stubbornness. You've been through hell, and whilst we're delighted you've returned, we need you back on your feet.' He paused and grinned. 'I'm only half joking when I say Flight Lieutenant McNabb now outranks you. I'm putting him in charge of your rehabilitation, to get you back to being a useful member of this squadron after your ordeal. You two have a lot of catching up to do, but seriously, Jox, I want you to get Ant fit and healthy. Get him back in the cockpit, competent and up to speed in our new Spits. I'll let you work out how to deal with the grumpiness and complaints you'll undoubtably face.'

Anthony growled. 'I know how to fight, by God. I've seen more than enough of what the Nazis are capable of. There's been plenty to stoke the fire in my belly.'

'No one's doubting that, Ant, but don't forget that when you left us, we were flying twin-bladed Hurricane Mark 1s. You've not been in a cockpit for almost two years, and we're now in Spitfire Mark Vbs, totally different beasts. I've no doubt you'll manage the conversion, but it'll take some adjustment and Jox is well placed to bring you up to speed.'

Anthony smiled grimly. 'So, you're telling me this laddie's going to teach me the ropes? Aye, well, I can live with that, but mark my words: I've a fierce desire to get back at the Jerries for what they've done to me ever since Dunkirk. I'll not be taking any prisoners.'

Jox patted the shoulder of his one-time mentor. 'When have you ever, Ant? All I want is to have you by my side again. We both have plenty of scores to settle.'

'Aye, right then. Lead on, Macduff.'

Jox began to laugh. It was infectious, and soon they were all joining in.

'What the devil are you cackling about now?' asked Anthony, happy tears rolling down his half-starved face.

Struggling to get his words out, Jox spluttered, 'I've just realised, the next time you see your wee brother, you'll have to salute Pilot Officer Cameron Glasgow DFM and MM. He may even be a flying officer by now, the way things move in Malta.'

'What? Oh no, it was bad enough hearing that the daft wee fella followed you into trouble all the way to Malta! Now you're telling me he's become a Rupert, a bleeding officer. Christ on the Cross, things sure have changed around here. A man goes away for a wee while and the world turns upside down. My baby brother, an officer! Lord alive, whatever next?'

'So how long has it been, then? Feels like a lifetime ago,' said Anthony, peering at his former protégé. They were having a lunch of egg and chips in Debden's NAAFI cafeteria, with lashings of sugared tea in chipped enamel mugs.

'You're not wrong there,' said Jox wearily. 'We lost you over Dunkirk in May 1940. It's now May 1942 — so almost two years.'

'We've both got some tales to tell, I'll be betting. So, let's get all that out of the way and we can crack on with getting me flying again. I can't tell you how much the thought of that has driven me to get back home to Blighty. I've travelled halfway across bloody Europe — walking most of the way, too. That's why my feet are so knackered.'

'I've been meaning to ask,' said Jox. 'I can understand the slippers, but what's with the bright red socks?'

Anthony smiled and raised his trouser leg to display a red Argyle sock. 'I swore to myself that if I ever got home in one piece, I'd only ever wear the finest and brightest of socks. You see, when I bailed out of the Hurricane, I lost my flying boots and landed in *la belle France* in nothing but my regulation black socks. I spent the best part of my first week as a prisoner of war in just my socks. They didn't last long, so I was on my bare feet, hobbling my way through France and Belgium. I eventually managed to find some boots, but they were way too big for me. Some French fellow had died in the filthy coal barges they'd stuck us in to transport us to Germany. Poor fellow was killed when RAF fighter-bombers attacked as we made our way up the waterways. I wasn't exactly popular with the others, when it turned out it was our boys bombing us.' He laughed suddenly. 'Did you know the pongos call us RAF laddies "crabs"? Any idea why?'

Jox shook his head.

'Let me explain, then. It appears the colour of our slate-blue uniforms is exactly the same colour as the ointment that the pongos receive from their medics for pubic lice — in other words, crabs. Consequently, I spent the next several weeks of my life in those stinking barges known as McCrabs. They all thought it was hilarious. Good lads, mind you. One of them, a Corporal Stephen Pidgeon from Sussex, Royal Artillery fellow, gave me his puttees to wind around my feet so that the Frenchie's boots might fit.' He paused. 'You know, during my whole time as a prisoner and when I was on the run, my biggest challenge was that I couldn't find any shoes to fit. I promised myself I'd never again wear anything but the finest socks and most comfortable shoes I could find. That's why I'm wearing red socks — and bloody marvellous they are, too!'

'I'm sure we can find you some fleece-lined flight boots to get you flying.'

'Aye, that'll be great,' said Anthony. 'We can get back to that, but now you must tell me your tale. Pritch and Badger filled me in a bit, and I know you've had quite a rough war, laddie. I was sorry to hear about your young lady, although I never had the honour of meeting her. I was glad that my brother Cam stepped up and was here to help you during the difficult times when I wasn't about.'

'They all have,' said Jox. 'The Treble Ones are a family to me. It was heart-wrenching for me to leave them, but my head just wasn't right after Alice was killed. I just needed to go for a while.'

'Aye, well, I'm glad Cam stood by you and went to Malta too. By all accounts, he's done well, getting his commission and everything. Christ, he's going to love having me salute him, but you know, it'll be my honour to do so.'

'Well, let's get you back on your feet first,' said Jox. 'By the way, did you get a chance to visit your mum? I still wear the tartan scarf she sent me whenever I fly. It's a present from when I helped Cam out a bit — when you were missing and he went a bit wobbly.'

'I've not heard anything about that. What happened?' asked Anthony.

'Not much to say. You were reported missing, and he got the wind up him for a spell. Wheelie Ferriss and I popped over to see him, and we had a chat and soon had him sorted.'

Anthony took a deep breath. 'Mike Ferriss, now there was a sound fellow. I was very sorry to hear we'd lost him. Badger told me you took care of the funeral. Well done, lad, that must have been tough. Badger also took me through the names of the other men we've lost. It's unbelievable. There's almost no one left that I flew with in France. Just you and Pritch, as far as I can tell. You're the old hands now, but I can still remember the two young squirts arriving, very wet behind the ears. War has made you grow up fast, laddie.' He had a faraway look in his eyes, but then seemed to catch himself. 'Only old Badger never seems to change. God bless him.' He forced a smile. 'Never mind, mustn't get morose. So, tell me about your war, Jox. I see the ribbons on your tunic, but what's the story? Come on, spill the beans.'

Jox was embarrassed. It was like bragging about your exploits to someone who'd taught you everything you knew and had kept you alive. It was Anthony, for example, who had taught him that most fighter pilots were right-handed and therefore instinctively looked left when fired upon from behind, most often then pulling left to evade. If you anticipated this jink, you usually had him. Jox had used this insight to bring down several Italians over Malta, adding the refinement of first aiming for the fuel tanks at the base of the wings, then pausing to let fuel leak out, then setting it alight with a second burst of tracer and cannon fire.

'I don't know where to start.'

'Start from the beginning. Tell me about your lassie. Her name was Alice, wasn't it?'

'That's right. She was my pal George Milne's sister. He died during training with Pritch and I, and also Mogs, who's now joined the squadron. We went to his funeral and that's where I first met her, then again during the Battle of Britain when she was a plotter over at Kenley. We got close, and pretty soon we were engaged. I was really happy, Ant. I knew there was a war on, and we were losing people left and right, but I'd never been happier.'

Anthony reached across the table and patted him on the shoulder.

Jox grimaced. 'We spent Christmas together in London, which was both wonderful and terrible. We saw the best and very worst of the Blitz — glamour and valour put in sharp contrast to the utter devastation we witnessed. I was posted back to Montrose and Alice stayed on in London. She was caught in a raid, and she disappeared. I fell apart completely, started behaving like an idiot and inevitably was brought down. I spent some time recovering from my wounds but also getting my head straight again. I still wasn't fully right when I volunteered for Malta, but thank God Cam was there to watch my back. Then, completely unexpectedly, I met someone who got me thinking it was worth living again. Her name is Julianna and she's Maltese. She's there, waiting for me, and I'm determined to get back to her. In the meantime, I've been transferred back to the squadron, thanks to the scheming of Badger and Tommy Thompson, who wanted me back with the Treble Ones.'

'Good old Tommy — I'm glad to hear he's alive and kicking. Just about the finest squadron CO I ever served with. A bit of a bull but with a big heart. I hear the new chap isn't a patch on him.'

'I think it's too early to tell. He is a bit of an oddball and seems to be in a terrible hurry to prove himself or something. I'm not sure why. We should give him the benefit of the doubt. He does have a good rep and has certainly seen plenty of action.'

'Aye, I suppose so. So, what's old Tommy up to these days?'

'I think he's Wing Commander in Malta — quite a big shot now. He's certainly pulled a few strings for me over the last few years.'

'Not the least bit surprised,' said Anthony. 'He always had a soft spot for you. I can remember how impressed he was with your shotgun skills on the clay pigeons. That's stood you in good stead, I've no doubt.'

'All right, your turn now,' said Jox. 'Let me get you another mug of tea and you can tell me how you got home. You said you were in those barges getting bombed — then what happened? All that we heard was that you were a prisoner of war. The Red Cross Capture Card said you were wounded, nothing more. So, where did you get hit?'

'That's probably just my feet they were referring to. Once we got to Germany, I spent some time at a transit camp called

Dulag Luft near Frankfurt, then I was put on a long train journey in cattle cars to Stalag 17b in Austria near a town called Krems. What a dump that was. Prisoners from all over, not just air force and not just Brits. The way Jerry treated some of them was appalling. The Poles and Russians got it the worst, and there were Frenchman and Belgians in the camp too. Weren't all that many Brits to start with, but the camp kept getting bigger month by month. We spent most of our time chopping down timber from the nearby forest or using the lumber to build more barrack huts. After a while, the goons realised I was handy with electrical wiring, so they got me working with a squad of sparkies overseen by a Jerry pioneer. All the different nationalities were kept in separate compounds but mixed during labour details. Each compound had four barrack huts, about a hundred feet by about two hundred and fifty, housing two hundred men in primitive and bloody freezing conditions. I'm from Scotland, but I can tell you that Austria's bloody cold in deep winter.

Each of the wooden huts was on a concrete base with a washroom of six basins in the middle of the building. There were triple-decked bunk beds and a stove for heating and cooking. We got about fifty pounds of coal a week, which wasn't enough in the winter, so occasionally we were allowed to scavenge for felled wood in the forests. It was on one of those scavenging trips that I hid behind a pile of grubbed-up root balls, then managed to make my escape. I only had the clothes on my back, which thankfully included my Irvine jacket that got so badly charred that no Jerry thought to nick it, and those bloody great French boots that made it hard going in the snow. I still had my compass and escape map sewn into the lining of the jacket, so I was able to navigate broadly southwards towards Yugoslavia, where I reckoned I might have a chance of hooking up with partisans.

'Long story short, I joined one of Tito's Proletarian Brigades and worked my way west. I was finally able to catch a boat to Venice, then crossed the top of Italy into France. Let me tell you, there are an awful lot of bloody mountains all the way. By the time I got to the Auvergne region of France, I was utterly exhausted, and the best part of a year had passed. I got lucky then and fell in with some fellows from the Maquis. They fed me up and got me back on my feet. It was thanks to them that I was delivered to one of those escape lines that promised to get me home. I was travelling with a French-Canadian chap, which was handy for the lingo, and we were sent to a remarkable woman, an Australian lady called Nancy Wake. She took a bit of a shine to me and was very nice.

'By then, I was wearing Russian boots, but the leather was hard as planks and the soles were flapping. My feet were in a terrible state, infected and stinking, wrapped in strips of linen that the Russians use instead of socks. They were in a real mess, but Nancy patched me up and sent me on my way. Of course, that involved a lot more walking, but thankfully some of the way was in the back of a lorry and then hidden amongst livestock on a train. We eventually got to Gibraltar through Spain. From there I caught a merchant ship home to Blighty, then spent some time convalescing in Scotland at Strathcarron House Hospital in Forfarshire. After that I spent some time with my mam. Once I was more or less back in shape, I was told to report back to the Treble Ones, stationed at Debden, so here I am. Pretty battered and bruised, but still reporting for duty, Flight Lieutenant McNabb, sir!' Anthony said with a final flourish, then chuckled.

It certainly felt good to have him back. Very good indeed.

CHAPTER SEVEN

On a grey and overcast morning, Jox and Anthony entered the squadron's cavernous engineering hangar. They were searching for Flight Sergeant Black, the canny Dubliner who was now the squadron's maintenance chief. He would advise them which aircraft they'd been allocated for Anthony's first flight in a Spitfire Mark V. Black was an old friend of Anthony's and was making a big fuss about seeing him again.

'You're a grand sight to see, Mister Glasgow, so you are,' said the mischievous Irishman. 'I've got two fine birds all primed and ready for you lovely gentlemen. They're parked out front in the blast pens. I've taken the liberty of allocating JU-X for you, sir, and for my old pal Mr G, what could be better than JU-G? Especially with a fine mug like yours, eh, Ant?' The tough Scotsman and equally tough Dubliner grinned at each other like schoolboys.

Anthony followed Jox out of the hangar. He was still limping, but his feet were in soft, padded flight boots. Earlier, he'd told Jox that he was dosed up on some painkillers but was determined to get this first flight under his belt. The ground crew erks for each of the Spitfires were on standby as the pair circled their respective aircraft for pre-flight visual inspections. Jox followed Anthony as he assessed his Spit with the seasoned eye of a veteran aviator.

'You'll notice that she's a good deal lower to the ground than the Hurricane, and the forward view from the cockpit is restricted because of her long nose. You'll find the cockpit is tight, but the knobs and levers of the dashboard are much the same, just more finely tooled.' Jox gave Anthony a hand up into the Spit's footwell and onto a wing so he could peer in. 'The undercarriage system is automatically controlled once you've selected the wheel positions, so there's no more of that pumping business. This propellor is a new constant speed type too, but otherwise, everything is much like what you were used to in the Hurricane, but perhaps with a little more refinement.' Jox still had divided loyalties between the two aircraft, both of which had saved his life.

Once they were installed in their respective cockpits, Jox continued to coach Anthony over the R/T. 'The start-up procedure is much the same as the Hurricane. The engineering boys will get us going with a charge from the trolley accumulator. Watch your engine temperature, though. The Spit doesn't have quite as efficient a cooling system as the Hurricane, so there's always the risk of boiling over. You take the lead; I'll watch your take-off, then I'll follow you up.'

'Roger, wilco,' replied Anthony. He taxied JU-G to the far end of the airfield and turned into the breeze. There, he paused, completing his cockpit check and no doubt steeling himself for take-off in the unfamiliar bird. He confirmed to Debden control that he was all set and received the green signal, proceeding to take off smoothly and confidently, passing east to west across No. 71 Eagle Squadron's parked Spits on either side of their own hangar. Anthony's aircraft rose effortlessly through the morning gloom as weak sunlight sliced through the fine rain.

'Aye, a fine *dreich* bit of Scottish weather for my first flight in a good while,' said Anthony's voice, sounding tinny in Jox's headphones as he followed after JU-G in JU-X. Jox was pleased to have noted that his Spit now bore the name 'Marguerite', as well as the emblem of a muscled arm holding up a claymore sword.

Up ahead, Anthony waggled his wings. 'Follow me,' he said, then banked sharply. Rising up over the verdant mosaic of North Essex countryside, he was heading towards the North Sea. To the south was the broad, brown expanse of the Thames estuary, boiling darkly beneath the Mark V's clipped elliptical wings. Those turbid waters were the grave of far too many of their squadron comrades, and the sight of them made Jox shiver. The Spitfire cockpit was notoriously chilly and that hardly helped.

Anthony throttled up the Merlin engine as he climbed towards the distant sea. He cut through the low grey cloud cover and the brooding sea disappeared, replaced by glorious sunshine and the wide blue expanse of the heavens. It was a joyful sight, and he celebrated by rolling his aircraft onto her back. There, above and starboard of Jox, he was hanging from his straps, head down to the hidden waves. He turned his head towards his friend and gave him an enthusiastic thumbs-up. He then eased back his stick and pushed her vertically downwards in a sudden rush of increasing speed. Punching the column hard over, the responsive little aircraft spun through a hundred- and eighty-degree aileron turn then began climbing. Anthony opened up the throttle, and she was back up in the sunlit sky, having completed a long, wide loop. All the while he was singing to himself, full of the sheer pleasure of his liberty.

Jox smirked into his mask as he heard Anthony's song.

'*Och aye pick a doolie, give it to your Uncle Moolie. He'll pick it and flick it into the porridge po-ho-ot. The porridge will taste really groovy, all because that little doolie…*'

Shortly after his reunion with Anthony, Jox wrote to Cam to let him know what had transpired.

111, N. Essex
May 1st, 1942

My dear Cam,

I hope you're holding up all right. I'm sure the sun must be shining on the island, but here it's done nothing but rain! Good old Blighty, eh? I thought I'd drop you a quick line to update you on things. I expect you'll have heard through official channels, but your gnarly older brother has turned up like the proverbial bad penny. I can't tell you how delighted and dumbstruck I was to see him standing there in front of me. I'm afraid I'd rather written him off, and then there he was, glaring at me the way you Glasgow boys do. I'm afraid he isn't in great shape but seems to be on the mend now, and as you know, God help anyone that tries to get in his way. He's absolutely determined to get back into shape, so he can get back to thrashing Jerry. He tells me he saw a lot of terrible things in the camps and on his long trek through occupied Europe. By the sound of things, he's lived enough for a dozen lives. As ever, he's so driven, but to be honest he also seems a little haunted. I think it's been a very long and lonely time for him.

I'm not sure that returning to his beloved Treble One squadron has addressed that, as there are so few familiar faces still around from back then. There's only really Badger, Pritch and me, and of course, thank heavens for old Blackie. He's made Flight Sergeant now and keeps Ant busy, chatting, laughing and distracted. Ant spends long hours with him and his engineering erks in the sheds. I think he appreciates their uncomplicated company. What I've no doubt about is that he's also missing you. I don't really understand all that twin business, but I'm sure you know what I mean.

You may have heard I ran into a bit of bother on my way back to Gib. It was just my luck that the cushy flight home to Blighty should get jumped by a night fighter. We ended up in the drink and lost half the crew and passengers. I was fortunate to have the knife that Julianna gave me before I left — she told me her father made it. Without it, I'm pretty sure I wouldn't have made it out of the flooding cabin.

So, how are things at your end? Easing up a bit, I hope. Have you seen much of Julianna or her little brother? I've not had a letter from her yet, but I expect the civvy post isn't up to much. Will you look in on her for me? You're a good pal. I wonder if Cocky Cochrane is still visiting Elias, her brother, now and then? I expect Cocky must be over his bout of 'The Dog' by now. He certainly wasn't looking too clever when I left. How about Screwball? He's making quite a splash in the newspapers over here.

We're being kept busy, but it's nowhere near as frantic as it was during the Battle of Britain, nor does it compare to the wild times we had together over Malta. We usually head out on big wing operations every two or three days, trying to get Jerry to come up and fight. That's certainly not a problem we had on the island! Here, Jerry seems content to hold onto the territory they have, or maybe they're just concentrating on the Russians. From what the papers are saying, things are pretty grim over there and the Reds are desperate for us to get stuck in and relieve some of the pressure. We've heard noises of a big ops in the offing, but nothing concrete has materialised.

As for the new CO of the Trebles — you know, the one that people seem to think is a bit off — well, I really don't see what the fuss is about. Sure, he's a bit of an oddball, very ambitious and rather too aggressive with the enemy, but he seems to have the squadron's best interests at heart. He is very experienced and really knows his stuff. He rather likes his drink, but there's not many that don't, and quite frankly if that's the medicine he needs to keep in the game, that's all right with me.

Right, better sign off. Take care of yourself, old chum, and I'll keep an eye on that brother of yours. Yours aye, Jox

To his delight, Jox received a letter from Julianna shortly after he'd sent his message to Cam.

Hotel Point de Vue
Rabat, Malta
April 1942

My dearest darling Jox,

It seems such a long time since I had you in my arms. How are you, my darling? I'm at work and it's quiet, so I thought I'd write you a quick line.

I miss you so very much. Our island home just isn't the same without you. How can this be? I've lived here all my life, but now because of you, it no longer feels like home. Come back to me, my darling. I know you have important things to do, but please remember your Maltese sweetheart is waiting for you here. You have all my heart, so be gentle with it.

Elias misses you too. He sees your friend Cocky every now and then, and they go and play on the beach. He makes Elias laugh and I'm happy for that. My poor little brother has seen so much death and destruction — no child deserves such a childhood. Cocky is such a lovely man, and so very kind. Sometimes, he comes to see us with that Scottish friend of yours and the dark-haired one from New Zealand. Also, one time he brought that tall Canadian who I think you said was a little crazy. Was it 'Screwball?' The first two are always quiet, but this Screwball man never stops talking. He has become quite famous on the island as he has shot down many of the enemy. The Times of Malta are calling him the 'Falcon of Malta' and even the 'Knight of Malta.' Why is my Jox not called something like that? Don't worry, darling — I'm only joking.

How is life in England? I cannot imagine what it must be like. You said you would show me one day and take me to Scotland, your home. I'm afraid it will be very cold. I'm not used to that.

Life on the island is slowly improving. There are some more supplies in the market, but supplies go up and down. Thanks to you showing your friends the gift my father made for you, there have been many requests for similar knives. It has kept him busy making many blades, but this is good; the family can earn some money and we eat a little better. Elias is not so skinny now and is almost the height he should be for his age.

The island feels busier, with many ships in the harbour and aeroplanes in the sky. The raids are less frequent and there is even some reconstruction. The streets are full of soldiers from all over the world. The children love the Americans for their chewing gum, and the women love them because they have money. Don't worry, I only have eyes for my Jox, although some of them can be quite persistent at the officers' mess where I work. We sometimes hear dance music now, and the cinema has been rebuilt and is reopening soon, so maybe things are truly getting better.

I often go to our Hospitaller beach to feel close to you. I look out to sea and imagine you doing the same in England. I'm probably looking in completely the wrong direction, but never mind. Can you remember our time here? You might remember I told you it was a childhood beach for me, but the memories were ruined by the sight of those poor boys, buried at sea. But now it is once again full of good memories, thanks to our happy times together here.

I think I must finish now. I will leave you with the memory of our bodies entwined in the sea. I long for you, my darling, and I think of you every day. Just know that your Julianna is waiting for you. Please write to me. Probably best to address any letters to the officers' mess at the Belle Vue, where they have the best chance of making it to me.

With all my love and kisses,

Your Julianna.

With Anthony flying comfortably once more, he and Jox soon took off on a 'rhubarb' mission — a small-scale Circus effort that was usually carried out by a pair of fighters, most often in bad weather. This was to capitalise on cloud cover and the element of surprise.

Today, the low-cloud weather conditions were perfect to disguise their approach to the continental mainland, the driving rain discouraging all but the keenest of flak gunners. The hope was to catch some targets of opportunity on the ground, or perhaps even enemy aircraft who considered themselves safe under the protection of rain clouds.

Jox was happy to fly as number two of the pair, supporting Anthony as his wingman. He dutifully followed him on his portside shoulder, just a little up and back, as Anthony descended through the cloud cover to follow the main road leading out from Rouen. They tracked several wood-powered vehicles leaving very obvious smoky trails, until they located a Wehrmacht convoy of three camouflaged OPEL Blitz trucks making their way up a steep country road overhung by large trees. What followed was a rather satisfying game of cat and mouse with the three-ton lorries. Anthony finally caught the lead vehicle with a burst of cannon fire, with Jox finishing off a second vehicle. The third cleverly pulled up beneath the leafy canopy of a large elm, the driver and co-driver abandoning their vehicle in sheer panic, running across a recently sown field. Anthony made a slow sweep back over the stationary target and raked the vehicle and tree with fire, until the truck's reservoir caught light. A plume of thick black smoke rose through the air as he banked back around, going after one of the drivers still running down the hill. Jox watched as Anthony ruthlessly lined up his sights and fired, toppling the driver like a scarecrow caught in a fierce wind.

Now gaining altitude, the pair circled the burning pyres before heading for home. Anthony was short of ammunition, and they were nearing their bingo fuel point. Below them, Jox caught some movement. Camouflaged against the woody landscape was a hedgehopping Fieseler Fi 156 Storch, a light reconnaissance aircraft, probably sent out from a nearby airfield to identify the source of the smoke. They were sometimes used to ferry senior officers or other VIPs about, making them legitimate targets. Anthony manoeuvred his aircraft to one side, letting Jox take the lead on this attack.

It was a relatively straightforward interception for Jox to line up the shot. The Storch was nimble and could turn on a six-pence, but it was also slow and this one had no idea it was being stalked by a pair of vengeful Spitfires.

Jox rolled his trigger button to the 'FIRE' position, lined up the illuminated gunsight and primed his gun camera to record his hits. The Storch's pair of small wheels jutted out on long legs, giving it the ability to land in the long grass of improvised airfields. With a single rotary engine, it had a large cockpit that provided excellent visibility for the pilot and an observer / gunner who was seated behind him.

When Jox opened fire, the fourteen-metre-long wing running across the top of the cabin folded up dramatically. The shots burst through the glazed cabin, and the Storch began falling earthwards. The smashed cabin and engine block fell faster than the separated wings, which now zig-zagged as they went down. There was no sign of the crew, but Jox was fairly sure of their fate, given the ease of the shot. It was grim, murderous warfare, but it was a job that needed to be done.

Not for the first time, it struck him that he'd become a stone-cold killer, trained by the war to feel nothing. It was a revolting thought, one he had to shake off. He focused instead on getting home.

The cloud base was pretty much continuous all the way — good cover for their retreat. Occasionally, they lost sight of each other but just followed the same heading. As they approached North Essex, the conditions began to clear, and they made their way into Debden. The airfield was busy, with aircraft taxiing on the ground and several landing in different directions. The other squadrons of the wing had obviously been on missions too.

They called in their assigned callsigns, WAGON Black 1 and 2, and asked for permission to land. Once this had been given, they began lining up west to east when instructed to do so by the Ops Room. Anthony was up ahead and Jox to the rear, some fifty yards behind, with full flaps applied, producing sufficient drag to slow their descent onto the runway. From a distance they looked like wildfowl landing on a lake, feet outstretched below them. Anthony touched down with the briefest shriek of rubber, and Jox landed just behind. The view of the aircraft in front gradually disappearing as the rear wheel touched down and the whirling propellor and the Spit's long nose rose skywards.

There was a sudden grinding sound, followed by some frantic thrashing. From the corner of his eye, on the starboard side, Jox saw a dark shadow cutting diagonally across the runway. His aircraft juddered and skewed off the concrete, skidding onto the wet grass. His wheels dug into the mud and the Spit tipped onto its nose, the spinning prop hurling thick clods of earth in every direction until the engine seized up.

Tail in the air, Jox was completely disoriented, but he had the presence of mind to loosen his straps and scramble from the cockpit, escaping from the aircraft that could burst into flames at any moment. He landed heavily on the grass and rolled away. Once he was at a safe distance, he got unsteadily to his feet, mud-streaked from head to toe. Lifting up his goggles, he tried to identify what it was he'd collided with.

Up ahead on the grass, at a right angle to the runway, was another Spitfire with a mangled portside wing and the lettering XR-B on its fuselage. This was an Eagle Squadron bird that had cut directly across Jox, practically landing on top of him. It was a miracle that Jox was still in one piece, but rather than worry about that, he ran towards the other aircraft, as he could see the pilot was still trapped inside.

Anthony Glasgow was already beside the unknown Spit. He scrambled up onto the damaged wing and hauled the helpless Yank out of the cockpit. The air was now turning blue with ripe Caledonian expletives.

'You stupid bastard! You nearly killed my wingman! Can you not see where you're going, you daft septic?' He was shaking a bulky fellow, who was desperate to escape from this vision of unbounded fury. He whipped off his flight helmet to reveal a shock of strawberry blond hair, a ruddy face and pale eyes. Jox instantly recognised Darren 'Bayou' Beans of Louisiana, one of the Americans he'd met the other night. Still shocked at being manhandled by the furious Scotsman, Beans was flailing back at him with both of his arms. This further infuriated Anthony, who promptly struck him with a haymaker blow. The larger man lay sprawled on the grass, the tips of his cowboy boots pointing skywards.

'Now look what you made me do, you bloody bampot,' said Anthony as he reached down and struggled with the considerable weight of the unconscious American, dragging him to safety across the bumpy ground. There was fuel leaking from the ruptured tank at the base of the Spit's mangled wing. It suddenly caught fire and quickly started to spread. Anthony was now joined by Jox, and together they pulled away the limp body. An ambulance and clanging fire truck came to a skidding halt beside them. Whilst the unconscious American was driven away, Jox and Anthony sat on the wet grass, trying to catch their breath. Anthony caught Jox's eye and before long, they were both howling with laughter and relief.

CHAPTER EIGHT

'But for Gawd's sake, he's assaulted a superior officer!' said Squadron Leader Chesley Peterson in his nasal accent. 'We can't just brush that under the carpet.'

'Any officer who cuts across the runway as two of my most experienced pilots are attempting to land — with clearance from the ops room, I hasten to add — deserves anything that comes to him,' Pete Wickham said icily.

'I realise Beans is at fault too,' replied Peterson. 'But he had no choice but to bring his crate down as he'd run out of fuel.'

'In which case, in my book, he is doubly at fault,' replied Wickham. 'No experienced pilot would ever leave things until they'd run completely dry. Should I also assume his lack of fuel hampered his ability to transmit on the R/T? Is that why the ops room had absolutely no knowledge of his presence over the airfield? Frankly, all I see here is his gross incompetence.'

'Hey, hold on, buddy. Darren is a damn fine pilot, who's been fighting for your country since 1940,' replied the red-faced American squadron leader.

'Well, considering the carnage he's created this morning, he needn't have bothered.'

'Steady on, Pete,' interrupted Wing Commander Duke-Woolley, CO of the Debden Wing. 'There have been more than enough hotheads this morning. Let's try to de-escalate things, please. You two shake hands and let's figure out how we deal with this situation.' The wing commander turned to Jox, who was standing nervously in the corner of the office. 'McNabb, what's your view on what happened this morning?' All eyes turned to him.

'Well, sir, he came out of nowhere and with no word of warning.' Jox took a deep breath as he collected his thoughts. 'I think Warrant Officer Glasgow's actions were entirely out of concern for my welfare. We go back a long way, and in my view, he was righteously indignant at seeing his wingman so nearly taken out. We had just returned from a successful combat patrol, and perhaps adrenaline levels were still running high. I know it's no mitigating factor, but we should remember Glasgow has just returned from two years as a prisoner of war and fugitive from the Nazis. For something like this to happen when he's finally back home must just have set him off. None of us can really understand how he must be feeling, other than perhaps Flight Lieutenant Coen here, who I believe has had a similar experience of making a "home run" back to Blighty.'

Oscar Coen was also present in the room with his CO. He looked up at the mention of his name and the short, heavy-browed officer nodded. He glanced at Jox, then at Petersen. 'I'm sorry, sir. I've got to agree with Jox. After being on edge for so long, the relief of feeling safe again is something unbelievable. To then have someone you feel strongly about threatened — well, that would probably make me react in exactly the same way. Put it like this: if you and I had just landed and Jox here had cut us up like that, writing off his own Spitfire and trashing yours in the process, I have little doubt I would be hot under the collar, and I'm pretty sure I would have punched the culprit too. Now, listen: we all know Darren is highly spirited and a tad undisciplined, and frankly he can be a menace. I for one hope this bump on the nose is the wake-up call he needs. He could so easily have been burnt to a crisp because of his foolishness. God knows his Spit is a write-off. In my view he got off lightly, all things considered.'

'McNabb,' said Duke-Woolley, 'are you concerned about Glasgow's temperament? His ability to fly?'

'Absolutely not, sir,' said Jox. 'Considering he was piloting an unfamiliar aircraft for the first time since his return, I think his performance was spectacular. On our rhubarb mission, he took out three Jerry lorries from under thick cover. That's not someone who's lost his edge — that's someone with a killer instinct. Might I also add, sir, that Anthony Glasgow is the man who taught me the art of combat flying? Without him, I have no doubt I'd have been killed long ago.'

'Your devotion is commendable,' said the wing commander. 'That's the sort of commitment to each other we need to foster between our men. *All* of our men are allies. We'll need to be strong together to succeed in the liberation of Europe.' Duke-Woolley drummed his fingers on his desk. 'This is how we will proceed.' He lit a cigarette and stood up before addressing the room. 'First of all, let's patch up our belligerents. Then march the silly sods into my office. Flight Lieutenant Beans will apologise to Flight Lieutenant McNabb for damaging his aircraft and endangering his life.' He looked for any dissent from Petersen, the youthful American. 'Warrant Officer Glasgow will then apologise to Flight Lieutenant Beans for his overreaction. I then suggest both men spend some time with the station medical officer to ensure their heads and attitudes are as they should be.' He smiled. 'I'm afraid the cost of those two Spitfire Vbs is coming out of your budget, Chesley. I'm told we may be able to patch up Jox's, but it will need a new front end and probably a replacement engine. It was brand new, too. I suggest some significant docking of Beans's pay so that it stings a bit. His actions today have cost this wing more than the entire day's actions against the enemy. Not exactly something to write home about, is it, gentlemen?'

The following day, Anthony and Beans were marched into the wing commander's office. One was sporting a fine black eye and swollen nose, while the other was wearing bright red socks and leather slippers. Both looked like petulant schoolboys with sullen faces.

'Somewhat unorthodox attire to report to the wing commander, wouldn't you say, Mister Glasgow?' said Duke-Woolley with an arched eyebrow.

'Aye, sir. Sorry, sir — special dispensation from the medical officer,' replied Anthony. 'My feet are still not right, and yesterday's excitement didn't exactly help, sir.' The garrulous Scotsman was clearly completely unrepentant for his behaviour, eyeing the big bruised American with undisguised contempt. Two years in the clink and on the run had obviously done nothing to cool the infamous Glasgow temper. 'I will admit that I may have overreacted, gentlemen,' Anthony went on. 'But you must understand, yesterday this fellow endangered both my and my wingman's lives. I did see red, but what I was actually trying to do was get him out of the cockpit, as the whole lot was going up in flames. That's when he took a swing at me. I just reacted because I was angry and in pain. I know I'm hot-headed and I apologise unreservedly, but given the same circumstances, I would do it again.'

Both Wickham and Jox looked heavenwards. This was absolutely not what they'd coached him to say.

'I suppose that's as near to an apology as we're going to get,' said the wing commander. 'Chesley, is honour satisfied?'

Squadron Leader Petersen nodded, and Beans bristled beside him.

'Sir, I...'

'Shut up, Beans,' said his young squadron leader. 'Learn when to shut up and when to speak. You've done significant damage to some valuable aircraft and even more damage to the relationship with our allies. I want to hear nothing more from you other than an apology to Flight Lieutenant McNabb, is that clear?'

'Yes, sir,' said Beans, stiffening his posture. 'Flight Lieutenant McNabb, Mister Glasgow, please accept my apologies for putting y'all in danger with my foolish actions. I hope you can forgive my inattention and we can move forward to future collaboration between our great squadrons. This is a time for allies, not for rancour, and I deeply regret my part in creating this unfortunate situation.'

Duke-Woolley grinned. 'Now that, gentlemen, is how you make a grovelling apology. Beans, if you don't get yourself killed in the meantime, you'll go far in politics, my boy.'

Wickham entered the squadron office later that afternoon, nodding to those present, which included Jox, the Treble Ones' other flight lieutenants and the adjutant Robertson. They'd been discussing flight rosters for forthcoming operations over the next few days. A lot of personnel movement was scheduled, with the Czech pilots heading off to national squadrons and a fresh contingent of sergeant pilots arriving from operational training units, who would need bringing up to speed.

'Right, chaps,' said the CO. 'It appears the Yanks are throwing a bit of a party tonight, in the spirit of fostering an *entente cordiale* between allies. We've been invited to a "cook out", whatever that means. I expect a three-line whip for all pilots; attendance is absolutely mandatory. No excuses will be accepted, nor will any form of antisocial behaviour be tolerated.' Wickham looked at Jox. 'Do you think you can keep that mad Scotsman on a leash?'

'Are you referring to him, or to me?' asked Jox tersely. 'I'm just as capable of losing my rag with that septic if I come across him. He bloody well nearly killed me, that damned fool.'

'All right, I get it, Jox, but let bygones be bygones. Are we clear on that?'

'Yes, sir,' said Jox, still bristling at the reference to his friend and mentor.

'There's a good chap,' said Wickham. 'Might even be fun. They've always got plenty of grog and good grub, so let's make the most of it. Seriously, we need to make this work and I want you senior chaps to set the example. The noises from upstream are that some big op is in the pipeline and the Yanks will have a key role, and so will the Canadians. Since Pearl Harbour, it seems that everyone is itching to get at Jerry, especially the Canadian ground troops who have been kicking their heels for ages. We're all friends now, so let's make the most of it.'

That afternoon felt like the first truly fine day of the summer. It was Sunday lunchtime, and the Americans were cooking outdoors. Cold bottles of American beer were on offer from tin buckets filled with water and ice. No. 71 Eagle Squadron were obviously making an effort, and the airmen of No. 111 Squadron were determined to enjoy it.

There were several metal barrels spaced out on the grass, which had been cut lengthways and filled with hot coals. A steel mesh was placed over the ash and barbequed meat was sizzling alongside several bubbling pots. The largest held what looked like a red soup, behind which stood the bruised figure of Flight Lieutenant Darren Beans of Baton Rouge, Louisiana. He wore a white apron and paper chef's hat with 'Born on the Bayou' crudely lettered across the front, and he was bossing around the catering staff manning the grills.

'Hey there, boys,' he called over cheerfully. 'Y'all in for a treat, my Limey friends. These fellers have found me some real fine crab, shrimp, mussels, cod fish and haddock, so we got ourselves a real Louisiana Creole gumbo on the go. It's going to blow your socks off. By the colour of yours, Mister Glasgow, that might not be such a bad thing. Y'all forget all the grey food you seem to be so fond of and try this stuff. It fires the blood and is going to win us this war, you mark my words.'

They approached warily and Anthony Glasgow eyed his recent opponent, then the fragrant pot. He nodded, as if making up his mind. 'Aye, I'm game for a go. I've always liked a good fish soup. Cullen skink's a fine use of haddock and has always kept the chill from my bones.' Jox and Pritchard were in agreement, having both had the Scottish delicacy made from smoked haddock, milk, onion and potatoes when training up at Montrose. 'Not too spicy now, is it? I'm not very good with all that heat,' added Anthony, who was known to have a very narrow interpretation of what qualified as acceptable cuisine.

'Let me fix you up a special bowl of gumbo,' said an enthusiastic Beans with a dangerous twinkle in his eye. 'I promise y'all will never be the same afterwards.' He handed over steaming bowls of shiny black mussels, furry red crab legs and plump shrimp floating in a crimson broth. Pritchard sniffed it suspiciously and started to cough, but that didn't provide enough warning to dissuade Jox and Anthony, who began slurping it up hungrily.

After a few mouthfuls, the burning in Jox's mouth became so overwhelming that he had no option but to spout the contents onto the grass. His lips were on fire as he looked at Anthony, whose face had gone bright red. There were beads of sweat forming across his top lip, but he was determined to finish his bowl. Jox watched with growing apprehension, realising that one way or another, things were about to kick off.

With a calmness very much at odds with the puce colour of his face, Anthony exhaled slowly. 'Not too bad. Got quite a kick to it, mind,' he said, his voice sounding hoarse. 'Not a patch on the bouillabaisse I had when on the run in France. Maybe you're missing a wee bit more garlic.'

'Garlic?' said Jox. 'What, from the fellow that wouldn't accept that French fries where the same as chips?'

Anthony smiled, his eyes streaming. 'A lot of things have changed over the last two years, laddie. You'd be surprised what you're willing to eat if you're hungry enough. I cannot believe some of the things they call food in Europe. Mr Beans's fish stew is positively delicious compared to some of the tripe, innards, dried sausage and stinking goat meat that I've been served by the good people who went without to feed me. I'll always be grateful for that. This is no different, I suppose, eh, Mr Beans?'

Darren Beans burst out laughing. The others soon joined in. 'You know what? For a little Scotsman, you're a lot tougher than you look, and by golly you're damned tough as it is,' spluttered Beans. 'I reckon you're a good old boy, and here's my hand on it.'

Anthony reached over and took his hand. 'You're not so bad yourself, septic, but I can see I'm going to have to keep an eye on you.'

'I can't deny that, but do tell me something,' said Beans. 'What is this septic y'all keep calling us?'

They all grinned. 'Septic tank as in Yank. It's cockney rhythming slang, a speciality of Flight Lieutenant Pritchard over here,' said Jox. 'It starts to rub off on you after a while.'

'Hmm, I see,' said Beans. 'Septic — well, I guess a swamp rat like me can't complain about that. Come on, boys, let's have us another beer.'

Smoke and the delicious aroma of grilled meat rose through the balmy air of the Essex afternoon. Someone had turned up the volume on a scratchy gramophone, and American swing music competed with the conversation and laughter. Some of the WAAFs from the ops room and a detachment of ladies from the VADS volunteers had been invited along, so the men were minding their manners and trying not to drink too much. A few couples were even attempting to dance, but the grass made their jive moves heavy going.

As the Andrews Sisters sang of the 'Boogie Woogie Bugle Boy', Jox felt a wave of relief. What tomorrow would bring, he didn't know, but for now he was content with getting to know these peculiar allies. Many of the Yanks had served with the RAF since the early days of the war, but he sensed many more would be coming before this war was done. He grinned, catching sight of Pritchard and Beans dancing a lively jive together, both competing to be the life and soul of the party.

CHAPTER NINE

Wickham's grey Hillman Minx wheezed around the periphery of Trafalgar Square, weighed down with three burly RAF officers.

They were running late for a hush-hush meeting set for two o'clock at Combined Operations Headquarters, off Whitehall. Wickham was driving and had delegated navigation duties to the Treble Ones' intelligence officer, 'Doc' Ridgway, sitting in the front with him. Jox was squeezed in the back with his feet going numb for lack of leg room. The drive through London shouldn't have been complicated, but with all street signs removed to confuse enemy parachutists, combined with Ridgway's lack of navigation skills, they were hopelessly lost.

Combined Ops were based at 1a Richmond Terrace, just a stone's throw from Whitehall, in the heart of central London. Downing Street was almost opposite, and the War Office was up the road, across from the Admiralty. With all these landmarks, they shouldn't have been lost at all, and Jox was wondering whether he should intervene. He knew the area well, since Alice had worked in the Cabinet War Rooms on King Charles Street, opposite St James's Park. Thinking of Alice made him feel rather maudlin, prompting him to interrupt the pair squabbling in the front.

'Head straight down here, past the cenotaph, then turn right opposite Downing Street,' he said testily. 'We should be able to park there, but we'd better get a move on. At this rate we're going to be late. Careful, that copper doesn't look happy.'

Ridgway had only told them the briefing was for 'Operation Rutter.' Pete Wickham had asked Jox along as a second pair of ears in case he missed anything. They were representing Duke-Woolley, who was out of action after a trip to the dentist, as well as Debden's other resident squadrons.

Combined Operations Headquarters was an unusual organisation comprised of personnel from all three services, working together to plan and execute operations in enemy-held territory. The entrance to 1a Richmond Terrace was impressive, as might be expected for a substantial stone building on Victoria Embankment. It emerged that the meeting was being held in an underground basement, devoid of sunlight. Feeling rather claustrophobic, Jox scanned the room. There were several tough-looking army-types with the Combined Operations badge of a red albatross over a submachine gun and anchor, plus several aloof naval officers with bored expressions, often associated with the senior service, who believed they'd seen it all before.

Amongst the slate-blue RAF uniforms present, Jox spotted several faces he recognised, having either served with them or seen their pictures in the papers. He spotted Paddy Finucane, the lauded Irish fighter ace whom he'd trained with at Montrose. He was here representing RAF Hornchurch, and they nodded to each other across the room. Wickham waved at a serious-looking wing commander, who smiled back. 'That's Brian Kingcome, Wing Commander of Kenley,' said Wickham. 'He's the chap who's invited us to that party I told you about. This must be quite a big show if he's involved.'

Sitting next to Kingcome was the bulky form of Jox's old Canadian pal, Maurice 'Moose' Grant. Since training together at Montrose, he'd joined No. 1 RCAF Squadron, but they'd served together at Croydon during the Battle of Britain. They'd spent a memorable Christmas that year, in the company of Alice and three wild and beautiful Albanian princesses during the London Blitz. Both Jox and Moose now wore the red ribbon of the Albanian Order of the Eagle, awarded to them by King Zog the First, amongst the other more conventional awards on their chests. The friends had been through a lot together, and with the exception of Pritchard and the Glasgow twins, Jox had no closer pal. Moose had spotted him too and the big Canuck's face split into the widest of grins. Through hand signals and nods, they agreed to meet after the briefing.

The room was called to attention, and with a scraping of chairs everyone stood as the panel filed in. They were led by a tall and athletic naval officer with a long face and lively eyes. He was in the uniform of a vice admiral, and Jox recognised him from the society pages of the newspapers. This was Lord Louis Mountbatten, the king's cousin and the newly promoted Chief of Staff for COHQ. It made him the youngest vice admiral since Horatio Nelson, and apparently he was a natural orator. He smiled warmly at the assembled group. 'My, my, what dastardly deeds we shall cook up together, gentlemen. Welcome to Operation Rutter.' His eyes swept the gathered throng. 'Please take your seats. I'd like to make a few introductory remarks, then I will hand you over to the briefing officers who have the requirements for each of the services.' Mountbatten clasped his arms behind his back and began striding about. 'You will all be aware of the press clamour for a "Second Front Now" — not least from our dear Lord Beaverbrook's *Daily Express*. The plain truth is that our Soviet allies are currently facing the brunt of the enemy's might and are barely hanging on by their fingernails. They are demanding that we should engage more vigorously, to take some pressure off their forces, and frankly, I can't disagree.' He smiled disarmingly. 'As a nation, we have more or less recovered from the ravages of the Blitz, and whilst things continue to be challenging in Burma, the Far East, Malta and the North African desert, here on home shores some might accuse us of sitting on our hands.' He lit a cigarette, adding to the fug already in the basement. 'Since Pearl Harbour, our American allies have been desperately keen to get involved in the European field of operations. There's really only so much training, refitting and building up of forces that one can do before men start getting jaded. We need some action. Our Canadian land forces in particular have been kicking their heels since 1940. This is why they will have pride of place in this great Anglo-Canadian endeavour we are about to embark upon.'

He turned and indicated to an aide, who pulled down a large-scale map of Northern France on a roller behind him and said, 'There you are, my lord.'

Mountbatten smiled. 'No need for that; Dickie will do. We're amongst friends. Right then, our objective is to capture the seaside town of Dieppe, here in the Pays de Caux in Normandy. This will be a "seize, examine and withdraw" assault, a "reconnaissance in force", if you will. We're currently aiming for late June or early July 1942. Intelligence sources indicate that the town is not heavily defended, and the beaches are suitable for landing infantry and tanks. Our intention is to hold the town and destroy identified targets for the duration of two tides, then withdraw back to Blighty in time for toast and cocoa.' He grinned at his audience. 'Well, perhaps we might manage something a little stronger for our valiant heroes.'

The room roared.

'Dieppe has been chosen because it's barely seventy miles from Newhaven, so easily reachable by an amphibious attack force under cover of darkness. It's also well within range and therefore the protection of our esteemed colleagues of Fighter and Bomber Command.' He placed his hands on hips. 'Gentlemen, we have less than six weeks to get this off the ground. I thank you for your attention and hand you over to others who are much more qualified to discuss our plans.'

The next to speak was a heavy-set, moustachioed pongo with a hound dog face, who introduced himself as Major General John Roberts, commanding general of the 2nd Canadian Division. He explained that the size and scale of the planned operation was too large for the Combined Operations Army and Marine Commandos to handle alone. After their recent St Nazaire raid, successful as it was, Combined Ops had learnt the hard way that going in under-manned would mean losing half the raiding force as casualties or prisoners. This time, the commandos would be participating to take out key installations, but General Roberts would be leading the Canadian forces providing the bulk of the raiding party put ashore.

An all-volunteer force, the Canadians had spent almost three years training and as General Roberts explained, 'My boys are chomping at the bit. My 2nd Canadian Division will lead the way, and I've chosen six infantry battalions and one armoured for the task. The Royal Regiment of Canada, The Royal Hamilton Light Infantry, The Essex Scottish, The South Saskatchewan Regiment, The Queen's Own Cameron Highlanders of Canada and The Fusiliers of Mont-Royal will be going in, supported by the Churchills of the 14th Calgary tank battalion. These troops are the flower of Canada's youth, and I'm damned proud to be leading them.' The emotion in his eyes was clear. 'Our objectives will be divided into six beaches, four in front of the town itself and two on either flank. From east to west, they are codenamed Yellow, Blue, Red, White, Green and Orange. An airborne landing will secure our flanks, provided by the 1st Parachute Brigade, targeting the coastal batteries at Berneval-le-Grand, behind Yellow Beach and at Varengeville-sur-Mer to the rear of Orange. The different phases of the operation are still being worked out, but let there be no doubt of the scale, ambition and resolve that will be needed to achieve what is planned. This is a significant task before us, but working together I'm convinced we will make it work.'

A Royal Navy admiral then stood up to explain that getting the landing force to and from France would involve over six thousand Navy personnel and a multitude of vessels. They would also provide supporting gunfire to neutralise enemy installations before the landing. The RAF's role was to protect the entire operation from the attentions of the Luftwaffe, as well as interdicting and destroying the defensive capabilities on the ground. A vast fighter screen would be employed to ensure air superiority over Dieppe, representing the largest deployment of fighter aircraft since the Battle of Britain.

Next to speak was Air Vice Marshal Leigh-Mallory, Air Officer Commanding No. 11 Group of Fighter Command. During the Battle of Britain, he'd led No. 12 group, often making himself unpopular by following his 'big wing' doctrine — wasting time, according to some, by gathering his forces before coming to the aid of the beleaguered No. 11 group. Many of the veterans in the room undoubtedly still held that against him.

Leigh-Mallory explained that there were forty-eight squadrons at his disposal. They were tasked with providing air cover and escort duties for the bombers targeting identified strategic objectives, as well as continuous protection for the ships and landing craft during the raid and their eventual return to home ports that evening. His air forces would also protect the beachhead against any hostile threats developing from inland, be that reinforcements, especially armour, flak and artillery or any aerial response sent against them.

Leigh-Mallory was a blunt, no-frills sort of man. The losses, he explained, were expected to be high. RAF planners estimated that up to a hundred fighter aircraft would be lost on the day, unsettling odds for all the pilots in the room. This operation, he promised, would be a hammer blow to the enemy. The Luftwaffe would have no option but to react to an incursion of this magnitude. To the other services, Air Vice Marshal Leigh-Mallory expressed his full confidence that the RAF would not let their comrades in arms down. He wished them good luck during the logistical, planning and training days to come.

There was a brief tea-break during which Jox had hoped to catch up with Moose, but he wasn't given the time as Ridgway was keen that he and Wickham should meet the wing commander delivering the Intelligence briefing on the town of Dieppe itself. They found him in an anteroom, preparing for his presentation.

He was a short, frail-looking RAF officer standing with his back to the door. Jox knew instantly who this was, and the man's eyes lit up at the sight of Jox. It was his old friend, Sandy Bullough: his large head and prominent ears and teeth were unmistakable. He had gone through basic flight training with Jox but had unfortunately been bowler-hatted out the service rather early on. Through family connections, he'd retrained as an intelligence officer, by all accounts making the transition successfully, given the wing commander's rings on his uniform. Sandy had also been a great help to Alice and Jox when they'd got into a spot of bother over Jox's violent reaction to a senior officer with lecherous intentions towards his fiancée.

The trio had again met in the rarefied and somewhat debauched atmosphere of the Ritz during the height of the Blitz. Bullough had become a habitué of the louche demi-monde of the 'West End Front', an after-hours world of bars and clubs where life was lived with an intensity that didn't follow any of society's rules or conventions. Having become a spymaster for British Intelligence, he had promptly recruited Jox and Alice, setting them on the trail of some unlikely enemy agents.

'Jox, my darling boy,' said Bullough in his high-pitched South African accent. 'I'd heard you were back from foreign climes but had no idea that you'd be here. Are you joining the little party we're brewing up? I spotted that gorgeous great lummox Moose in the audience, but not you. How have you been, my dear fellow?'

'Sir, may I introduce Squadron Leader Wickham, CO of No. 111 Squadron, here representing the Debden Wing today,' Ridgway interrupted. 'You obviously know Jox, who is here as second in command.'

'Yes, of course, Timmy. Jox and I have had quite some adventures together. Sadly, there have also been countless trials and tragedies too, not to mention a few spicy revelations — isn't that right, Jox, my dear boy?' said Bullough with a salacious wink. 'I forget myself — very nice to meet you, Squadron Leader. Are you taking good care of these boys? Jox and I go way back, and young Ridgway here was my star pupil on the Intelligence course at RAF Station Highgate, Caen Wood Towers. He joined us straight from medical school. You've got a sharp one here in Doc Ridgway, let me tell you.'

'Very pleased to meet you, Wing Commander,' replied Wickham. 'I look forward to your lecture and finding out more about our target.'

Ridgway beamed with pride, while Bullough fixed Wickham with a steely gaze. He frowned, as if puzzling something out. 'You're from East Africa, I'd say,' Bullough said eventually. 'The accent has something of Kenya. Am I right?'

'Well, yes. I left when I was very young, so I'm surprised it's still in there.'

'Oh, it is,' replied Bullough. 'You'd be surprised at the legacy our forefathers leave, hey? Look, I must run. You chaps take your seats and we'll catch up afterwards.'

Bullough began his lecture by explaining that Dieppe was a coastal town in the Seine-Inférieure *département* of France. The town was built along a long cliff-face overlooking the English Channel, with the river Scie to the west and the river Arques flowing through the town and out to sea through a small harbour.

In recent months, portions of the town's seafront buildings had been dynamited to provide clear fields of fire and unencumbered views for artillery spotters. The cliffs dominated the town's beaches and were dotted with machine gun emplacements. Spies amongst Dutch and Belgian workers brought in to build the concrete fortifications along the coastline reported that the town and its sea approaches were covered by two large artillery batteries, codenamed Goebbels and Hess. They would need to be taken out as a priority.

'Let's make no bones about it,' said Bullough. 'Dieppe is a hard place to attack and an easy one to defend. Given the cliffs and limited access off the beach into town, we mustn't view this operation through rose-tinted lenses.' He frowned. 'I also have concerns regarding the pebbles on the beach. They're smooth, flat and about the size of a child's fist. Our vehicles, whether tracked or wheeled, may well struggle to find purchase on them. Dieppe's beaches slope steeply, and the tide is constantly shifting the pebbles, leaving unpredictable structures, ridges and obstacles that will need to be negotiated. They may well act as natural tank barriers leading up to the cliffs that loom over the beaches like castle walls. Our access inland is through narrow funnelling ravines that will undoubtedly hold wire entanglements and mines, and will be covered by gun emplacements and mortar pits. We should expect every inch of the town's beaches and promenade to be covered.' He used a pointer to indicate what he was referring to.

'Our intelligence on the ground indicates the town is half empty, possibly pre-warned about the forthcoming battle. I do worry that someone somewhere knows we're coming. I'm sure I'm not making myself popular by being so candid, but I want to provide my full view from a purely Intelligence perspective.' He grimaced. 'On a more optimistic note, the ground forces we are facing are from the 302nd Infantry Division from Pomerania. The French Resistance tell us they've been in situ since April 1941. Apparently, life has been rather too good for them, and they've grown flabby in *la belle* France. Combat effectiveness has been diluted by the demand for manpower from the Eastern Front, so many of the best troops have been transferred out. Replacements are mainly half-trained drafts, lured or pressed into service by the Reich. We can expect to run into Poles, Czechs, Belgians and even some Russians. It's unlikely they'll have much stomach for a fight.' He smiled encouragingly. 'That's the biggest weakness in Jerry's defence, or at least let's bloody hope so.'

It struck Jox that the pilots of No. 111 Squadron included several men from those same countries, and all of them had proven to be able and hardened fighters. He didn't think that their compatriots, albeit having chosen the opposing side, would be any different.

'Up in the air,' continued Bullough, 'we can expect to meet the Jagdgeschwader 26 Schlageter, covering the east of the river Seine, northern France and Belgium and then JG 2 Richthofen, covering the west including Normandy and Cherbourg. Many of you will have tussled with them before, their nearest base being only thirty miles northeast of Dieppe, about ten minutes of flying time. The plan will be to deliver a devastating bombing raid on the airfield before dawn, courtesy of our new friends of the United States 8th Army Air Force and their big beasts, the B-17s. Make no mistake: what is planned will be an air battle unlike any other since the massed enemy raids of two summers ago. Dieppe will be our most significant showdown with the Luftwaffe, and I expect continuous streams of aircraft to be fed into battle from both sides. These will not only be fighters: once Jerry realises the scale of the amphibious assault, they will no doubt include bomber forces equipped with Dorniers and Heinkel 111s against our ships, coming from Kampfgeschwader 2 in Holland. The narrow skies over Dieppe will be a continuous air battle for the duration of the operation, and airmen should expect multiple sorties starting before dawn. I have no doubt the enemy will throw everything they have at us, as they have also been waiting for an opportunity for an all-out slugging match. This, gentlemen, is the big one.'

CHAPTER TEN

The Red Lion had stood at 48 Parliament Street between 10 Downing Street and the Houses of Parliament since 1749. Under normal circumstances, the pub would be full of Members of Parliament, their staffers and civil servants of various obscure departments. Amongst these political warriors, uniforms were rare, but today the pub was awash with them. After the claustrophobic briefing at 1a Richmond Terrace, all manner of military personnel were now wetting their whistles. It was just a short walk to the pub, giving the servicemen an opportunity to re-oxygenate and concentrate on lightening the mood, despite the dire warnings about absolute secrecy.

Mingling with the crowd, Jox had the opportunity to catch up with several old friends and be introduced to some new. He'd quickly worked out that Pete Wickham was the sort of chap who came into a room with you, companiable and full of bonhomie, but was always on the lookout for someone more interesting or important to meet. Ridgway was off discussing something undoubtedly top secret with his mentor Sandy Bullough, so Jox feared he would have to make his own company. *Where the devil is Moose when I need him?* he wondered.

'Brian!' Wickham called out across the bar. 'Let me introduce you to Jox McNabb, my new second in command. Jox is the chap I'm bringing along to your party.'

'No need for introductions, Pete. I've heard a great deal about the famous Jox McNabb from Moose, my own enormous second in command. He's over at the bar,' said Brian Kingcome. 'If you're quick, McNabb, you can get some drink orders in with him. He's big enough to ensure that he gets served quickly, even amongst this thirsty mob. Tell him that I sent you over and that his Rams, 401 RCAF, are paying for the round. Oh, and be warned, Moose is likely to get rather overexcited at seeing you.'

Jox barely had time to shake Kingcome's hand before there was a bellow from the bar and his big Canuk friend came limping towards him. Moose had lost a couple of toes to a 20mm cannon shell fired by a FW 190 over the French casino town of Le Touquet. Jox took a deep breath, knowing full well what was coming.

'Jox McNabb!' roared Moose, sweeping him up in his arms and spinning him around the crowded space. A number of beers were spilt, but this raised no rancour as it was touching to see such a reunion between brothers in arms.

'Put me down, for heaven's sake, Moose. We're going to get into trouble. There's far too much top brass around here,' said Jox, grinning from ear to ear.

'So how are you bearing up, eh?' asked Moose. 'You didn't look too clever the last I saw you at Babbacombe. I was surprised when I heard you'd disappeared off to Malta. I'm glad to see you're back in one piece. I heard Cam Glasgow pulled a few strings to get out there to keep an eye on you.'

'Yeah, that's right,' replied Jox. 'He's a bit hacked off at the moment, since he's still stuck out there and I'm back home. Mind you, he'll be over the moon when he hears that his brother Ant has made it back from being a POW, after a hell of a long walk. I've somehow managed to replace one Glasgow twin watching over me with another.'

'I can think of worse wingmen,' chuckled Moose. 'What I'm really asking, though, is how you are. I was so sorry to hear about what happened to Alice. She was so lovely, and you two were perfect together. It broke my heart to see you destroyed like that.'

Jox could see the grief on his friend's face. He clapped him on the bulky shoulder and said, 'I'm all right, I really am. I won't pretend it hasn't been tough, but I'm out the other side now.' He broke into a grin. 'Actually, I've got a confession. I met someone in Malta, and it was like the sun coming out from behind the storm clouds. Her name is Julianna, and she's waiting for me on the island. Once we get this damned op out of the way, I need to figure out a way back. Maybe getting my own squadron might help.'

'That's fantastic news, Jox. I'm really delighted.' Moose stood up straighter and took a deep breath. 'Actually, it's going to make what I'm about to tell you much easier.'

'Come on, out with it, Moose.'

He looked sheepish. 'The thing is … you remember Alice's friend, Stephanie? They worked together at the Cabinet War Rooms. Tall girl, great fun with a lot of red hair.' He bit his lip. 'Her and Alice were good pals. Actually, they were supposed to meet at the cinema on the night that Alice was killed. Steph was delayed at work because she had to re-type something or other, so she was running late and arrived to find a scene of utter devastation. She's blamed herself ever since.'

Jox looked at him, pity in his eyes. 'That's just silly. If anything, she was lucky. If she'd been there, she'd have shared the same fate, along with all those Polish troops. I would *never* hold her responsible. She was only ever sweet to me, and I remember she was a great pal to Alice. She always made her laugh.'

'I can't tell you how relieved I am to hear you say that.'

'Why?'

'She's going to be my wife. I've proposed and she's said yes. I'm getting married, Jox.'

'Oh my God, that's fantastic! Congratulations.'

'I feel bad. We should really have been celebrating your wedding.'

'That's in the past now, Moose. Weddings are all in the past for me, at least for now.'

'What? Even with this Julianna?'

'It's too early for that, but we'll have to see. I just need to get back to her, and then we'll see where things take us.'

Moose stood at his full and considerable height, looming over the diminutive Jox. 'Listen, my friend: I want you to be my best man. Will you do that for me? It would mean a lot to me and Steph. I don't have much family over here, just my brother Willie, who's with the Royal Hamilton Light Infantry. I'm guessing he's involved with this new op, so he may not even make it, but I want you to be there, brother.'

'It would be my honour, Moose. When and where is it?'

'Wednesday the nineteenth of August at a church near Kenley called St. Luke's at Whyteleafe.'

'Isn't that where…'

'Yes, it's where the Kenley's airmen's chapel and plot are. Many of the chaps lost on the Kenley raid are laid to rest there. Steph wants to place her wedding bouquet on their graves. I know you and Alice were there during the raid, so maybe it's a way of having her involved too.'

'Of course, it seems somehow fitting. What a lovely idea. I'm honoured, thank you for asking me.'

Moose picked Jox up again and spun him around. It was his usual way of expressing joy, but this time there were rather more complaints as beer was spilt for the second time. Moose didn't care, as he was happily howling across the smoke-filled room.

'Dieppe? Why on earth Dieppe?' said Pritchard to Jox, Chalmers and Franti Vancl, the squadron's gathering of flight lieutenants. They were in the corner of the Treble One dispersal hut, discreetly discussing the recent briefing in London. Jox was on the sofa with Vancl, with wee Georgie the Border Terrier between them, torn between whose attention he most wanted.

'Where is this Dieppe?' asked the Czech airman, unsurprisingly unfamiliar with the French town.

'Actually, I know it quite well,' replied Pritchard. 'My family used to holiday there when I was a child. I've spent countless hours going back and forth on the ferry between Newhaven and Dieppe. It's really just an ordinary bucket and spade sort of resort, but with better food because it's in France.'

'Go on Pritch, paint us a picture,' said Jox.

'Ah right, let's see. It's about seventy miles from East Sussex and has a fairly similar landscape. The seafront is bound on one side by the port filled with fishing boats, and then there's the casino overlooking the water and the old chateau up behind it. A wide boulevard runs along the front and there's another parallel one on the town side for about a mile. In between there's the *esplanade*, and on Boulevard de Verdun are many hotels, boarding houses and some quite large villas. The beach is pebbled and slopes quite steeply. The stones are kept back by a sea wall that's above head-height, or they butt up against the tall, rather grubby chalk cliffs that are streaked with orange oxide from the agricultural fields above. If I'm honest, I can't even see where troops might land unseen since everything is overlooked.'

'What's the actual town like?' asked Chalmers.

'It's a quiet, not terribly exciting place, with a few people with a bit of money playing golf, gambling on the horses or up at the casino, then enjoying drinks on the terraces of the seafront cafés or dining rather well at one of the restaurants. There isn't anything even remotely strategic there, as far as I can see. Even the St Aubin airfield is just a pokey little grass strip. I can't imagine why it's been chosen as the target.'

'Because it's there is probably reason enough, but mostly because it's in range,' said Jox. 'For us and for the boats, so everyone can get there and back in a day. I think it's only a four-hour steam each way.'

'Yes, but surely if we know that, the Germans do too. They're not so stupid,' said Vancl darkly.

'That's what worries me,' said Jox. 'I fear we're going to get rather more than we bargained for.'

'Never mind that brooding,' said Pritchard. 'We need to plan for the next few weeks. As you know, many of the Czech chaps are being posted away, but this fine fellow Franti has elected to stay with us, and for that we are very grateful.'

Vancl grinned. 'I like this squadron and you are my friends, so I will stay, at least until forced to go by Czech authorities.'

'Where are your men being posted?' asked Jox.

'All over the place, but Jiri and Zou will go to No. 310 Czech Squadron, I think. They are not so happy because it is far away, in Cornwall. They think they will miss all the action.'

'For God's sake, let's talk about something more cheerful,' said Jox. 'Tell you what, I ran into Moose and Sandy Bullough when I was in London. The big fellow was in fine form and terribly excited about his forthcoming wedding. Old Sandy's gone stratospheric in rank and is a Wing Co now, compared to us lowly flight lieutenants. He's got quite the following and delivered an illuminating briefing on Dieppe and the surrounding area. He expressed some misgivings that I'm not sure made him terribly popular with the higher-ups. There were certainly plenty of brass in the room to get upset.'

'Well, at least they're listening,' said Chalmers. 'Sandy was never short of an opinion. Takes all kinds to win a war, I suppose'.

'Speaking of which, there's a fresh bunch of sergeant pilots due in,' said Pritchard. 'Badger was telling me that with the Czechs transferring out and this big op on the horizon, we need to staff up. By the time we're in shape, the Treble Ones will have nineteen or twenty pilots on the roster, not just the paltry dozen we scraped together during the Battle of Britain.'

'Yeah, and we were reporting for duty half-trained with very few hours on fighters,' said Jox. 'These new chaps are better prepared than their elders ever were.'

'Elders? Hardly, Jox,' said Pritchard. 'You're barely in your twenties and I'm just a couple of years older. The only really experienced fellows we have here are the ones like Franti, who's been flying forever.' He lit a cigarette and picked a fleck of tobacco off his lip. 'By the way, one of the new chaps says he knows you. You went to school together, apparently. He was wearing a cricket jumper.'

'Really? What's his name?'

'Now, what was it? Campbell, I think. Yes, Ralph Campbell.'

CHAPTER ELEVEN

Ralph Campbell! thought Jox. They hadn't seen each other since the inebriated youngster had spewed his frothy few pints of McEwan's 80 Shilling onto the school boarding housemistress's prized Paisley carpet.

It was a moment that had triggered a sequence of events that had led to Jox McNabb becoming the fighter pilot he now was. At the time, it hadn't felt terribly momentous; it had just felt like a ridiculous reason to get chucked out of school. Jox was surprisingly nervous at the prospect of seeing his school friend again. He felt no residual anger towards Ralph, whom he recalled was a fine sportsman and always up for a laugh, but he rather feared the change that Ralph might see in him. Was he now a cynical, scarred veteran, unrecognisable as the carefree lad he'd once been?

He needn't have worried. Ralph was effusive in his welcome and seemed desperately proud to introduce his school senior to the other sergeant pilots joining the squadron. When introduced to them, Jox barely retained that one was an Aussie called Harry Cooper and the other was named Nigel Steevenson.

Ralph was a little taller and stockier, and still as excitable as a puppy with two tails. He had slightly protruding eyes, a boyish fringe across his forehead and a gap between his front teeth. Watching him interact with his friends, Jox couldn't help thinking they looked like sixth formers, not at all like dashing fighter pilots. It dawned on him that he and Pritchard hadn't been so different when they'd joined the squadron.

Morose Mike Longstaffe preferred to ignore the trio, not wishing to risk getting too close to anyone who might be brutally snatched away in an instant. Others, like deadly Axel Fisken, considered them too flippant and lightweight to take seriously. Others acted haughtily, like the aristocratic de Ghellinck or the vastly experienced Franti Vancl, who dismissed them as mere boys. It was Pritchard and Chalmers who welcomed them the most warmly, despite being their flight commanders and seniors. Everyone knew these newcomers had to prove themselves in a fight before they would be fully accepted. It was up to them to survive long enough.

That afternoon, Ralph and his friends were given the opportunity to show what they were made of. Each was paired with a senior wingman: Ralph with Bubbles Broughton, Harry with fellow Aussie Kanga Reeves, and Nigel Steevenson with French-Canadian Flight Sergeant Ernest Mouland. Pete Wickham and Pritchard would lead this composite A Flight on a patrol over the Isle of Wight, where assorted ground forces earmarked for Operation Rutter were training under increasingly realistic conditions. Down on the ground, Lord Lovat and the various Commando battalions were playing the role of the Jerries, defending against the landings of predominantly Canadian troops, with the Royal Hamilton Light Infantry, Les Fusiliers de Mont-Royal, the Queen's Own Cameron Highlanders of Canada and the Calgary Regiment of Tanks.

Separately, Jox and Anthony, with Vancl and Fisken, were tasked with playing the role of interceptors, stalking the training patrol and taking the new chaps through their paces.

The half squadron of Treble Ones took off first, circuiting around the airfield before heading south in two ragged Vs. Jox could imagine Wickham chiding the new boys along, insisting they keep in a tight formation.

Once Jox was beside his aircraft, now fully christened *Marguerite* and with his J-UX lettering, he was helped into his parachute. The four straps were clicked into the circular buckle at his stomach, and he put his foot into the stirrup, then the other onto the wing, taking the short step along it to place his right foot into the cubby in the fuselage, and finally lowering himself into the cockpit. A nimble-fingered rigger passed the Sutton harness straps over his shoulders and clipped them in across his chest: one, two, three, four, then put the pin through and tightened the adjustment pieces. Jox pulled on his leather flying helmet and clipped the mask across his face, turning on the oxygen supply as he plugged in his microphone cable. He primed the engine, flicked the switches on, then gave a thumbs-up to the ground crew before reaching for the starter button.

Gathering momentum, the four 'hunters' lifted away from Debden together, their spinning wheels first thundering along the tarmac, then falling silent, save for the whistling of the undercarriages as they passed through the air until retracted. Taking a circuitous route down to the Channel, they flew counterclockwise around London's periphery and over Reading. They then headed for Southampton and the busy Solent. They were keen not to be seen by the flight of Treble Ones until they were intercepted over the island.

It was a fine day, with visibility for miles. It would therefore prove challenging to sneak up on the flight, so Jox opted to climb for altitude and the doubtful cover of some cloudy wisps of over the sea. He knew his 'opponents' were assigned to patrol the dramatic chalk cliffs of the Needles to the far west of the Isle of Wight and then fly over Compton beach, where a massed landing exercise was underway. He decided to lead the other three Spits clockwise around the island, but well out to sea, so as to approach the operational area from the sea like any raiders would.

The Spits skirted the heel of the island, and Jox spotted that the southern shoreline of Compton beach and the cliffs on the Needles headland were partially veiled by a rolling bank of smoke. Under it he could see the curving, frothing wakes of multiple warships manoeuvring, with a multitude of craft heading towards landing beaches. The Canucks were rehearsing their landings for the umpteenth time, and he could see tanks churning up the beach as they headed inland. It occurred to Jox that since he was observing the exercise, completely unchallenged, it was entirely possible that the enemy's high-altitude reconnaissance aircraft could do the same. It was well known that they kept a permanent surveillance on Britain's shoreline. He scanned the heavens nervously.

'Black Two to Black Leader,' said Anthony Glasgow's voice in his ear. They were on a different frequency than that usually used by the squadron's WAGON call sign. 'Eight WAGON bandits up ahead. Spits at two o'clock below at Angels ten. I'm fairly sure it's them.'

Jox's eyes searched the area ahead and beneath his right wing, tilting it slightly to remove the blind spot. He scanned quickly and methodically, examining the slice of horizon where his number two had reported seeing their 'targets.' It didn't take long to spot them — a formation of tiny gnats against the blue-grey water. They were approaching from an opposite course to theirs, about five thousand feet below, appearing and disappearing through the billowing smoke barrage created by specialist rocket ships and a flight of Hampden light bombers who had dropped smoke cannisters earlier.

'Black Leader here, I'm turning portside and formatting for the attack,' Jox said into the microphone. 'Close up and follow.' He wheeled about and dove towards the untidy formation of No. 111 Squadron Spitfires. The four 'intruders' gathered speed as they crept up on the unsuspecting aircraft, which were steadily holding their course. Jox could identify the inexperienced newcomers amongst them from the way their machines wobbled as they concentrated on keeping tight to their respective wingman's tails. Jox knew his veteran foursome were already selecting which of the newcomers would be their victims.

Jox picked one and wondered if it was Ralph. Whoever it was, he was about to get the shock of his life. The chosen Spitfire flew on unawares about fifteen hundred feet below him. Jox barrel-rolled, losing more height, then levelled out about a hundred and fifty yards behind and slightly on the starboard side. Coming in for a quarter beam attack, Jox waggled his wings, the agreed signal for the four hunters to shout loudly into their mics, having already switched over to the WAGON frequency.

'BANG-BANG-BANG, you're dead,' he said, parroted by the other three fellows, before erupting into raucous laughter. The flight reacted like sticklebacks jumped by a jack pike. All semblance of order was lost as they broke away in varying directions, desperate to escape. It was a miracle there were no collisions, but that was exactly the point that was being made: the need for constant vigilance.

'You new chaps drop out of formation. It's time for you to head for the showers,' Jox added for good measure. He heard a sharp expletive from Wickham, and it was equally clear to the other more experienced Treble One pilots they'd been well and truly 'bounced.'

'WAGON leader here,' said Wickham through gritted teeth. 'Well done, boys. You got us good. We clearly need to tighten things up, especially with the new chaps onboard. Pritch, take them home and give them a good bollocking for this cock-up. Black Flight, you come with me. Let's take a closer look at what the pongos are up to down on the beaches.'

The CO pulled his Spitfire sharply away from the rest of the formation and dropped landwards. The four Black 'intruders' followed him down. Several vessels sounded their horns in a confident greeting as the Spits flew past slowly and deliberately to ensure recognition.

Jox knew Moose's brother was down there somewhere, sweating it out with the infantry. Dropping lower, they identified several Churchill tanks churning up the gravel beach, then breaching verges of vegetation as they headed inland. Advancing, they fired two-pounder guns and machine guns, shredding the boughs of several trees. The Churchill was designed to support dismounted infantry by suppressing strong points and obstacles. Jox had read somewhere that it was rather heavy, weighing in at forty-five tons with multiple bogies supporting a long chassis. Its engine was reportedly underpowered for such a big beast, with the exposed caterpillar tracks susceptible to enemy fire. Living conditions inside the hull were very hot and so noisy that radio communication was often impossible.

Once back at Debden, Jox was summoned to the CO's office. He was greeted by Wickham with a face like thunder.

'I really don't appreciate you making me look like a bloody fool out there,' he said acidly. 'Especially in front of the new men. How do you expect me to lead them when I get shown up like that? Can you imagine the effect on their morale?'

Taken aback, Jox spluttered, 'I see it as my mission to develop their resilience and awareness of the threats they will encounter. In fact, those were your instructions to me. Their morale is of no concern to me; I am more invested in their ability to survive first contact.'

'And you think scaring the wits out of them is the way to achieve that?'

'They're new and inexperienced,' replied Jox. 'Yes, their survivability is always in question for the first several missions. You know that as well as I do. In fact, if anything, the benefit of this morning's exercise was to show the more experienced pilots, my "intruders" for example, how easily they can get at inexperienced opposition. They're the real killers in the squadron, and the ones who will have the greatest impact over Dieppe.'

'I'm sure Pritch doesn't appreciate being considered inexperienced, nor do I.'

'You know full well that's not what I mean, sir,' said Jox testily. 'Pritch will appreciate the wake-up call, as we all need to guard against complacency, particularly before going on a big shout like we will shortly.'

Wickham fixed him with a glare, then blinked a few times and nodded. 'You're right, of course, but I still don't appreciate being embarrassed like that, particularly by one of my own men. Listen, Jox, I need to know that I can count on you.'

Jox considered what he was about to say very carefully. 'You can count on me, Pete, but I'm not here to make you look good. I'm here to help pull this squadron together after it's been in a tight spot for a while. What I do is for the good of the squadron. You heard the level of casualties they're expecting for this op. I see it as my job to ensure that a minimum are Treble Ones. We've lost far too many on my watch as it is. I can't speak any plainer than that.'

Wickham nodded. He wasn't happy, but hopefully he knew where Jox stood.

By the following morning the weather had turned, and the squadron was stood down from readiness. This coincided with being advised that another 'innovation' was being trialled on Operation Rutter.

Because of the scale of the raid and the combined services involved, there were real concerns about friendly fire occurring, especially given the understandable propensity for naval forces to fire at any aircraft that appeared overhead. In addition, several new and unfamiliar light bombers and American Mustang fighters would be deployed for the first time. It would be easy for them to be mistaken for enemy aircraft, especially since many Allied gunners were comparatively new to their AA gunnery roles.

To aid recognition, identification marks were to be painted on the aircraft of participating squadrons. For No. 111 Squadron, these would be four vertical white stripes on the long noses of their Spits, with two more on each horizontal stabiliser. In addition, the nose spinners of the Spitfires were painted white instead of the usual sky-blue. This was a laborious task for ground crews to execute, and the new paintwork on the aircraft divided opinions amongst pilots. Some were concerned they were now too visible and almost clown-like in appearance, whilst others were simply happy to reduce the chance of getting shot at by their own side.

CHAPTER TWELVE

Operation Rutter had been earmarked for some time between the 4th and 8th of July, depending on the weather and tide. However, early on the morning of the 7th of July, a convoy of vessels anchored off Yarmouth on the Solent, west of the Isle of Wight, was spotted by the Luftwaffe. Four Focke-Wulf 190 fighter-bombers attacked the troopships HMS *Prinses Astrid* and HMS *Prinses Josephine Charlott*. Both vessels were pre-war Dutch passenger ferries, which had been converted into troop ships and were loaded to the gills with young Canadians. Both ships were hit but no bombs detonated onboard, one miraculously passing through two decks and out the other side before exploding. Remarkably few men were wounded, and it was a very lucky escape for the Canuks crowded on board. There was now no doubt, however, that the enemy knew something was up. As the weather conditions worsened, the planned air- and glider-borne elements of the plan were also scrapped, and finally the difficult decision was made to cancel Operation Rutter.

Jox, Pritchard and Chalmers were sitting together when Badger came out of his office to share the news.

'Sorry to be the bearer of such tidings, but there you are,' he said. 'Maybe it's an opportunity for the young pups to get a bit more experience before they're properly blooded.'

He sat down and began flicking through the newspaper he had under his arm. Jox and the others resumed their conversation when he suddenly looked up.

'You lot know Paddy Finucane, don't you?'

'That's right,' replied Jox. 'He was on the same course as us at Montrose. Lovely chap. I saw him in London the other week. He's doing marvellously well — he's a wing commander now up at Hornchurch. He makes the three of us look like real slackers.'

Badger had a sour expression on his face. 'Looks like you'll have the chance to catch up, then.' He read aloud from the paper. *'The famous Irish ace Brendan 'Paddy' Finucane has bought it whilst on a ramrod raid on the Wehrmacht army camp at Étaples.* Apparently, the attack was timed for midday to catch enemy troops having lunch, which seems rather sneaky to me. He's got quite the record, though, with thirty-two downed, and he's the youngest wing commander in the RAF. Pretty impressive, I'd say.'

'Oh Christ, that's a blow,' said Jox. 'Another good chap gone.'

'I remember Paddy,' said Pritchard. 'He was a Dubliner but grew up in south London like me. What on earth happened? Any more details, Badger?'

'It says here he was hit by ground fire off Le Touquet. It was a fluke shot to his engine, which then overheated, forcing him to ditch into the sea. Apparently, his last words to his wingman were, "This is it, Butch," then he crashed and sank without a trace.'

'Bloody hell — snuffed out, just like that,' said Chalmers. 'Say, Le Touquet, wasn't that where Moose lost his toes?'

'That's right,' said Jox. 'Just up from Dieppe. The silly sod always says he put the "toe" in Le Toe-quet.' He fell silent for a while. 'Paddy Finucane, bloody hell. The few are getting fewer every day.'

'Cheer up, chaps. I'm afraid it comes with the territory,' said Badger. 'On a brighter note, you'd better put this in your diaries. Their Majesties the King and Queen are coming to pay us a visit on Friday the twenty-fourth of July. I'll want everything and everyone bright and shiny, spick and span. You know the drill: if it moves, salute it. If it doesn't, pick it up. If you can't pick it up, then just paint it.'

'Why are they coming to Debden?' asked Chalmers.

'Haven't you heard? Some of our esteemed colleagues are being decorated,' said Badger.

Jox could feel his ears reddening.

'Who's that, then?' asked Pritchard nonchalantly.

'Well, for a start, our beloved Squadron Leader Wickham will receive the DFC.' He glanced at Jox, laughing at his discomfort. 'And of course, our dear old chum Jox is being decorated for valorous services in Malta.'

'You're getting a Bar to your DFC?' exclaimed Pritchard. 'You'll have more baubles than a flipping Christmas tree at the rate you're going.'

'No, sir, not a DFC for my boy,' said Badger. 'Our dear Jox has managed to hook himself a Military Cross, by God. He must have done something significant to impress the pongos to that extent. Now, dear boy, do tell us, how on earth did you manage that?'

'Well, actually, it was the Navy,' said Jox. 'You sure you want to hear this? I warn you, it's a long, rather tedious story…'

The citations published in the London Gazette stated:

The KING has been graciously pleased to approve the under mentioned awards, in recognition of gallantry displayed in operations against the enemy:
— Awarded the Distinguished Flying Cross.

Acting Squadron Leader Peter Reginald Whalley WICKHAM (33403) Royal Air Force No. 111 Squadron. This officer is a fine leader and a courageous fighter. Whilst serving in the Middle East he destroyed at least 9 and damaged many other enemy aircraft. Since his return to this country, Squadron Leader Wickham has completed many sorties during which he has displayed fine leadership and a magnificent fighting spirit.
— *Awarded the Military Cross.*

Flight Lieutenant Jeremy Argyll Easton McNABB GC DFC (41276) Royal Air Force No. 111 Squadron. For conspicuous gallantry and devotion to duty whilst under enemy aerial attack. This officer took forward a team of his men and succeeded in getting an anti-aircraft gun into action. Under intensive fire, the gun successfully brought down three enemy aircraft. His gallantry and devotion to duty during recent operations was most marked.

His Majesty the King was as tall and slim as Jox remembered him, wearing the uniform of a Marshal of the Royal Air Force. His queen was shorter, almost squat, in a powder-blue dress with a string of pearls about her neck and a wide-brimmed hat pinned up on one side. She carried a pair of white gloves and had a handbag at her elbow.

'We … we've met before, haven't we, McNabb?' said the king, after Jox was introduced by Wing Commander Duke-Woolley.

'Yes, sir,' he replied, flattered at being recognised. 'Just after the Battle of Britain, you were good enough to award me with these.' Jox indicated his left breast, below his pilot's wings where the ribbons of his gallantry medals were ranged. He noted the king had the same wings above a vast array of colourful ribbons on his rather grander uniform.

'I … I don't believe I gave you that red one,' said the king in a distinctive reedy stutter. 'That's a new one on me.'

Jox blushed at being singled out of the presentation line. He sensed Pete Wickham standing to attention beside him, quietly fuming. 'It's an Albanian Order of Merit, sir. I had the pleasure of meeting His Majesty in London during the Blitz.'

'Ah yes, Zog!' said the king. 'He's quite a character — slippery sort of fellow, as I recall. N-now then, on to business.' He turned to his equerry, who was holding open a leather presentation case. The king picked up the Military Cross, its ribbon a single vertical stripe of rich purple with white on either edge. He pinned it to Jox's tunic and as he did, Jox noticed how closely it resembled the Maltese Cross, and for that matter the Iron Cross.

'S-so what mischief were you up to, to deserve this, McNabb?'

'I saw some action on the ground in Malta, sir.'

'Ah yes, Malta. They're having quite a time of it. We keep trying to get convoys through, but they're getting clobbered almost every time.' He spotted the deep blue ribbon of the George Cross on Jox's tunic. 'Yes, I've awarded the brave people of that island the very same George Cross as you've got there, McNabb. I really hope it encourages them to keep their spirits up, much as it drove you to greater endeavours, what?' He laughed. 'Do please remember, though, McNabb: no man is an island. I couldn't possibly manage without Her Majesty the Queen. You think I jest, but I do sincerely hope you have someone special.'

'Yes, sir,' replied Jox, surprised to find himself discussing such things with the king of the Britons. 'I do, sir. Actually, she's on the island of Malta.'

'I see, well that makes things rather tricky. We must see what we can do about getting you back to her.'

The king turned to introduce Jox to Her Majesty the Queen, who was chatting with Wing Commander Duke-Woolley. She walked past Pete Wickham and straight up to Jox. She held up her hand. 'Very nice to meet you Mister McNabb, and my congratulations on your award. We've all endured so much, and it's brave men like you who have led the way. Thank you.' She glanced at Wickham. 'And to you, Squadron Leader. Thank you all, gentlemen.' She put a hand on the king's forearm. 'We mustn't keep Mister McNabb, Bertie. I know you love to linger and chat with our military men, but it plays havoc with our timetable.' She bustled him along, but then stopped and turned back to Jox. 'Nice to meet you, Mister McNabb. I feel sure we shall meet again. Good afternoon, gentlemen.' The assembled officers stiffened to attention and saluted as the royal party headed for their waiting cars.

'What is it with you and always having to monopolise the attention?' growled Wickham. 'The rest of us never got a look-in.'

'Oh, I don't know, the queen seemed rather taken by the Dook here,' said Jox, trying to lighten the mood.

'Come on, chaps,' said Duke-Woolley. 'Don Blakeslee and the other Yanks want to buy you fellows a drink to celebrate your new gongs. He's shipping out of No. 71 Squadron over to No. 133, another of the Eagle squadrons. Jox, your dear friend Darren Beans is off with him as second in command. The Eagle squadrons are having a bit of a reshuffle before USAAF squadrons start arriving here in earnest. I don't suppose it'll be long before they get absorbed into Uncle Sam's Army. Worth celebrating, don't you think, boys?'

Wickham was still bristling, unhappy that he'd failed to make much of an impression on the king, but he certainly wasn't one to pass up a drink.

'Right you are, Dook,' he said with a forced smile. 'Sure, let's go.' He turned to Jox. 'We'll pick this up some other time.'

Several days later, Jox and Wickham were driving over to Biggin Hill. The atmosphere between them had been somewhat chilly since the investiture. Being in such close proximity meant that whatever bad blood existed had to be dealt with.

'Look, I really don't know what you expected me to do,' said Jox. 'It's not as if I could refuse to speak when I was addressed.'

'Yes, but you didn't need to monopolise their attention with your stories. We're all trying to make a good impression and having you about doesn't make it any easier.'

'Look, Pete, I really don't understand why you feel so threatened,' said Jox. 'I was asked to come back to help you get the squadron back on its feet. It's in better shape now and yes, the big op we were preparing for has been cancelled, but surely there'll be more. It's not as if we're running out of war. You know very well that all I want is to get back to Malta. Whether I do that with this squadron or another is quite immaterial. I'd rather we worked together until that eventuality occurs, but if that's not possible, we can just keep out of each other's way. Frankly, I'd prefer to be friends, but it's your choice.'

Wickham fell silent as he navigated along the twisting country lanes of Kent. By the time they'd reached the outskirts of Biggin on the Hill, the turbulent waters had calmed. They'd both been honest about their ambitions and realised they should be allies, rather than rivals. Pete had shared that with the number of Americans in the war increasing, he saw a future for himself in a role like that of Wing Commander Duke-Woolley, in a liaison capacity between the RAF and the USAAF. He liked the Americans, finding them more straightforward, less convention-bound and political than working with their British or Commonwealth counterparts. Jox wasn't sure he agreed but left it at that.

The plan was to meet up with Moose, Brian Kingcome and Tony 'Bolshie' Bartley — another of Wickham's friends — for lunch at the famous Battle of Britain pub, the White Hart, just a few miles east at Brasted. Bartley was another Biggin Hill ace who'd fought in the Battle of Britain. Afterwards, Jox, Wickham, Kingcome and Bartley were expected at the Red House for the party that evening. Bartley was a great friend of that evening's hosts, the indominable Macneal twins. Moira and Sheila were referred to by one and all as the 'Biggin Hill Belles', and the evening promised to be a wild one.

CHAPTER THIRTEEN

From the outside, the White Hart was an unremarkable country pub. Inside it had a low ceiling, exposed wooden beams and smelt of stale beer, woodsmoke and cigarettes. There were horse brasses hanging on the pillars that held up the ceiling and a long bar with stools ran down one side of the room, with a large brick fireplace running down the other.

What made it remarkable was a large blackboard hanging on the wall, with a carved wooden frame with RAF wings across the top. The board was covered in chalk signatures, many of which Jox recognised. The great and the good of Fighter Command had at some point passed through the White Hart and left their scrawl as evidence. High and to the left, he spotted Moose Grant's tiny signature. Tony Bartley's was top right, large and bold. Brian Kingcome's effort was equally flamboyant and right across the middle.

The landlord was a friendly, bearlike chap called Teddy Preston, who seemed to know everyone and had stories to tell about them all. With his jovial chatter and the delicious lunch prepared by his charming wife Kath, the afternoon passed swiftly.

Jox finally got the opportunity to catch up with Moose during one of the many long reminiscences between Bartley, Kingcome and Teddy, whilst Wickham hung on to every word.

'So, how are things on the run up to the big day?' Jox asked his friend, who was dwarfing the barstool he was perched upon.

'Not too bad, Jox. Steph and her mother have been getting things organised. I got hold of a Jerry parachute, so that's taken care of the material for the dress, but now they're fretting about the wedding cake. Did you know you can hire a fake cake with tiers? You then insert a fruit loaf into a drawer and you serve that to your guests. That's all we could get hold of with rationing and everything. Ingenious, though, eh?' He smiled. 'Remember that great grub we had when we spent Christmas with the Albanian princesses? There was no sign of rationing then. Princess Myze sent me a wedding gift, you know.'

'Really? What did she send you?'

'A silver elephant about the size of my hand.' Moose held up his large fist. 'It must have cost her a small fortune. I had quite a bit of explaining to do with Stephanie. She doesn't like it if I mention the Albanian princesses. She gets jealous, you know.'

'But why an elephant?'

'That's what the princess called me: "*son éléphant*." I tried to explain I was a moose, not an elephant, but that was her pet name for me.'

'Are you planning to invite her to the wedding?'

'Not a chance. Steph would kill me,' said Moose. 'That's one adventure best left in the past.'

Jox nodded before changing the subject. 'How are your No. 401 Squadron boys holding up? There must be plenty of new faces since I knew them back at Croydon.'

'Some old, some new. Si and Neil are still with us, but we lost Phil and Nick.'

'You must have been pretty excited about the big Canadian-led operation. I know it was cancelled, but it's likely to happen in one form or another, especially after all that training.'

'Well, my boys in the squadron have seen plenty of action,' replied Moose. 'It's really the ground troops we're concerned about. You remember I mentioned my little brother Willie is in the infantry? He's been kicking his heels for almost two years.'

'Let's hope they get another opportunity,' said Jox. 'And that it doesn't become some wild goose chase.'

'Surely you mean a wild moose chase, eh?' grinned Moose.

By the time evening was upon them, half the party were well lubricated. Jox held back on the free-flowing drinks because he wanted to keep an eye on Pete Wickham, who was really getting stuck in with Kingcome and Bartley. Moose was also uncharacteristically spartan in his consumption, since he was meeting his fiancée at the party.

When the Macneal twins arrived at the White Hart, they did not disappoint. Over six foot tall, dark-haired and coiffured, they were bewitching and charismatic. Moira was the more forthright one, with Sheila arguably the prettier and more thoughtful twin. They both had the confidence of the upper class and the Swiss finishing school poise that only a very wealthy father could afford. Sir Hector Macneal was a close friend of Lord Beaverbrook and was charged by the PM to oversee the nation's aircraft production.

Friends sometimes struggled to tell Moira and Sheila apart, as both had dark eyes and long-fingered hands that lingered flirtatiously on the shoulders and laps of besotted men. At first, Jox watched them in action from afar, nervous of getting pulled into their sphere. Earlier, Kingcome had shared that Moira, the eldest by ten minutes, wore a wedding ring since she was married to an RAF officer stationed out in the Middle East. Sheila was the widow of Squadron Leader Freddie Shute, a fighter pilot killed early in the war, leaving her with a young daughter, Lesley. It was Moira who noticed Jox first, beckoning him over with a vermillion-painted finger.

He shuffled up nervously. 'Hello, I'm Jox. I'm a friend of Moose's, who flies with Brian Kingcome.'

'Oh yes,' said Sheila, who slinked over to her sister's side. 'He's the big Canadian chap. Such a lovely boy — engaged to Stephanie Clarke, more's the pity.'

Moira fixed Jox with her dark gaze. 'So, you're a Scotsman. Not much of an accent, but it's still in there, Mister Jox…?'

'Jox McNabb,' he stuttered like a besotted schoolboy. 'That's right, from Edinburgh.'

'McNabb, Macneal … you know, we could be related. Now, wouldn't that be fun? We're from Edinburgh too, originally,' purred Moira. 'Went to school there before getting packed off to Geneva. Of course, that's where we discovered quite how much trouble we could get into with you lovely boys…'

Looking for an excuse to escape, Jox spluttered, 'Can I get you ladies a drink?'

As one, they answered, 'Pint of bitter, please.'

'Teddy Preston knows which one we like, and we'd like it in our pewter tankards, please,' Sheila added. 'Ask him for some Ballantine's whiskey chasers too. We've got a bottle stashed behind the bar. Tell him it's for the Macneals from up at The Red House.'

When Jox got back with the drinks, Sheila had her arms draped around Pete Wickham, who looked like he'd died and gone to heaven. They made a handsome couple. Moira was in deep discussion with Moose and Kingcome, and Bartley was chatting up a group of WAAFs that had come into the pub.

Jox joined Moira, who eventually said, 'Right then, who's for The Red House? Time for some dancing, I think. You do dance, don't you, Jox?' There was a predatory gleam in her eye.

The party moved to The Red House, a large Victorian villa, just a short walk from the White Hart. It was a second home for Biggin Hill's pilots, and even after they'd been stationed elsewhere, they often returned. It had a club house feel to it and it had become a bit of a sanctuary from the war.

There were even a number of convalescing RAF officers staying, with scars on their hands and faces and the golden badge of McIndoe's Guinea Pig Club on their dressing gowns. Unofficial residents at The Red House, they included Bob Holland on the piano playing along with the gramophone, and Richard Hillary making cynical wisecracks, amusing one and all. Pete Wickham was now dancing with Moira, and Sheila came over to Jox to introduce her best friend, Janet Montagu, a slim and elegant woman with an assured air and friendly smile.

'Ah, there you are, Jox,' said Sheila. 'This is my Netty. We're the tragic widows around here, so you must dance with us all night long.' Never much of a dancer, Jox did what he could to keep up and soon realised he was rather enjoying himself. With two lovely socialites to keep entertained, he was soon exhausted, begging for their mercy so he could catch his breath. Unperturbed, they danced on, arm in arm, watched by every man in the room.

Jox found a stool to watch the spectacle. He was joined by Bartley, who filled Jox in on the flirtatious pair. 'Janet was married to William Montagu, son of the ninth Earl of Sandwich, but he was killed in a Harvard in 1940. She's Sheila's best friend, and since they've both lost their husbands, they call themselves the "Merry Widows". Her father is Lord Beaverbrook, owner of the *Daily Express*, and her brother is Max Aitken, CO of No. 68 Squadron — night fighters. She's the perfect socialite and a first-class deb, but as my friends all say, "Buyer beware."'

'Oh, don't worry, I'm not on the market,' replied Jox.

'Oh, I rather think you are, old boy,' said Tony with a laugh. 'I know fresh meat when I see it. You're in play, my old son.'

Bartley went off for a drink and his stool was filled by a squiffy Pete Wickham.

'Those Macneal girls are simply marvellous,' said Wickham. 'I'm going to marry one of them, you mark my words.'

Jox laughed. 'Which one?'

'D'you know, I haven't decided yet.' He giggled. 'But the night's still young.'

Jox was grateful for the distraction when Moose arrived hand in hand with a tall, striking redhead that he recognised as Stephanie Clarke, his fiancée. They hadn't seen each other since that wild week between Christmas and New Year, almost two years ago, when Alice was still alive. As their eyes met, Stephanie burst into tears. Checking first with Moose, who nodded, Jox took her in his arms, saying soothingly, 'It's not your fault. We all lost her that night.'

'Oh, Jox, she was the best of us,' Stephanie sobbed.

'I know, but those left behind have a duty to keep living. I was so happy to hear that the two of you are getting married. It feels right, and I'm honoured that you've asked me to be your best man.'

'Thank you, that means a lot. I wanted your blessing,' said Stephanie, composing herself. 'Gosh, look at the state I've got myself into. Moose, get us a bottle of something nice, so we can toast our dear Alice. I'll go and fix myself up. I don't want to embarrass you in front of all your fighter pilot chums.'

'You could never do that, darling. Old Moose is the one that's embarrassing, eh?'

'I can certainly confirm that,' chimed in Jox. 'He's been embarrassing me for years. Tossing me about like a baby, every time he sees me.'

Stephanie laughed for the first time. 'Yes, he does that. A girl likes to be swept off her feet, but he does rather take it to extremes, does my lovely boy.'

The next few hours were a blur of laughter, dancing and wild capers. It was the wee hours of the morning before Jox, Moose and Stephanie decided to call it a night. They had rooms booked at the White Hart, and Moose knew where the key for late patrons was hidden.

Jox excused himself to look for his hat, which he'd left in the other room. He entered to find it was dimly lit by candles. Someone was playing the piano quietly. People were snoring on various armchairs, and a few couples were giggling in dark corners.

He searched amongst the huddled forms for his missing hat, wondering where Wickham might be and hoping he hadn't overdone it. Perhaps he'd decided which of the Biggin Hill Belles would be his bride. Jox approached the large damask sofa in the centre of the room. Sprawled elegantly across it, like a panther in a tree, was a long, languid figure.

'Are you looking for something?' asked a husky voice that Jox recognised as belonging to one of the Macneal twins.

'I left my hat somewhere around here.'

'I know, dear boy. It's underneath me,' she replied.

'May I have it?'

'Only if you pay the toll, my dear Jox.'

'Toll? And what might that be?' he asked nervously.

A long slim arm with a red-nailed hand reached up. 'Shut up and kiss me, you fool.'

CHAPTER FOURTEEN

'It appears the party's back on again,' said Wickham, looking breezier than he had any right to be. He and Jox had travelled back to Debden from the White Heart early that morning and were now sitting in his office. 'Operation Jubilee is a go.'

'What on earth is Jubilee?' asked Jox, who felt like death warmed up. 'And why in God's name are you so chipper? My head feels like it's about to explode and my mouth is like the bottom of a parrot's cage.'

'Quite a soiree, wasn't it?' said Wickham with a grin. 'What you need is a big bowl of marrowfat peas. Never fails as a hangover cure.'

'Ugh, I can't imagine anything worse,' replied Jox. 'So, what's this about Operation Jubilee?'

'It's the new codename for the Dieppe operation. It's back on and scheduled for mid-August,' said Wickham, glancing through the papers on his desk nonchalantly.

'Moose isn't going to be happy,' replied Jox. 'That's when he was planning to get married. St Luke's Church is already booked, with catering, flowers, the dress and everything. You remember — you met Stephanie last night. I'm to be their best man.'

'Oh yes, that lovely woman with fiery red hair. She's terribly clever. She's going to run rings around Moose.' Wickham shrugged. 'Can't be helped. Needs of the service and all that. I'm sure it's nothing that can't be rearranged. In any case, the Kenley Wing are sure to be involved. Moose is up there with the Canadians, isn't he?'

'That's right — he's A Flight leader with No. 401 RCAF. Been with them since the beginning.'

'Which reminds me — it says here that we're relocating to Kenley too, so as to get closer to the action for the big op. So, it's "Ta-ta for now" to our American friends and the East India boys. Actually, the plan is for all three American Eagle squadrons to be brought together here at Debden under the Dook's command, but before that, they may well move south for the op too. As we've discussed before, if I'm trying to find a role with them, I'll be hoping to return here at some point. It should leave a gap for you to step into my slot and lead the Treble Ones. How does that sound?'

'Yes, I suppose it works,' replied Jox. 'But to be honest, it's rather too much to think about with the fuzzy head I've got this morning. Crikey, what a do! Those Macneal twins are quite something.'

'Speaking of which, I've decided which one of the Macneals I'm going to marry,' said Wickham. 'Sheila's the gal for me. We had a bit of a kiss and a cuddle last night, and that's clinched the deal for me.'

Jox began to laugh. 'Well, that's cleared up a mystery for me too. I was wondering which one of them jumped me, latching herself onto my face.'

'Really? Gosh, they really are rather game, aren't they? What on earth did you do?' asked Wickham, intrigued now.

'Kissed her back, of course. Rude not to, but then I admit I ran like the coward I truly am,' added Jox, looking sheepish. 'I used the excuse that Moose and Steph were waiting for me. I was terrified she'd eat me alive. I must warn you, Pete: you're going to have your work cut out if you're setting your sights on Sheila. She's no shrinking violet either. And you do realise you'll have to contend with that father of theirs? Are you man enough for the job?'

'Absolutely,' said Wickham, not entirely convincingly.

'Rather you than me, old boy, but I wish you the best of luck in your endeavours.'

They laughed and shook hands.

By mid-morning, most residual hangovers had been dealt with and everyone was more or less back in shape. The Debden squadrons were being briefed on a Ramrod mission — a raid with a specified ground target — for that afternoon they were after the port of Ostend in western Belgium.

They were tasked with escorting light bombers going after destroyers, motor torpedo boats or indeed any other fast launches, vessels that could conceivably be called in at short notice to harry Operation Jubilee's flotilla. Ridgway said there should be plenty of targets of opportunity within the harbour, and there was a good chance that the attack would provoke an aggressive response from nearby fighter airfields in the Low Countries. He warned that flak defences over the harbour would be heavy and advised getting in and out as quickly as possible.

To hopefully avoid radar detection and deliver a surprise attack, the 'beehive' of participating aircraft were specifically ordered to cross the Channel at wave height. The raid shouldn't take more than two hours, and Ridgway stressed the 'hit and run' nature of the operation. In any case, they wouldn't have enough fuel for much more than about twenty minutes over the Flemish port.

Jox scanned the room. He caught the eye of Axel Fisken, who smiled, then pointed a finger at the large map behind Ridgway. On that hand, the little finger and the next were missing to the first knuckle, the result of torture when he'd been a prisoner of the Nazis in Norway. He mimed shooting at the map, clearly relishing the prospect of dishing out some revenge.

Beside him was his friend Olivier 'Ghillie' de Ghellinck, the Belgian aristocrat. He was understandably concerned about civilian losses but keen to strike against his homeland's oppressors. Over in the corner, Ralph Campbell and his fellow sergeant pilots looked nervous. In contrast, Pritchard, Chalmers and Ant, grizzled veterans, were the image of calm, blasé professionals. Broughton and Reeves were whispering to each other, whilst Vancl and Longstaffe listened impassively, both lost in their thoughts. These were a solid bunch of men, as good as you could get. Jox relished going to war by their side, and if things went as he hoped they might, perhaps he might be leading them into battle soon. There would be no greater honour.

Approaching the enemy coastline at wave height looked far more terrifying than it actually was. For experienced pilots it was a simple enough to hold formation, as long as they didn't bunch up with the heightened anxiety of imminent action. Scant yards above the shifting slate-green sea, the formation gave a solitary fishing skipper one hell of a fright as he pulled in the last line of mussels for the day.

No. 65 (East India) Squadron were in the lead and first to attack, shooting up the harbour master's tower and the pair of flak posts on the long concrete mole. Dirty smoke appeared amongst the swooping Spitfires, indicating Jerry was aware of their presence and was shooting back. An aircraft spouted a long, fiery streak and disintegrated, landing in the oily, grey water of the harbour. Too low for his parachute, the young airman's life was snuffed out like a candle.

The East Indians were followed by two squadrons of powerful twin-engine Bristol Beaufighters, gunning after the shipping along the quaysides. Each was armed with four 20mm cannons, some with rockets, others with torpedoes, and the devastation was absolutely terrifying for the poor matelots and fishermen below. Wooden civilian craft were smashed to driftwood, whilst assorted military fast-strike vessels were sieved and sent to the muddy bottom or exploded spectacularly as onboard munitions detonated. The bombers didn't escape unscathed. One of the Beaufighters was struck by a rising wall of fire from the flak ship moored at the harbour entrance. It caught fire and began dropping in slow motion, smashing into an innocent trawler that was unloading its catch at the quayside. Another bomber arched away for the open sea, a smoky trail blossoming across the opaque sky from a stricken radial engine. The pilot was trying to coax some height from his sole functioning prop; Jox could see his frantic movements through the glazed nose panels of the pugnacious aircraft. For the Beaufighter's two crewmen, it would be a long and harrowing flight home. Jox said a silent prayer and wished them well.

It was the Treble Ones' turn to strike at the moorings and quays, already a scene of billowing smoke and mass devastation. Through the masking haze, Jox picked out a target and glanced over his shoulder to check Ant Glasgow was there, his ever-faithful wingman. Before them, lashed together in long rows in a sheltered corner of the harbour, were dozens of plump-looking flat-topped vessels covered in grubby tarpaulins. They were moored four deep alongside the quay and from Ridgway's briefing, Jox recognised them as invasion barges. They were converted commercial vessels from the inland canals of the Low Countries. Originally assembled for Operation Sealion, the postponed amphibious invasion of Great Britain, their time may have past, but they still represented enemy infrastructure and were therefore a legitimate target. Jox opened fire and was joined by Ant, their guns and cannons wreaking havoc on the unarmoured wooden hulls and flimsy canvas.

The pair pulled away gracefully from their trail of destruction. Their attack positions swiftly taken up by successive pairs of Treble One Spitfires, spreading the mayhem upon the helpless landlubbers, so out of place in this maritime warzone.

The need for stealth was over and the Treble Ones climbed, swiftly gaining altitude to face any aerial threat that might materialise. They were fortunate, as no such response came. The mission was a perfect hit and run, aside from the losses incurred. With greater altitude, the view before Jox opened up, just as a few rays of watery sunshine cut through the cloud cover. It was enough to reflect weakly off the white cliffs of Dover and Kent in the distance, a toothy welcome grin from old Blighty.

Before long they were back at Debden, orbiting the airfield and waiting for clearance to land from the ops room. Once they were wheels down, the pilots assembled, still high on the adrenaline of combat, some for the very first time. Ralph Campbell came bowling over to Jox, talking a mile a minute. Jox laughed and tried to calm the young sergeant's enthusiasm. Thankfully, Ridgway came to the rescue, navigating between them and trying to separate fact from fantasy to form an accurate picture of what had been achieved. He had his work cut out from the roar of far too many talking all at once.

A few stragglers hadn't made it back. Jox and Pritchard joined Badger Robertson outside the dispersal, as he scoured the horizon for the latecomers. He looked tense.

'Who's still missing?' asked Jox.

Robertson lowered his binoculars. 'Morgan Chalmers and Mike Longstaffe are unaccounted for. They're wingmen, so they have probably stuck together. I think that's Bubbles Broughton coming in just now.' They could hear the ragged burble of a faltering engine before the familiar silhouette of the Spit appeared low above the treeline bordering the aerodrome. As it approached, white smoke flared from its exhaust stubs and there was the ominous flashing of flames. The pilot landed heavily and rather too fast but was obviously in a hurry to get the crate down. With haste that would normally have earned him a reprimand for being heavy-handed, he spun the stricken aircraft off the runway into the knee-high grass and skidded to a clumsy halt. The young airman tumbled from his cockpit as a thickening cloud of smoke rose from within and sheets of flame began to take hold. Broughton rolled through the damp grass until he stilled, his chest heaving. Fire and ambulance crews were helping him up by the time Jox and Pritchard reached him. They'd left old Badger puffing far behind, as they'd sprinted to provide whatever assistance they could.

Broughton was mud-streaked and dishevelled, but he gave a tired grin, creasing the features of his impossibly young face. His clothing was charred, and there was smoke rising from it. A cautious fireman gave him a final squirt of white powder from his extinguisher.

'It was getting too bloody hot up there,' spluttered Broughton, succumbing to a flurry of coughs.

'You all right?' asked Jox.

Without saying a word, Pritchard seized Bubbles, spun him around and began patting down the smoking patches of his charred clothing with his hands.

'Take it easy, Pritch,' wheezed Broughton. 'No need to beat me up — just give me a second to catch my breath and have a sip of water.' He was handed a canteen by the ambulance medic and swallowed several deep gulps. 'Thanks, doc,' he croaked.

Badger caught up with them, panting almost as heavily as Broughton. 'That's more than enough drama for one afternoon. Are you quite sure you're all right, young Broughton? Let the medics give you the once-over, there's a good lad.'

Robertson returned his attention heavenwards, scanning the hazy grey skies once more. 'Where the devil have Longstaffe and Chalmers got to? They're well past due.'

When the stragglers appeared through the brume, they were in a staggered pair. Jox identified Chalmers' Spit from the white letters on his patterned fuselage, circling around the other like a mother mallard worried for her fledgeling. In contrast, Longstaffe's aircraft was a flying wreck. Even at this distance it was obvious that a single wheel was hanging like a wounded leg below the starboard wing. As it got closer, it became clear that there were several sections missing from the wings and the tail assembly looked like something had taken a big bite out of it. Like Broughton's aircraft, the engine was intermittent, coughing and spluttering as it glided towards the runway. Chalmers waggled his wings furiously, indicating his companion was in trouble. The airwaves on the set in the fire truck remained resolutely silent.

Trying to land on a single wheel was always going to be a challenge. The high-pitched shriek of the single rubber tyre skidding along the concrete runway was almost mournful, swiftly followed by a deep grinding sound, increasing in volume as a shower of sparks rose from the portside wing scraping across the runway surface. The sound stuttered as the ruined wing dug into wet grass, sending the whole aircraft tumbling violently over itself. The force of the movement detached a large piece of it, sending it flying through the air before landing with a thump. The rest of the wreck ground to a halt, steaming and ticking in a shattered heap. Unidentified liquid poured from the exhaust stubs and streaked down the Spit's ruined nose, its propellor bent like a giant black daisy. Trembling fuel haze rose from the vacant cockpit, empty like the top of a hollowed skull.

As the ambulance and fire truck reached the wreckage, Chalmers continued to circle anxiously. On the ground, the rescuers tumbled from their vehicles. Firefighters hosed down the wreckage as flames whooshed and it started to burn. The medics ran over to the broken figure lying prone on the wet grass some twenty or so yards beyond. Longstaffe had been thrown clear of the wreckage, but was lying very still, his limbs splayed at unnatural angles.

Jox and Pritchard exchanged worried glances and sprinted towards the crash.

CHAPTER FIFTEEN

It felt strange to be back at Kenley. For Jox, it was the scene of so many significant moments and the ghost of Alice lingered everywhere.

Approaching low and from the north, he passed over the Wattenden Arms, the village pub where they'd had their first lunch together and subsequent confrontation with Squadron Leader Drummond. Crossing the perimeter fence, he recognised the airfield's odd shape, reminiscent of the head of a teddy-bear. Gliding over to the portside of the crossed runways, he recalled how the cable rockets had fired across this end of the airfield during Kenley's 'Hardest Day' — 18th August 1940. They'd clawed at the enemy Dornier 17s passing overhead on their low bombing runs, bringing several tumbling down. Jox had tried to land amidst the chaos, his Hurricane ending tail-up in a bomb crater. He vividly remembered the cold, metallic taste of fear as he'd raced across the devastated airfield on foot, desperate to find Alice.

The subsequent events came back to him in snatches: the fight with Drummond, the relief of finding Alice unhurt, and then his ill-timed and completely unrehearsed proposal. He smiled, remembering the instant joy of her acceptance in the horrendous pink room that served as Kenley's WAAF officers' sitting room.

Once back on the ground, Jox powered down, then slid back his canopy and took in the familiar surroundings. From every angle he felt the past rushing at him, setting off a deep sense of melancholy.

The physical damage to the airfield was long gone, the only remaining scars on certain buildings and patches of earth that betrayed where the fires had been. The craters had been filled in and the crushed rubble spread. Kenley was buzzing, far busier than he recalled, but that wasn't all that surprising, considering it now housed five up-manned squadrons in the run-up to Operation Jubilee, with the surplus personnel, aircraft and logistics that entailed.

Leaving Debden had been quite upsetting, not because Jox was particularly fond of the airfield but because the squadron had left Mike Longstaffe behind. Thrown clear from his wrecked Spitfire, he was badly hurt. His broken body had been strapped onto a stretcher, and he'd been swiftly transferred into a waiting ambulance by medics, tight-lipped with anxiety for their patient's welfare. He was such a serious case that he hadn't stayed long at the wing's infirmary, and a large modern ambulance had come to transfer him to a specialised care unit.

Longstaffe wasn't bound for Archibald McIndoe's experimental burns unit at the Queen Victoria Hospital in East Grinstead, like so many other airmen. Rather, he faced the equally terrifying prospect of the spinal injuries unit at Stoke Mandeville Hospital near Aylesbury. Rumours were already circulating that Longstaffe might be paralysed. This grim prospect had hung over the squadron as they'd packed and readied themselves for the transfer to Kenley.

It took the Treble Ones a few days to acclimatise to their new environment. Time was spent training with Kenley's other squadrons, plus those stationed at the nearby satellite airfield of Redhill. Despite the uncertainty that came with operating from a new base and with new comrades, the squadron felt ready and were looking forward to getting stuck in.

On the morning of Wednesday, 19th August 1942, the Kenley Wing, callsign SAPPER, was up well before dawn. The Treble Ones were paired with their old friends of No. 65 (East India) Squadron, now flying out of RAF Eastchurch. When they took off, it was 04:15 and still dark. The early start meant many pilots had spent little time in their beds, kept awake by over-stimulation, anticipation, terror and the simple determination not to fail in their duty.

The previous evening they'd been assembled at the station cinema to be addressed by the Station Commander and Wing Commander (Flying), who confirmed the operation was a go. The mission objectives were recapped, and the only new and useful information provided was that anyone who got into trouble over Dieppe and needed to land urgently, should make their way to the nearby racetrack. The Hippodrome de Dieppe was in the Bouteilles neighbourhood, recognisable from the air as a large green park in the middle of town, beside the river that fed into the harbour. It would be one of the first objectives to be seized by ground troops, and any downed pilots would be withdrawn from there at the end of the raid. Jox wondered what would happen if the racetrack wasn't captured or if they were hit nowhere near Bouteilles, but it seemed churlish to ask, given the confidence that was in the room.

After a rushed early breakfast, duty rosters for those flying the first mission of the day were issued. The Treble Ones would provide cover for two squadrons of Boston light bombers, who were tasked with attacking coastal artillery covering the landing beaches. These Bostons would also be dropping smoke bombs along the gun emplacements on the eastern heights, so the landing beaches would be shrouded in a thick covering of smoke.

As they climbed up through the dark stillness of sleeping Kenley and nearby Whyteleafe, Jox spotted the church where Moose and Stephanie should have been getting married that day. The stars were still shining before the pre-dawn, and no horizon was yet visible. The squadron was vectored towards the rendezvous point with the bombers over the Channel and were scheduled to reach Dieppe at 04:40. The Spitfires of No. 65 Squadron would join them five minutes later, and together they would greet the sunrise over France at 05:50.

Between 05:09 and 05:44 the Bostons dropped a hundred and fifty 100lb smoke bombs and were amongst the first exposed to the wrath of the newly awakened anti-aircraft guns, throwing up a storm of fire. The smokescreen, a thousand yards long, began to drift out to sea, where a flotilla of landing craft could be seen approaching. The artificially generated smoke was thickened by a burning cliff-top wheat crop, set alight by the various pyrotechnics of both sides as this decisive new day of the war dawned.

Out to sea, the dark waters were streaked with boats streaming towards the shore. Looming behind them were the destroyers ORP *Slazak* and HMS *Albrighton*, which began the naval bombardment of the beaches and the covering gun emplacements. They were swiftly joined by every capital ship of the flotilla, creating a creeping barrage that would soon begin landing on the town itself.

For the Treble Ones, the first sortie of the day would prove to be a wasted effort. Their presence was no doubt reassuring to the crews of the Bostons and a heartening sight overhead for the seasick Canadian troops before the landings, but it was really too dark for them to make a meaningful contribution. They couldn't pick out any ground targets, nor did they see any signs of a Luftwaffe response, so for forty impotent minutes they patrolled up and down the pebbled beaches as the sky lightened from the east.

For Jox the only memorable moment of that first sortie was recognising Kenley's Wing Commander Brian Kingcome's voice on the R/T when handing over patrol duty to Wing Commander Myles Duke-Woolley of the relieving Debden Wing. 'SAPPER Leader to GARTER Leader. I say, Dook, my dear fellow, what on earth are you doing up so early?'

The Dook and his Eagles chuckled as they took up their positions and Jox and the Treble Ones headed for home. Kenley's Spitfires were back before 06:30, having completed their first and what would prove the only blank sortie of the day. Once parked up in their brick blast pens, the ground crews swarmed over the aircraft and the pilots were gathered for a debrief. They were joined by Group Captain Harry Broadhurst, Senior Air Staff Officer for No. 11 Group, who'd also just returned from a solo sortie over the beaches.

'Good morning, gentlemen,' said Broadhurst to the assembled airmen, many still sweaty and crumpled from the confines of their cockpits and yet already preparing for a second sortie. Others were pristine, getting ready for their first, and still others were in unfamiliar uniforms. 'It's a fine day for battle. For those who missed out on the Battle of Britain, I've no doubt that today will provide the high point of your military careers. A tale to tell your grandchildren, and one I've no doubt they'll be mightily bored to hear.' He raised his hand to stifle the polite laughter. 'Dieppe is waking to a day unlike any in its history. The first sortie was a bit of a milk run, but the Germans have definitely woken up now and the boys on the beach are in for a hot time. When we return, the enemy will be out in force.' His face was strained. 'Remember, gentlemen, we are on their home turf now and they don't like it one bit.' He scanned the room of fidgeting young airmen, anxious to get on with it. 'I'd like to welcome some newcomers amongst us. Our friends of the 308th Fighter Squadron from the United States Army Air Forces have joined us and will be coming along for their first combat mission. I wish you and them good fortune and fair winds.' He nodded to a cluster of elegantly attired, gum-chewing Americans. 'I believe you're familiar with some of our chaps, having trained with No. 111 Squadron, but a warm welcome to you nonetheless.' Jox knew Ralph Campbell and the squadron's junior pilots had recently been practising interceptions with the Americans.

'I've asked Squadron Leader Wickham to lead the 308th Fighter Squadron out today,' continued Broadhurst. 'We're having a bit of a reshuffle of responsibilities. To allow him to gain additional combat leadership experience before he takes over his own Czech squadron, Flight Lieutenant Frantisek Vancl will lead the Treble Ones for this next mission.' He glanced at Jox. 'McNabb, I know you're second in command, but I've got another job lined up for you. Our Belgian friends of No. 350 Squadron over at Redhill are down several men, including their CO. I want you, Warrant Officer Glasgow and Flying Officer de Ghellinck to head over there and lead them out. I believe you speak some French, and Ghillie can certainly help with any "lost in translation" issues. They're a smashing bunch of fellows. The squadron was originally set up by Tommy Thompson — I believe you're something of a protégé of his.'

Jox reddened at being singled out before such a large group but nodded mutely.

Broadhurst laughed. 'Don't be embarrassed, Jox. Everyone needs a mentor. Who do you think taught old Tommy the ropes in the first place? It was me when I was leading the

Treble Ones up in Scotland. Right, that's settled then. Everyone happy? Then it's time to crack on. The best of British luck to you all. And remember, gentlemen: *Per ardua ad astra.*'

It was a short hop over to Redhill in Surrey to catch up with No. 350 (Ambiorix) Squadron as they prepared for their first sortie of the day. Jox already knew many of them, friends of Olivier de Ghellinck, as there weren't all that many Belgians serving in the RAF.

Some were aristocrats like de Ghellinck, notably Flight Lieutenant Count Yves du Monceau de Bergendal, nicknamed 'The Duke', who led B Flight. Others, like Flight Lieutenant Alain Boussa leading A Flight, were professional pre-war soldiers. Jox had always found them to be earnest, well-trained men intent on achieving the liberation of their little nation.

After a swift round of handshakes and snatched conversations on the ground, Jox led the Belgians out to rendezvous with Pete Wickham and the American 308th FS leaving from Kenley at 07:15. They would provide top cover for the novice Americans, and they circled the airfield until they got airborne. As they circuited at about five thousand feet, the 308th clumsily pulled themselves together under Wickham's barked instructions.

Together they headed over the Channel, 308th FS at Angels Five and No. 350 at Angels Ten, crossing the jagged line of Dieppe's imposing cliff-face just before 08:00. The waters off the sloping pebble beach were already a chaos of bucking landing craft, interspersed with larger Landing Craft Tanks disgorging Churchill Mk II tanks. From altitude, they were like armoured beetles, peeking through the moving banks of smoke, followed by scurrying legions of foot soldiers. Rather too many appeared to be clumping together and not moving forward, either pinned or struck down, neither situation portending a successful outcome to the landings.

To the west there was a massive flash against the dark half of the horizon. Jox realised it must be the Hess battery at Cap d'Ailly, the objective of No. 4 Commando led by Lord Shimi Lovat. Something large and clearly powerful had exploded, the first positive indication that one of the ground mission objectives had been achieved. The Belgians banked and followed the clifftops eastwards until they reached Dieppe. Large swathes were in flames and the howl of gunfire was audible through the bubble of Jox's cockpit.

Sweeping over the shattered townscape, Jox recognised the sheltered waters of the harbour and the landmarks of the imposing chateau and casino. Both already looked rather ragged and battle-scarred compared to the pre-war holiday snaps they'd been shown in the pre-mission briefings. Up ahead and approaching from inland, a number of smudgy dots appeared. Sharp-eyed Ant Glasgow was the first to spot them. 'AMBIORIX Squadron, this is Blue Two. Bandits at one o'clock high. Estimate twenty to thirty at Angels Eleven.'

The Belgians reacted with a flurry of French and Flemish. 'That's enough!' cried de Ghellinck, furious at his countrymen's lack of R/T discipline.

'Thank you, Ghillie,' said Jox in a placating tone. 'AMBIORIX Squadron, this is AMBIORIX Leader. Stand by for contact.'

What appeared to be two full *Staffel* of Focke Wulf 190s were diving towards No. 350 Squadron, splitting up into a two-pronged attack, one going after the top squadron and the other diving on through to make a swooping pass at the Americans.

In a flash, a single aircraft from the 308th dropped out of formation and moments later a parachute popped.

Infuriated by the loss of one of their flock, the Belgians struck at the marauding wolves with the vengeance of faithful sheepdogs. In the ensuing dogfight, the Belgian duke downed a FW 190, which crashed into a cow pasture, then went on to share a probable with his B Flight mates, Pilot Officers Henri Picard and Emile Plas. Another Focke Wulf was damaged.

The three Treble Ones amongst the Belgians stuck together. At first contact, Jox, Ant and de Ghellinck peeled off as one, Jox feeling confident that his experienced wingmen were by his side. There was no shortage of targets and together the trio fired several rounds into at least five of the interceptors. Banking hard to pull away from a particularly aggressive Butcher Bird, Jox saw streaked cannon fire pass him by, as if scratching at the sky. His response was to return fire, a quarter deflection shot at a range of about two hundred and fifty yards. He smiled inside his mask, seeing the strikes register on his opponent's fuselage, right across the black cross in a bright yellow square, and on through to the mottled blue tail that bore a smaller swastika. The impact of his cannon shells blew the vertical tail assembly right off and his adversary spun repeatedly, falling from about two thousand feet, past the face of the contested cliffs before smacking into the shallows amongst the pitching landing craft. Jox broke off immediately as he was being engaged by his victim's wingman, the number thirteen visible on his flanks. *Unlucky for some*, thought Jox, knowing his veteran wingmen would be on him.

Ant and de Ghellinck fired in rapid succession from no further than a hundred yards away. At near enough full deflection, the tracks of their fire converged, and their opponent staggered in the morning sky. He attempted to pull up but failed, starting to drop in a long, slow dive, smoke pouring from the nacelle of the FW 190's radial engine. Olivier de Ghellinck followed him down, firing a final burst moments before his foe smashed into the vertical cliff face dominating the beaches. He looped away and executed a flamboyant victory roll as he climbed to re-join his squadron mates.

Back together, Jox quickly inspected the silhouettes of his companions' aircraft, looking for any signs of obvious damage. They appeared unmarked, so he waggled his wings and pointed a gauntleted hand vaguely homewards. The pair tightened up either side of him as they banked over the wide-open bay of Dieppe, the cliffs now bathed in morning sunlight. In the gaps between the rolling smoke, the pebbled beaches and shallows were visible. Heading back across the Channel, the sea below boiled with ships of every size scurrying about on urgent and deadly missions.

It was barely 09:00 and they would be back again soon. The battle was just getting underway, and things would only get hotter as more enemy forces were thrown into the fray. The troops on the ground were scheduled to pull out by 15:00 that afternoon, which was only a scant six hours away, but six hours during which they would be hard pressed and dependent on both the junior and senior services. Jox for one was determined that he and his men wouldn't fail them on that account.

CHAPTER SIXTEEN

Returning for a third time, Jox approached the now familiar clifftops and was met by a horizontal curtain of orange tracer fire plunging down at the sea from the heights. It appeared to bounce off the water's surface in a way that didn't seem possible. It was only when ricochets rose vertically, having struck some of the bobbing and weaving vessels, that he realised this was very real. Surely, no one could survive the maelstrom of fire down there.

Jox was leading yet another new squadron, although not an entirely unfamiliar one. The Eagles of No. 133 Squadron were nominally led by Flight Lieutenant Don Blakeslee, who Jox knew from Debden when he'd still been serving with No. 71 Squadron. The tall Ohioan with film star looks was a gifted leader of men, but by his own admission he had limited combat experience and often claimed to be a lousy shot. Accordingly, Jox and Ant had been assigned to 'ride shotgun' with the Yanks on their next trip. During the flight across the Channel, Jox also recognised the unmistakable accent of Darren 'Bayou' Beans dominating the R/T chatter amongst the talkative Americans.

As they approached the flotilla of ships fanned across the bay of Dieppe, their Spitfires had a grandstand view. Several offshore Landing Craft Tanks (Rockets) were now in range of their inland targets and without any warning, began to fire. Jox had seen them in action before, during the exercises on the Isle of Wight, and knew they carried over a hundred mortar-like rockets each, fired in spectacular salvos in under a minute.

'Well, I'll be damned!' exclaimed the startled voice that could only be Beans. 'It's like the Fourth of July down there.' They couldn't see where the rockets were landing, but their fiery tails held the deadly promise of devastation — none more so than when a salvo passed straight through the loose formation of Spitfires. By some miracle, no-one got struck, but several came uncomfortably close. A hit would have been catastrophic, so hoping to diffuse any resulting tension, Jox piped up, 'Well, with friends like that, who needs enemies?' There was nervous laughter on the R/T.

On their previous sortie, Jox and Ant Glasgow had seen only enemy fighters. Now, over the smoke-wreathed town came a formation of something much larger. They could only be bombers after the Allied shipping in the bay. The squadron had been assigned the task of top cover and providing fire to protect landing craft that were picking up the wounded of earlier waves. It seemed fairly clear the bombers were keen to break through the protective screen of fighters and go after the 'sitting ducks' just off the shingle beaches.

Jox signalled they should climb to intercept the bombers above them at Angels Twelve or more. As the opposing forces neared, the German aircraft became discernible as Junkers Ju 88s and Dornier Do 17s, accompanied by a strong escort of fighters, principally FW 190s. Jox and the Americans were roundly outnumbered, but Jox still instructed Blakeslee's flight to go against the bombers, whilst he, Ant and the flight led by Beans would take on the fighters. Climbing steeply to meet them, Darren Beans exclaimed, 'Born on the bayou!'

In the ensuing melee, Blakeslee's flight claimed first blood, a Ju 88 falling almost immediately, trailing black smoke. The sky was filled with the stuttering flashes of tracer and the agonised roaring of engines.

Jox tried to get a bead on an agile FW 190 with an unusual black spiral propellor cone. He got separated from Ant, who went after another. Pursuing his quarry over the town's harbour, Jox yawed the Spitfire to check the blind spot behind, just to make sure he wasn't being lured into an ambush. The movement attracted the attention of his opponent, who immediately arched over and came snaking round after him. Coming at each other almost head-on, they both began turning hard left on opposite sides of an ever-decreasing circle. Jox opened up his throttle and held the aircraft in the tightest, shuddering vertical turn he could manage. His eyes began to grey out and he feared he would lose track of his opponent. Where the devil was the brute? Jox imagined he could feel the glare of the gunsights on his back. Verging on panic, he threw his Spit into increasingly desperate manoeuvres, but the German stayed hard on his tail. Jox felt the cold hand of doom resting on his shoulder.

He pulled frantically at his stick, shoving it hard over so as to plunge into a near vertical dive — a manoeuvre as dangerous as it was desperate. Pulling up at wave level, his stomach lurched, and he was low over the ships off the beaches, the clifftops above him. Flashing by, he glimpsed lumbering tanks, burning pyres and the thick smokescreen. Through it pulsed waves of men, ant-like amongst the gravel. Offshore, a destroyer bristling with guns loomed through the smoke. At the pre-sortie briefing, they'd been warned to stay above four thousand feet, but he was well below that, as was his pursuing nemesis. Jox jabbed the emergency booster tit, desperate for that surge of power as he headed straight for the ship.

When almost overhead, he broke hard to starboard, and his opponent cut off in the opposite direction. Just then it seemed like the entire flotilla opened fire on the pair. The Focke-Wulf

190 got a tremendous clobbering, disintegrating into a mass of trailing cables, a spinning propellor and a riddled fuselage, which splashed into the shallow coastal waters.

Meanwhile, Jox's cockpit had filled with the acrid stench of a glycol leak as his stricken overheating engine roared. He pulled on the stick, desperate for altitude so he might give his parachute a chance to deploy if forced to bale out. Fumbling with the canopy, he was barely conscious of scraping over the clifftops dominating the chaos on the beach. He was then over green fields beyond, gaining height, before slowly corkscrewing the dying Spitfire. The momentum propelled him from the cockpit, flinging him into the void. Tumbling away from the stricken aircraft, he felt his heel clip the rear assembly in an explosive burst of pain. The crunching impact sent him spinning away, as did the ferocious blast of air on his flailing body. Thrown clear of the noise and fury of his dying kite, he was now in utter silence, save for the rasp of his throat as he struggled to breathe. Buffeted by the fierce flow of air, he tried to reach the cord of his parachute. For a terrifying split-second, he feared it had failed, but then with a satisfying crack it snapped open, his fall arrested with a sinew-wrenching jerk.

Jox swung in the harness as the ground approached at a dizzying rate, his attention distracted by the agony from his throbbing ankle and the fear of further pain when he landed on it. As he fell, he was dimly aware of odd kidney-shaped forms on the ground, pale against green pastures between banks of shrubby gorse and ferns. He landed with a gut-wrenching thump that took his breath away, straight into a thicket of yellow broom, dusty and prickly in the summer heat. He cried out as his ankle jarred against the hard ground, sending a fresh surge of pain up his leg as the silken canopy became entangled in the branches. It flapped in the breeze as he concentrated on containing the pain. Catching his breath, he realised that for the first time in his flying career, he was a member of the Caterpillar Club, his life saved by distant Indian silkworms. He was in no mood for gratitude.

Sitting up gingerly, he scanned his surroundings. From the north he could hear the roar of battle on the beaches, and above the clear blue sky was a mass of twisting contrails. The map in his head told him more or less where he was. He'd passed over the chalky promontory of the Côté aux Hérons, west of Dieppe, and was fairly sure he'd ended up on the genteel fairways of the Dieppe Pourville Golf Club, one of the oldest golf courses in France. In other words, nowhere near the Hippodrome de Dieppe racetrack.

He had to get away. His parachute was flapping in the breeze and would surely attract attention. The clifftop defensive positions were not far away. He quickly unclipped his harness and slipped out of his highly visible yellow Mae West jacket. He checked his pockets, gave the porcelain doll's arm a reassuring rub, and confirmed his Maltese switchblade was still in his trouser pocket. He also pressed the hard lump sewn into his flight tunic for reassurance, knowing it contained two gold sovereigns, a map printed on silk and a compass. He would take a look once out of sight, reasoning that there must surely be a holiday villa alongside the golf course with outhouses or garages where he might hide and get his bearings.

The sound of gunfire told him which direction not to head in and he began limping inland. As he passed a kidney-shaped, sand-filled bunker, he picked up a rake and began using it as a makeshift crutch, his progress becoming a little swifter. He lifted his head at a new noise. Could he hear dogs barking, or was it just his imagination? He wasn't going to hang about to check and quickened his pace.

On the edge of the course, he came across an impressive Victorian wrought iron fence line. It must surely belong to the house of someone with connections, as a fence like this in England would have gone for munitions or some 'Spitfire drive' long ago. He reached the ornate gate, was relieved to find it unlocked and slipped through. Closing it behind him with a metal groan, he was sure he heard dogs again. Had they caught his scent? He cut through some flowerbeds of plate-sized dahlias and reached a long gravel drive, which forked left to a grand mansion and right to garages and stabling. He headed for the green doors of the garages but found them all locked. Slipping around the back, he passed a pile of manure and spied a row of small windows in the rear brick wall. Using the handle of the rake, he smashed a single glass pane and reached in to open one of the windows. With difficulty because of his ankle, he then pulled himself through, landing roughly on a wooden workbench covered in tools. He was lucky he hadn't impaled himself on something sharp, as all manner of woodworking chisels and tools were scattered across the bench. A rack on the wall held a row of wooden-handled screwdrivers of varying sizes. He lifted the largest and assessed it as a weapon. It had a two-foot-long octagonal pale wood handle and a metal shaft, about a foot long, with a corkscrew curl halfway up and a blunt square-cut tip. It was a thing of beauty but could also double as a useful club at one end and a stabbing blade at the other. Holding it in his hand felt reassuring.

Jox peered into the gloom. He was in one of four garages, interconnected by arches, that had perhaps once been stabling. The room he'd broken into was a workshop, the woodworking bench along one wall and a mechanic's post up against another. The other rooms were garages and Jox could see several vehicles shrouded under protective dust sheets. He'd have a look underneath in a moment, but first he wanted to catch his breath. He collapsed noisily onto a chipped bistro chair by the bench, where he testily flexed his sore ankle. He gasped at the unexpected surge of pain.

Once he'd recovered, Jox peered at the luminous dials of his wristwatch. Almost ten o'clock in England, so it must be eleven in his current location. The operation was due to wrap up by three, but from what he'd seen on the beaches, things weren't exactly going to plan. He expected the powers that be might well pull the plug earlier, so he really needed to make contact with friendly forces on the beach or in shattered Dieppe itself before it was too late.

He heard a scraping sound. Something was moving between the vehicles, too large to be an animal. Jox froze, desperately trying to quieten his breath. Sweat trickled down the small of his back from the stifling heat in the garage. The smell of motor oil and petrol seemed to get stronger as he strained his senses. There was definitely a footstep and the sound of low breathing. He felt for his switchblade but dismissed it as too noisy.

Something glinted in the slanting ray of sunlight coming through the little windows across the top of the garage doors. Jox raised his newfound club. The shape of a hand clutching a large wrench cut through the light. The hand was missing the two smallest fingers, the stubs stark and pale against the dark metal.

'Axel,' said Jox incredulously. 'Is that you?'

From the darkness came a familiar Norwegian accent. 'Bloody hell, Jox!' A bedraggled-looking Axel Fisken stepped into the light. His little round spectacles glittered, but not as brightly as his smile. He looked a little pale and there was blood on his sleeve. The men embraced like long-lost brothers.

'By God, you're a sight for sore eyes,' said Jox. 'Damn it, I was this close to braining you with this thing. Say, are you hurt? What's that?'

'I took some shrapnel in my forearm, I think. Not too bad, but it will scar,' he said matter-of-factly. 'How about you? You're favouring one leg — have you hurt the other one?'

'Banged my ankle on the way out of the kite. Don't think it's broken, but it's bloody sore. How about you?'

'I got hit by groundfire during our second sortie. Just unlucky. Pancaked in a cornfield a few kilometres away and then made my way towards the sound of the guns. For a while I watched the troops trying to land from a spot hidden on the cliffs. Things are not going well, I think. All along the beach they were pinned down with many dead, lots of burning landing craft and tanks too. I saw many prisoners taken.' He gave a strange little smile.

'What is it?'

'Amongst all the carnage on the beach, I could hear bagpipes playing between the firing and explosions. I think you Scots are totally crazy.'

'That'll be the Canadian Scots, but you're not wrong there. "Gets the blood up and the job done," as the Glasgow twins would say.'

'Ant will be frantic with worry that he's lost you.'

'Probably,' said Jox. 'Let's see what we can do about getting back to him. I think we should assume that patrols are out looking for us. I'm pretty sure I heard some dogs on my way here.'

'I think they're using them to catch stragglers. We must be careful. I broke in here hoping to find a vehicle to get past them and down to our troops. What do you think?'

'Sounds reasonable, but first I could really do with some water.'

'I'll find water and you think of a plan. I'll check under the dust sheets to see what we have to play with.'

'You think you can get them started?' asked Jox. 'I don't see any keys.'

'Keys, no keys, I can get anything started,' said Fisken with a glint in his eye. 'My family run a transport company with a fleet of trucks. I've worked with engines all my life. Let's see what we have at our disposal.'

Fisken disappeared into the gloom and Jox checked on his ankle again. It was throbbing now and felt painfully tight in his flight boot. He didn't dare investigate, knowing he would never get the boot back on again. Fisken was moving about in the other rooms, disturbing dust that floated into the workshop. Jox heard the sound of a tap and the Norseman returned, holding a metal dog bowl filled with water. 'Sorry, couldn't find a better cup.'

'Don't worry, I'm parched,' replied Jox. They sat quietly as he drank. 'So, what did you find?'

Fisken brightened. 'Two complete wrecks, but a real beauty too. One is on blocks and of no use, the other has no engine, but our beauty is something to behold.'

'Look, I don't know anything about cars, Axel,' said Jox. 'I've only ever owned one.'

'What we have is a beautiful 1929 Bentley Speed Six tourer,' he replied. 'A car like this won the Le Mans twenty-four hours in 1930. Our Daisy is a real beauty.'

'Daisy?'

'That's her name. It says so in silver lettering on the side of the bonnet.'

Jox laughed. 'Well, that's a good omen. My kites have always been named after little Marguerite. In French that means Daisy. She's surely our ticket out of here.'

'We do have one small problem: her tank is empty.'

'There's a jerry can on the mechanic's bench. Can't you smell the petrol?'

Fisken shook his head. 'Since my capture, I don't smell things so well, because of my broken nose. Can't play the piano either, but I'm still quite good at hunting, so I'll find the fuel.'

'No, I'll get it. You fix the car.' Jox got to his feet and limped to the bench. The jerry can was almost full. He expected fuel consumption in a Bentley Speed Six would probably be appalling, and this wouldn't get them very far, but hopefully it was enough to get them to the harbour.

Fisken pulled back the dust sheet to reveal a beast of a sportscar with large, spoked wheels and a spare tyre on the right-hand running board. It was a deep green, almost black, with chrome fixtures, a large radiator hood and silver letters on the bonnet spelling out 'Daisy'. She was a convertible, with a collapsible canvas canopy on slatted wooden frames and an open cab that was shielded by a flimsy-looking plate glass windshield. Driving the monster wouldn't be so different from handling a Hurricane or Spitfire, thought Jox, especially with the hood down. The ride would doubtless be just as exhilarating.

Jox lugged the fuel can over to Fisken, who was tinkering under the hood. He looked up to indicate where it should go and then strapped an oil can he'd found under the mechanic's bench, onto the left-hand running board. The engine came to life at the first attempt and Fisken beamed.

'Now we can see what the fates hold for us,' he said.

He strode to the green doors of the garage, unlocked them with a key he'd found hanging on a hook, then swung them back. He and Jox climbed into the front seats, pulled down their flight goggles and put on their leather flying helmets. They also put on some sheepskin coats they'd found in the boot. Fisken drove the car out of the garage, heading down the mansion's arching drive.

They looked like simple motoring enthusiasts out for a spin, but then one might well have asked what they were doing driving in the middle of a warzone. With a throaty roar, the engine spun the car's spoked wheels, fishtailing onto the open road.

CHAPTER SEVENTEEN

Speeding down the steep hill towards Dieppe, the Bentley hit a thick bank of smoke with the distinctive stink of cordite high explosives. As it cleared, the scale of destruction it revealed was utterly mind-boggling.

Slowing down to make their way through rubble-filled streets, just a few walls were above shoulder-height. Through the choking brume, they glimpsed shadowy groups of grey-clad troops, but advanced unchecked. It was only once they neared the harbour that the road ahead was blocked by a burning vehicle. It was a Daimler Dingo scout car that had been hit by an anti-tank PAK shell, which had ripped it open like a sardine can. The vehicle's rubber tyres were burning, filling the ruined street with sooty smoke. One of the car's crew was hanging from his hatch, painfully still and with flames licking at his charred uniform. The side of the Dingo had the word 'BEEFY' painted on it, a suitably nauseating description of the smell that was emanating from the carnage.

They could advance no further, so had no choice but to abandon *Daisy* to her fate. They crept forward and took shelter behind a brick wall freshly pockmarked with shrapnel strikes. On the other side of it, angry German voices and dogs barked above the crackle of flames and the occasional gun report. A ragged line of wet men appeared through the smoke, some with their hands in the air, others with mushroom-shaped Canadian helmets on their heads. Several were shoeless, others wore no trousers, and none appeared to be armed. It dawned on Jox that they must have kicked off their equipment when their landing vessels had sunk offshore. These men had swum through the churning surf to get to the beach, reaching the shoreline in no shape to fight.

They limped along in dejected clusters, the stupefied looks on their faces speaking of their shell shock. A few held up exhausted brethren, whilst the worst of the wounded were carried in blankets, unconscious heads lolling. Those that were too far gone were simply abandoned by the roadside.

Their captors could be identified by the weapons they carried, and the two large dogs on long leather leashes. Harsh guttural voices screamed at the prisoners as a stocky German in an oversized greatcoat approached a lad who towered over him and clubbed him between the shoulder blades with the butt of his rifle. The boy's bright blond hair was still wet from his swim for survival. Tears were streaming down his face, tears of fear and shame. As he groaned in pain, the Alsatians began a growling, snapping frenzy.

Fisken roared with fury and rushed past Jox, charging the assailant like a Viking berserker. He launched himself at the boy's attacker, kicking out with his heavy flight boots. At the same time, he swung a wooden-handled screwdriver, partner to the one Jox had found in the garage. His blow connected with the back of the German's helmet with the resounding clang of dense wood striking metal. He struck again at the downed Jerry, twitching on the cobblestones like a dying fish. Cowed prisoners watched unmoved, their fighting spirit leached out by the waters. Not one made any move to escape.

Jox grabbed Fisken. 'Come on, Axel, we don't have time for this! We have to find the harbour!'

Fisken kicked the unconscious man a final time, then followed Jox down a dank alleyway smelling of old fish. There was the sharp crack of rifle shot and the screwdriver was snatched from Fisken's hands. Another shot toppled the blond-haired lad, red gore spreading across his chest. He fell beside his assailant, their spilt blood merging on the cobbles. More shots rang out as angry German voices shouted, followed by the sound of running jackboots. Several Germans appeared out of the smoke, led by an officer wearing a peaked cap. The dogs were released and began tearing at the cowering prisoners, many falling to their knees, desperate to make their surrender more obvious. In others, a spark was ignited, and they made a break for it. The officer raised his pistol and fired at a pair of bedraggled soldiers who limped in pursuit of Jox and Fisken.

'Don't leave us, lads,' boomed the burlier of the two, in an accent that Jox recognised as that of an East Neuk Fifer. He wore a commando's woolly helmet-liner, and a brown leather jerkin with red Royal Marine shoulder tabs and a corporal's stripes. He was limping from a wound to the thigh, a crimson patch seeping through dark khaki. His face was determined, hook-nosed and rugged, and he moved surprisingly quickly, considering the wound. Beside him, he supported a younger companion, who had his eyes bandaged, and a wounded arm strapped to his webbing. He played no part in the decision to run; he was simply being propelled along in the tight grip of his burly companion.

Their faces were grimy, streaked with burnt cork, sweat and the pallor of exhaustion. The lad's battle dress was too big, with CANADA written on his shoulders, and he wore a netted Tommy's helmet on his head. Calling out, he pleaded to be told what was happening in heavily accented English. Jox thought he must be French-Canadian.

As they reached the quayside, the four men dashed into the bombed-out ruins of a fishmonger's shop. Squatting on the shiny, blue-tiled floor, they caught their breath before peering anxiously through the shattered front window to see if they'd been followed. The harbour was deserted; their pursuers' attention focused on rounding up the other prisoners.

The port anchorage was protected by long concrete moles of the quays, enclosing a mooring for several small fishing boats. Feeding into it was the inner channel, the lower reaches of the river Arques, which had been dredged out and widened to allow large vessels like the Newhaven ferry to manoeuvre into the ports. Beyond the moles, choppy waves were visible and to the left was the gravel beach. The entire sweep of the bay and the beach was under towering cliffs, divided by concrete breakwaters that reached into the waves. The beach was bordered by a high seawall, designed to protect the shoreline from the worst of the Atlantic breakers and tidal surges.

Savage signs of battle were everywhere on the beach, but Jox was struck by how very static the tableau seemed to be. Out to sea there was movement, but apart from the waves, the beach was deathly still. Fallen men and dismembered limbs were gathered in soggy clumps at the high-water mark, tangled with discarded nets, lost equipment, seaweed and the flotsam of battle on the open sea. Bodies seemed to have concentrated at the foot of the seawall, perhaps caught there in the murderous crossfire between the pillboxes built into the villas at either end of the shingle.

Leached-out body parts rolled in the surf, alongside countless sprats culled by underwater explosions. Further out to sea, the bay's rocky bottom was carpeted with many bodies, shifting in the current like legions of mermen.

Up the incline of the beach, the egg-sized stones had clogged the tracks of several stricken Churchill tanks. They were scarab beetles crushed by a giant's feet, the perfect target for PAK gunners on the bluffs. Practically none of the armour had made it off the beach. Miscellaneous other broken vehicles and abandoned landing craft were ringed with the twisted corpses of those who'd vainly sought to find cover behind them. Even within the harbour, a lonely body floated face-down, rocking in the current, the maple-leaf red of a CANADA shoulder patch winking from below the water's surface.

'So, what's the plan, boys?' demanded the burly marine. 'I'm Corporal Billy Robertson, by the way, and this laddie here is Louis from Quebec.'

At the mention of his name, the blind boy reacted. '*Louis Philippe Grenier des Fusiliers de Mont-Royal*,' he said with evident pride.

Jox shook their hands. 'Looks like you've been through the grinder,' he said. 'But strewth, haven't we all? I'm Jox McNabb and this is Axel Fisken. We're both from No. 111 Squadron, Spitfire pilots. Tell you what, stick with us and we'll all try to make it out of here. The plan is to swim to one of those fishing sloops moored out there. Axel here is a genius at getting any engine started. In the confusion, we should be able to sneak out of port unnoticed and hopefully we can catch up with the Royal Navy before it heads back to Blighty. Sound like a plan? We'll need to hurry, though; from the stillness of the beach, it looks like everyone's pulling out already. The place will be crawling with Jerries soon, and I don't fancy getting caught up in the net.'

'You want us to swim?' said Billy. 'I don't really think Louis or me are in any shape to be swimming.' He placed a meaty hand on his own sodden lap and winced.

'I can see you're both wounded, but just one last effort and we'll be in the clear. We're both hurt too — it's just something that's got to be done.'

'Aye, but my leg's bad. Louis can't see a thing and has a busted wing too. I'm sorry, fellas. I think we'd better take our chances down on the beach.'

'Wait, Jox,' said Fisken. 'Why don't you and me swim out? We can get the boat and come back for the boys. It shouldn't take long.'

Jox considered it and agreed.

'Aye, we'd sure appreciate that,' said Billy. 'A right fine thing for two RAF officers.'

'Oh, come on — we're all on the same side,' said Jox.

He and Fisken stripped to their underclothes and left their heavy outerwear — including the sheepskin coats — with Billy and Louis. The pair would wait in the shop until they returned. Jox kept his flight tunic on, quickly checking that the doll's arm and his Maltese switchblade were still in the buttoned-down pockets.

He slipped into the briny water and was surprised it wasn't as cold as he'd expected. If anything, the chill was soothing on his throbbing ankle. Swimming out to the moored vessels didn't take long and they checked three different craft in quick succession, before Fisken was confident that he'd found one he could get going. The biggest challenge proved to be actually getting aboard the craft from the water. It took a while to work out that the best way was for Jox to haul himself up with the aid of his knife, which he stabbed into the wooden hull to provide a foothold. This allowed him to climb up the mooring chain by pulling himself up with his arms. Once aboard, he found a rope, looped it down to Fisken and hauled the larger man up. Despite claiming it was only a scratch, it was clear the Norseman's wounded forearm was painful and there was only so much he could do with it.

After a good deal of cursing and some noisy clattering from below, the sloop's engine coughed to life with a black plume of smoke and the stink of diesel exhaust. Jox felt a twinge of seasickness as he pulled up the anchor, before Fisken swung the vessel at a steady speed around the harbour, keeping the lowest possible revs to stay quiet and discreet as he pulled up to the quayside. It was mid-afternoon, and the slanting sunlight was still wreathed by the smoke of the fires burning across the shattered town.

As they slowed, the harbour water around them suddenly erupted in violent splashes and thrashing foam. Several rounds thumped into the wooden slats of the decking and wheelhouse. They'd been spotted by a gun position high up in a large white villa overlooking the harbour. With the characteristic ripping sound of a fast-firing MG34 machine gun, a vicious weight of fire spat towards them. Ricochets whined off the concrete of the quayside as the deck was punctured by several rounds. From the doorway of the fish shop, Billy waved them off, before ducking back into its shelter.

On the fishing sloop, Fisken spun the ship's wheel and gunned the engine to a maximum. It was old but dependable, and they'd soon built up their speed, allowing the pair to pull out of range and slip from the sheltered harbour onto the bouncing sea. They lingered for a moment at the entrance but realised there was no way back without attracting further fire. A lorry had pulled up on the quay and there were soldiers swarming like ants all over it. Whether Billy and Louis would make it off the beach, Jox would never know, but in the meantime, they were making good progress towards the receding flotilla. It suddenly occurred to Jox that they had no idea where the safe channels through Dieppe's defensive minefields might be. Hurtling along, they ran the risk of explosive contact at any moment.

'Slow down, Axel. We're out of range!' shouted Jox over the din of the struggling engine. Some of the incoming rounds must have hit something important. 'We're in more danger from mines or trigger-happy Royal Navy gunners than the Jerries, so slow down!'

Fisken powered down to a more considered pace, and the sound of the flotilla firing at enemy aircraft and quite possibly their own defensive fighter screen could be heard. An old fishing boat like theirs was no threat to the Navy ships, but Jox still felt anxious as they steered towards them. He searched desperately through the deck lockers for any way of sending up a signal. He found a tarnished old flare gun with two stubby cartridges, salt-encrusted and looking like they'd seen better days. With no alternative, he took the chance that the flares might still work rather than explode in his face. Jox loaded nervously, turned his face away, raised his arm and fired.

The brilliant trace of the red flare rose brightly across the darkening sky. Jox reloaded and repeated the operation, feeling the warmth of the flare as it climbed. It was getting chilly in their sodden underclothes, so they put on the fishy oilskins from the deck lockers.

They'd been spotted and a light-grey motor launch bristling with double-barrelled machine guns circled aggressively. Through a loudhailer, a high-pitched voice spoke terribly accented French, giving them stern instructions to steer away. Fisken slowed the battered sloop and waved amicably, as Jox cupped his hands and shouted at the top of his voice, 'We're British RAF officers! We were shot down and managed to evade capture. Stand down, stand down! We're British officers.' The crewmen manning the launch's intimidating weaponry appeared to relax, but kept their weaponry trained upon them.

'Turn your engine off,' instructed someone with a West Country accent. 'Prepare to be boarded. Keep your hands visible at all times. How many of you are onboard?'

'Just the two of us,' replied Jox.

'Identify yourself.'

'Flight Lieutenant Jeremy McNabb, and this is Flying Officer Axel Fisken from Norway. We're Spitfire pilots from No. 111 Squadron, based at RAF Kenley.'

Fisken removed the yellow sou'wester from his head and waved it enthusiastically.

'Why doesn't he speak?' asked the voice. 'Looks like a Jerry to me. Keep your hands up.'

The launch's skipper, standing beside the speaker, focused his binoculars on the pair. He spoke to his bosun on the loudhailer, who asked, 'Why are you out of uniform?'

'We had to swim for it. Didn't get a chance to go back to collect our clothing. A Jerry Spandau on the bluffs spotted us and almost shot us to pieces. We had to scarper to save our tails. I'm afraid we had to leave two poor chaps behind — a pair of wounded pongos, who'd already been through a lot. I just hope they make it off the beach.'

'There are rescue launches picking up stragglers, so they might have a chance,' said the sailor. 'Prepare to catch a line. Two of my crewmen will come aboard and we'll take you in tow. We're heading back to Blighty, so we'll be home soon enough. It's been a hell of a day, and you should count yourselves lucky. Our orders were to blow you out of the water.'

CHAPTER EIGHTEEN

The return to England was long, cold and very bumpy. Jox was thoroughly seasick by the time they'd transferred to the destroyer HMS *Albrighton*, and it began making its way back to Newhaven in East Sussex where many of the Canadians onboard were stationed.

The pair of them were provided with Royal Navy roll-neck jumpers, bell-bottomed rating's trousers and rough blankets to warm up, helped along by a fiery tot of Pusser's Navy rum. Having been classified as lightly wounded, they remained on the crowded deck of the destroyer with a jumble of survivors taken off the beaches. Jox's ankle had been given a perfunctory examination by a harassed medic and had then been bound tight. Fisken's shirtsleeve was cut off and after some painful probing with long-nosed forceps, his arm was bandaged and immobilised in an impressive sling.

The journey home reminded Jox of his return in similar circumstances from Dunkirk at the beginning of the war. This time, though, the men around him seemed much angrier and were desperate to find someone to blame. Even so, Operation Jubilee was being talked of as a success by senior officers onboard, despite the evidence to the contrary.

Jox and Fisken paid little attention to the grumbling around them. They both dozed in spite of the ship's incessant vibrations and the stomach-churning surge of the waves as she steamed homewards. Survivors and the walking wounded huddled where they could, to shelter from the stiff sea breeze.

A ginger-haired lieutenant from the Essex Scottish, his arm and shoulder in a bloodied bandage, growled, 'I tell you, they damned well knew we were coming. Those guns waited for the first wave to hit the beach.'

'Calm yourself, Lieutenant Kilpatrick,' reprimanded his superior, a rotund major with a haggard face in the same grimy uniform. His legs were strapped together in a makeshift splint, and he was pale from blood loss. 'We have no way of knowing that. Perhaps we just attacked at the wrong time. Dawn was bound to be when the enemy would "stand-to" — no different to what we did in the last war. A break in the weather and favourable tides probably told them we were likely to be coming.'

'What?' said the hot-tempered lieutenant. 'You're saying we never stood a chance of catching them by surprise?'

A sergeant-major of the Fusiliers de Mont-Royal interrupted the bickering pair. 'My apologies, *mon Commandant*, but I believe you may be wrong. We captured some of the enemy on Red Beach and they boasted they'd been brought in especially for the raid and had been waiting for a week. The lieutenant is correct, I think. They were obviously warned.'

'How else would they have had such accurate mortar fire? The firing zones were clearly already set,' said Lieutenant Kilpatrick. 'Most of my casualties were hit by those damned mortars landing on those blasted pebbles, which sent stone fragments into everyone.'

A grimy, bare-headed tank crewman, with corporal's stripes and a face streaked with soot, added, 'When we came ashore, the artillery was very accurate. We got stuck on the stones and were hit almost immediately. The Churchill caught fire, so I baled out and hid under the tank until things quietened down. That's when I noticed a wooden stake painted yellow, hammered into the ground beneath our tracks. I then spotted several others as I made my way down the beach. The whole area was pegged out into fire zones, so they certainly took their time to prepare for our arrival. We didn't stand a chance.'

'I agree,' said another second lieutenant, again from the Fusiliers de Mont-Royal. 'I was leading my platoon into the town over the esplanade. We took shelter from heavy fire in a fisherman's house. Inside, we found two terrified old ladies. Their husbands had been taken away by the Germans for work parties. They were kind and gave us water and some food. They said the Germans have been preparing for weeks.'

When they finally docked at Newhaven, Jox and Fisken ran into some trouble upon disembarkation, trying to convince the Canadian military policemen of their identities, given the mismatched nature of what they were wearing. Thankfully, the sodden RAF wings on their tunics did the trick and they were shown to a reception area reserved for downed RAF personnel, who had returned from Dieppe without their aircraft. Most had been picked up from the sea, having managed to stay afloat in their dinghies or thanks to their Mae Wests for long enough to be rescued by R-boats.

Amongst the fed-up and exhausted airmen in the cramped room, they found the familiar face of Squadron Leader Chesley Peterson, the youthful but rather pale-faced CO of No. 71 (Eagle) Squadron. They knew each other from Debden, so waiting for transport, the pair exchanged war stories about their travails over Dieppe. Jox told him about his French adventure with Fisken, then settled in to hear about his.

'My guys were assigned the job of going after bombers attacking the ships in the bay,' said Peterson. 'I got close to a Ju 88 and clobbered him pretty hard, right across the starboard wing and setting that engine smoking. My curiosity made me follow him, dumbly watching his rear gunner fire at me the whole while. The guy must have known they were going down but stayed at his post. Bravest damned thing I've ever seen.' He smiled apologetically. 'He got me good too — set fire to my engine. I was struggling to get my canopy open, the flames already licking at my feet.' He looked down at his charred boots. 'I managed to climb out and jumped quite high. It took me about ten minutes to float down onto the sea. Time enough to see my Spit hit the water with a great splash, then the bomber with an even bigger one. It suddenly struck me that I had my brand-new revolver tucked in my flying boot. I'd only just got it and hadn't even fired it once. Well, I was damned if I was going to lose it without even firing it, so I emptied the chamber into the sea. Once it was empty, I let it drop and watched the grey waters of the Channel swallow it up. Just a few moments later, I hit the water too.' He rubbed his hands, trying to coax some heat back into them. 'I guess I was lucky, because an R-boat came along pretty quick and got me. But when we were heading back, we got attacked by a lone fighter. He tore up the boat and the guy beside me, who'd been picked up just before me, was killed outright. He was a Canadian fellow called Morty Buckley. It was a shame — he was a real nice guy. His body lay beside me under a blanket the whole way back. I spent the rest of the trip staring at his shoeless feet and watching the red stain spreading through that blanket. I don't think I'll ever forget that.'

The airmen were collected by a lorry and taken to the nearest airfield, where transfer flights were arranged to shuttle aircrew back to their home bases. The flight to Kenley was in a new C-47 Dakota transport laid on by the USAAF. Peterson was dropped off at RAF Gravesend, No. 71 Squadron's temporary station for the Dieppe operation, before they flew on. Once finally back on home ground, they made their way stiffly back to the squadron dispersal for a debrief and the thankless task of writing up after-action reports. They were greeted with noisy relief but great hilarity since they were still dressed like a cross between Naval ratings and Norman fishermen, and doubtless smelling like the latter too.

As they were talking through their adventures with Ridgway, Ant Glasgow came barrelling into the hut looking agitated. Spotting Jox, he cried, 'Och, thank God!' and gathered him up in a tight embrace, not caring about his pungent clothing. In his wake came Pritchard and de Ghellinck, evident relief etched across their faces.

'I'm so sorry I lost you,' said Ant. 'The sky was swarming, but we should have stuck with you. Jox, I let you down.'

'Please accept my sincere apologies as well,' added Jox's other wingman, a very sombre-looking de Ghellinck.

'What on earth are you two talking about?' said Jox. 'We all had our hands full — there is no blame. It was just my turn to be unlucky. Actually, once I was on the ground, my luck changed and I hooked up with Axel. He was also hit by ack-ack fire — though he was downed by the enemy, whereas I was struck by our own Navy. To be fair, though, I did go through their screen of fire to shake off a particularly nasty FW 190 who was stuck on my tail. He was bloody good and had me banged to rights. If the Navy gunners hadn't bagged him, I'd be toast. They winged me too — accurate fellows, but they do need to work on aircraft recognition. By the way, you can put that in your report, Tim.'

Ridgway replied, 'I can put it in, but I don't suppose the Admiralty will be listening, especially given the scale of the cock-up that Jubilee is turning out to be.'

'How bad is it?' asked Jox.

'I suppose you'd say the squadron's escaped lightly. We've lost Teddy Gallon and one of the new sergeants, Edward Hindley. Teddy brolly-hopped over the sea, but there's no sign of Hindley. Sergeant Tyrell was also shot down by ack-ack fire but was thankfully picked up by sea rescue and returned via Dover, strafed along the way for good measure.'

'There was a fair bit of that going on,' said Jox. 'We bumped into Chesley Peterson of No. 71; he got shot up too.'

Ridgway cleared his throat, not happy being the one delivering bad news. 'Sergeant Hindley went down on the third sortie, flying as wingman to the CO.'

'How did Pete Wickham get on?'

'I believe he's all right,' said Ridgway. 'Been very busy, actually. He flew a total of five sorties, a few with us and then more with the Yanks. It's probably some kind of record. I've had a call and he's safely down at Redhill.' The intelligence officer leafed through the pages of his notepad. 'On the plus side, we've got claims in for three Dornier 217s and three FW 190s, including the one shared between you, Ant and Ghillie, plus the one you claimed when flying with the Yanks.'

'How did the Eagles of No. 133 get on? I'm afraid I didn't do a great job leading them, getting myself shot down like that,' Jox said.

'Don Blakeslee did rather well, with claims in for a FW 190 and a Dornier 217,' replied Ridgway. 'With his previous victories, that now gets him to ace status. I understand the American press plan to make a big splash, since about forty US Army Rangers took part in the operation. Apparently, a young lieutenant called Edward Loustalot is the first American killed in combat on the European mainland and the papers are going to make him a hero. I don't suppose it'll make much of a difference to him.' Ridgway checked his notepad. 'Actually, I see No. 133 have done rather well, if their claims are to be believed: seven FW 190s and six Dornier 217s, with no losses at all. That's a remarkable turn of fortune, but maybe their claims are not as stringently checked as Wing Commander Bullough demands. In any case, they've been well and truly blooded.'

Jox laughed. 'Yes, I can certainly remember Sandy making himself unpopular during the Battle of Britain regarding evidence for valid claims. How about our Belgian friends? How did Ambiorix's lads fare?'

'Even better than the Yanks,' said Ridgway. 'Over four sorties, they clocked up ten FW 190s and one Ju 88. Flight Lieutenant Boussa was wounded but bagged a Focke-Wulf, as did Flight Lieutenant du Monceau de Bergendal. Casualty wise, they've had two wounded and one missing in action — Pilot Officer Marchal. By my reckoning, they've got off lightly too.'

'Certainly more lightly than the pongos on the beaches. I can tell you, it was a massacre down there, wasn't it, Axel?' said Jox.

Fisken nodded, and no one had any doubt there would be more grim statistics to come.

By the time Jox got back to the accommodation block, he was desperate for his bed. He found two letters waiting in his locker. One was a white card announcing that the wedding of Maurice Grant and Stephanie Clarke had been rescheduled for Saturday 22nd August at St Luke's Church, Whyteleafe. Jox had checked earlier and heard the No. 401 Squadron Canucks had bagged an impressive eight victories during the day, but more importantly Moose was still in one piece for his bride.

The other was a tattered envelope, covered in inky stamps, indicating that it had taken a circuitous route to reach him. He recognised the handwriting, turning it over in his hands and savouring the moment before opening it. His weariness had evaporated.

The Officers' Mess, Hotel Point de Vue,
5 Piazza Sakkaja 5, Rabat, Malta
August 1942

My darling Jox,

It's been so long since I've heard from you. I miss you terribly.

We've had such an awful time of it on the island lately. Things got better, then got worse. Only the thought of you keeps me from despairing. Food and supplies are so very short, and the people's will to keep fighting is eroding. You know how we Maltese love our bread, but with no flour and so little wood left, even baking this staple of our life is becoming impossible. Perhaps the Germans have finally figured out that lack of bread, not fuel or ammunition, is how they can defeat us. They harass anything that moves. Farmers like my grandfather dare not care for their crops or livestock out in the open, but to be honest there are so few animals. Most have been eaten long ago and there's so little to feed those that remain. The fishermen don't set out to sea either, as the Messerschmitts machine gun even the smallest of fishing boats. We are stranded in pitiless war and it truly breaks my heart.

Your friend Cameron sometimes comes to visit with Cocky Cochrane. He says what we are enduring here makes the Battle of Britain seem like child's play. Malta has become hell's playground. Cocky has been very kind. He visits often and is like a big brother for Elias. He's so sweet to the family, bringing food when he can. We are fortunate that you have such a fine friend. Between what little we manage to grow, the scraps I get from work at the hotel and the community 'soup' from the Victory Kitchens, we manage, but you'd be horrified at how skinny I've become. It's only the little treats from Cocky that keep us going.

Cameron is good to us also. Behind his angry face and that accent I find so difficult to understand, I know there is a good heart. He never says so, but I know he misses you. Sometimes I see him with that strange Canadian one, Screwball Beurling, at the officers' mess. One minute that Screwball is talkative, the next he just sits and glares. I suppose the war affects people in different ways. He has become quite famous on the island, with many victories. The Times of Malta have taken to calling him the Knight of Malta. They say he's shot down twenty-seven enemy aircraft in just fourteen days. But he is a strange one, not at all big-headed and very shy and reserved. Screwball and Cocky have become quite good friends, I think, but will often just sit together saying nothing. What a strange life we are living.

Cameron says he will arrange for this letter to get to you. He told me to write whatever's on my mind and not to worry about the censor. He has a friend returning to England who will post it there. I think he said you know him too, Sally Salvesen, but maybe I've got that wrong. Sally is a girl's name, no? He was wounded, but Cameron says his life is not threatened.

The big news is that an important convoy made it to Valletta's Grand Harbour, arriving on the feast day of Santa Maria. It had a really terrible time getting here but limped into port after being attacked all the way. Cameron told me to tell you that HMS Eagle, the carrier you flew from to get to Malta, was part of the convoy but was sunk by a U-boat. He says over a hundred sailors and sixteen Spitfires were lost but thank God almost a thousand were rescued from the water before she sank. Such a terrible price to pay to get food and fuel to our poor, suffering island.

Elias and I went down to Grand Harbour to see the convoy come in. The biggest ship was a tanker called Ohio and was terribly damaged, its decks awash with water. It was held up by tugboats strapped on either side and was towed in by a destroyer. The walls and quays of the port were lined with islanders, waving and cheering at this miracle of Santa Maria. I will not forget the sight of so many Maltese mothers and grandmothers crossing themselves over and over to thank our holy mother for this deliverance, which I know the sailors are calling Operation Pedestal. I pray the supplies are distributed quickly, because I don't know how long our people can hold out. Our backs are against the wall, and we must find the courage to keep going.

Malta is proud to have been awarded the George Cross and we realise it is a great honour, but we cannot eat honour. It is good to know the king is thinking about what we are enduring and that we are not alone.

Cocky, Cameron and the others who were with you at Marsaxlokk Harbour have all received their medals. I expect you've had yours in England. Cocky explained that you have already been awarded the George Cross by the king. I had no idea, but now I realise what an honour it represents, I am in awe, and that you should be my man is more than I could dream of and is what keeps me going. Thank you for being my rock.

I'd better sign off now, before I get upset. I am praying for the moment we can be together. I find myself praying a lot these days.

Your Julianna

CHAPTER NINETEEN

It was the stench that hit him first. A powerful combination of urine and corruption made Jox gag, forcing him to breathe through his mouth.

Mike Longstaffe's bed was in the far corner of the paraplegic ward. He shared it with seven other broken men, strapped in their beds, either on their backs or face down. They were flipped over at two-hourly intervals to avoid pressure sores, but it was already too late for many. Hanging from each bed was a length of brick-orange rubber hose snaking from the covers and dripping urine into gallon jars on the floor.

Longstaffe was on his front, his face pointing to the ground through an oval hole cut into the mattress. The back of his hospital robe was open to the air, the bed sores on his shoulders and buttocks plainly visible, red, angry and weeping with the blue-black edges of necrosis. This was the source of the smell, and the men in the ward all appeared similarly affected.

Sitting beside Longstaffe's cot, Jox felt ashamed of his discomfort when faced with such evident misery. He was trying to distract his friend, and indeed himself, by reading out loud from the newspaper. His ankle, now encased in plaster, was propped up on a second chair. The medical officer had told him he'd cracked the bone when tumbling from his aircraft over Dieppe.

'The Reds have launched a major offensive to recapture the city of Stalingrad on the banks of the Volga,' said Jox. 'I quote: *Even Leningrad and Moscow are not as important as Stalingrad. Leningrad was the stronghold of the Russian Revolution and is still a great port and arsenal. Moscow is the nerve-centre of the colossal Russian Empire, and there can never be an adequate substitute, but both cities might have fallen without irreparable injury to the fighting strength of the Russian armed forces. Both were in great danger last year. Stalingrad is in even greater danger now. The Russians even admit the danger. They have been grimly honest in their recent comment that Stalingrad is the key to the war.'*

'What paper is that?' asked Longstaffe.

Jox checked the masthead. '*The Gloucester Citizen* of the twenty-ninth of April 1942, but they're quoting from *The Daily Telegraph*. I found it on a train seat on the way up here.'

'Does it say anything about Jubilee?'

'Not much. I'm sure there's a hush-hush job going on, especially as it was such a mess.' Jox flicked through the pages. 'Wait a second, here's something in the foreign news section, quoting an article from the Spanish papers. The headline says: *Rundstedt at Dieppe — Von Rundstedt, German C-in-C in Western Europe made a minute inspection in the last forty-eight hours of the shore defences at Dieppe penetrated in last week's British raid. Patrols all along the coast are likely to be tightened up.* Well, it doesn't sound like we achieved all that much, considering the carnage on the beaches.'

'Especially if the stated objective of the raid was to divert Jerry's attention from the Russian front and give them a bloody nose in a quick "smash and grab" operation,' Longstaffe agreed. 'I'd say we failed on both counts.'

'I've been meaning to ask,' said Jox gingerly. 'How are you bearing up? I've got to be honest, Mike; it doesn't look too good.'

'Doesn't smell too good either,' replied Longstaffe. 'Listen, I know I stink. It's my back that's broken, not my nose.'

'So, what are the doctors saying? What's the long-term prognosis?'

'Not great, to be honest. I can't feel anything below the middle of my back. Officially, I have what's known as a thoracic spinal injury at the eighth vertebra at mid-back level. I'm told it could be worse — at least I can breathe unaided and use my hands, although they often have pins and needles. Can't feel anything below my stomach, so you can imagine what that implies. The first few weeks were truly horrendous. Would you believe they transferred me here to Stoke Mandeville in a coffin-shaped box filled with sand? Apparently, it was there to catch any loose liquids. I woke up pretty much naked in a coffin and unable to move — the fear was bad enough, but the indignity made it my worst possible nightmare.'

'Sounds horrific. I'm so sorry, my friend. You really don't deserve that.'

'Well, things have improved a little since, especially since Poppa took over, but it's still grim. It's the hopelessness that gets me. You know, nothing ever seems to get better, and I do get myself into the most dreadful dark funks.'

'I can see why. Who is Poppa?' asked Jox.

'He's a German Jewish professor who escaped the Nazis and is now in charge of the National Spinal Injuries Centre at this hospital. His name is Professor Sir Ludwig Guttmann, but we call him Poppa. He's a no-nonsense sort of chap and tells us things straight. The first thing Poppa did was establish that the principal cause of death amongst those with spinal injuries is urinary infections and sepsis from infected bed sores. That's why we're getting turned every couple of hours and plugged into these charming piss bottles under the bed. It's exhausting, but at least we're doing something to improve things.'

'I see,' said Jox, depressed by the bleakness being described.

'The worst thing is the relentless indignity. The nurses are very kind and clean us up, but I can't feel a damned thing and don't even know if I've soiled myself. It's excruciatingly embarrassing. All I notice is the stink, and that could be from any of the boys in here. This is no way of living and to be honest, Jox, I wish I'd never made it back. Better to go with a glorious bang, snuffed out, rather than this lingering death.'

Jox was silent. He didn't feel equipped to provide words of comfort. What did he know about such terrible things?

'The only thing that brings us any comfort is the care from the nurses,' Longstaffe went on. 'There's one here from your neck of the woods — her name is Sally and she's very sweet. She reads me poetry sometimes, but not for too long as my attention tends to wander. Hearing her soft Scottish voice is like a soothing balm to me. When she hasn't the time to read to me, she'll prop a book up for me and come by regularly to turn the page. I struggle to turn the pages myself, especially when face down like this. Sally's my angel.'

'She sounds wonderful. Can I meet her? Is she around?'

'No, off duty, I think. But she'll be back — thank God. She's the only bright part of my day. Except for you lot coming, of course.'

The wedding of Maurice Grant and Stephanie Clarke took place on Saturday 22nd August at St Luke's Church, Whyteleafe, near Kenley aerodrome.

The small Victorian redbrick church was built in a wooded glade. Inside, the pews were crowded and most of the congregation wore RAF uniforms, some still bandaged and plastered from recent action and injuries. The bride's family were present, but there was no one from the groom's side.

Moose's younger brother, Willie, was missing in action on the shingle of Dieppe. His service family were there in force, though, with Jox, Pritchard, Chalmers, Ant and Badger all present and correct from the Treble Ones alone. There were also his comrades of No. 401 Squadron RCAF, the Kenley Wing CO, Brian Kingcome, and a number of the Biggin Hill Red House set. Pete Wickham was present with Sheila Macneal on his arm, her twin Moira winking lasciviously at Jox as he walked past on his best man duties. The groom progressed down the flagstones of the central aisle, his gait uneven, but no one was laughing. Everyone knew it was the legacy of injuries suffered in the defence of this country.

Everywhere Jox looked, he felt as if ghosts were watching. It was strangely comforting to have them be a part of this happy occasion, despite the bitterest of circumstances. The ceremony was quick: Moose fluffed his words, and Stephanie looked beautiful in her parachute silk dress and shed some happy tears. Jox was fretting about his best man's speech and after the ceremony, the wedding party threw homemade newspaper confetti. The hole-punchers from Stephanie's office had worked overtime, since rice was far too precious to waste. After the ceremony, the bridal bouquet was placed on the grave of Charlie Cox, a Canadian armourer who'd served with Moose. Pritchard placed a single rose on the grave of Violet Effingham, a kind-hearted WAAF whom he'd been fond of. Jox laid a second rose beside it for Alice, since she had no known resting place.

The wedding reception was held in an army surplus tent, doubling as a marquee. It was pitched in a meadow behind the church; it would have been an idyllic scene if it wasn't for snarling aircraft passing overhead from the aerodrome. Moose had the party in stitches with his speech and in a break with tradition, the new Mrs Stephanie Grant did too. It was the bride's father who provided the highlight, however; since he was a brewery owner, there was no shortage of beer.

Jox had spoken with his contacts in the American squadrons, and they'd agreed to help out with the catering. After mumbling his way through his own speech, he noticed that Don Blakeslee and Darren Beans of No. 133 Squadron were both present and raised a glass. He crossed over to them and was greeted by a grinning Beans. 'Good job you're a better pilot than you are a public speaker, Jox. You very nearly killed the buzz for the whole party.'

'Hello, boys,' laughed Jox. 'Glad to see you're still in one piece. Sorry, the last time I was with you, I left rather abruptly. Got shot up by our own dear Royal Navy. Riddled a perfectly good Spit, so I had to make my way home after a refreshing dip in the Channel. How did you get on? Rather well, I understand, Don.'

'Not too bad, thanks, Jox. Finally seem to have got my eye in and managed to hit something,' said Blakeslee. 'Got me a Dornier and a probable FW 190, damaging a couple more, so I can't complain. My boys have done good too.'

'So I'd heard. Our spy was singing your praises, but more importantly, you all came back in one piece. Not everyone was so fortunate. I'm told one of the Hurribomber squadrons lost eleven out of seventeen pilots — that's a hell of a rate of attrition.'

'That's terrible.'

'How about you, Darren? How d'you get on?'

'Can't complain, Jox. Got me a piece of Dornier 217 like Don and a couple damaged Shrikes. My kite did get chewed up.'

'As I recall, that's rather a speciality of yours.'

Beans grinned. 'Well, if you're not flying by the seat of your pants, you ain't doing it right. Now then, never mind all this shop talk — this here's a party. Where's my boy, Pritch? He's usually where the action's at. In the meantime, can y'all advise me which of these delectable young ladies is worthy of my attention? More specifically, who is likely to reciprocate my affections?'

This was an opportunity to hit two birds with one stone, thought Jox. He searched the crowd and spotted Moira Macneal eyeing him like a cat watching a mouse. He discreetly pointed her out to Beans, who smiled appreciatively and set forth, saying, 'Born on the bayou!'

Blakeslee sighed. 'Well, I guess it takes all kinds to win a war.'

'So what have you been hearing about the Dieppe op from your side?' asked Jox. 'Things are being kept pretty hush-hush at our end.'

'There's some talk about how bad the numbers are. Some are saying that what happened is a lesson on how not to run a war. I'm not one for gossip, but I'm told very few of the troops on the ground actually made it off the beaches. In eight hours of fighting, something like six thousand men went in and over thirty-five hundred are reported killed, wounded or missing, presumed captured. That's over half, Jox. Apparently, we lost more than a hundred aircraft, and the Royal Navy sustained over five hundred casualties. So, however you cut it, it doesn't look good, and the poor Canucks bore the brunt of it.'

'I suspect their eagerness to get stuck in will be reined in the next time,' said Jox. 'Moose's younger brother, Willie, is missing in action. He went in on White Beach, just in front of the casino, with the Royal Hamilton Light Infantry. He landed west of the esplanade, straight into the heavy street-fighting. I'm told they did manage to secure the casino, their objective

— they were one of the few units to achieve that. I was on the ground there for a while, but I couldn't identify any particular unit. Nearly five hundred RHLI went in and only about two hundred came out, with over half wounded.'

'My God, that's awful,' said Blakeslee.

'That's bad, but on Blue Beach, out of an entire battalion of the Royal Regiment of Canada, only six men made it back. That's a complete massacre. Moose is desperately hoping that Willie is a prisoner. Maybe he's grasping at straws, but miracles can happen. You know Ant Glasgow made it back from being a POW.'

'Wow, but that's a hell of thing to wish for,' replied Blakeslee. 'Especially on your wedding day.'

CHAPTER TWENTY

The windows of the spinal injuries ward were flung wide open, and a cool summer breeze blew away the oppressive air hanging about the patients. Music was playing somewhere and there was the buzz of quiet conversation and even laughter.

Mike Longstaffe was sitting up in bed, looking a good deal happier than the last time Jox had visited. Jox was limping, his foot still in plaster, and Axel Fisken had his arm in a cast and sling. They made such a sorry sight that Longstaffe burst out laughing. Never usually the jolliest of chaps, it took them both by surprise. Morgan Chalmers, Longstaffe's flight leader, was also with them, and was delighted to see him in such good form.

'You're certainly in better spirits than the last time I was here,' said Jox. 'What a tonic it is to see that.'

Longstaffe smiled. 'Thanks, I am feeling a lot more optimistic. Poppa Guttmann has been making changes around here and everyone is seeing the benefit.' He waved his hand, indicating the ward. 'It may not seem like much, but it's a world of difference for us. With these windows open, the sunshine pouring in and the wireless playing some jolly tunes, we feel almost alive again. If I decide I want to smoke, that's up to me, and in the evening, Poppa comes around with a bottle of malt whisky and offers us a nightcap. You've no idea how much little kindnesses like that help to raise the patients' morale.' He grinned unexpectedly. 'Would you believe that the other day we even had a troop of those Windmill Theatre ladies come up from London to see us? They posed in their saucy tableaux, leaving very little to the imagination. It's all perfectly legal apparently, as long as they don't budge an inch. It did strike me as rather bittersweet for a static bunch of fellows like us, but the ladies were awfully kind and really quite stunning. We've had all sorts of actors and starlets coming to see us.'

'Yes, we had them visit at Babbacombe too when I had my spell there. Can't say we ever got any nudie women coming to visit, mind. It's marvellous to see you so chipper, Mike,' said Jox.

'It will be a long road for you, my friend, but you are a strong man, Mike Longstaffe,' added Fisken.

'The truth of it is, I've come to accept what I can no longer do, but I also realise there's still an awful lot I *can* do and learn,' said Longstaffe. 'Poppa has been marvellous, but this new optimism is really down to Sally. She's taken me under her wing. You remember, Jox — she's one of the nurses here. I told you about her the last time you came.'

'We must meet this remarkable woman.'

'You're in luck. Here she comes,' Longstaffe replied, his face lighting up.

Jox and Fisken looked up to see a petite nurse with chestnut-coloured hair tied up in a bun under a stiff white bonnet. She was smiling at them, wearing a light blue cotton dress with a white apron and plastron pinned over her chest. On the left was a red cross badge and the right a timepiece. As she walked towards them, her sensible lace-up shoes tapped a dainty tattoo on the parquet floor. She was pretty, with high cheekbones, a fair, freckled complexion and blue-green eyes.

'Oh, I'm so glad you gentlemen have come to visit Michael,' she said. 'We've been so pleased with the progress he's making. He never stops blathering on about his Treble Ones. I suppose that must be you.' Her voice was matter-of-fact and had a soft

Scottish burr to it. 'My name is Sister Verden-Anderson, by the way, but you can call me Sally. And you are…?'

'Jox, Jox McNabb,' he replied, a bit flustered. 'I'm Mike's flight leader, or at least I was. Mogs here is his flight leader now. I'm supernumerary to the squadron — oh, it's all rather complicated, but yes, we all fly together.' Jox was rambling and making rather a fool of himself. 'And this fine fellow is Axel Fisken from Norway.'

Axel bowed his head and shook her hand vigorously. Mogs Chalmers did the same but a little more gently.

'How lovely to meet you all, Jox, Axel and Mogs. Yes, I think I can remember that. Michael speaks of you so often,' she said brightly. 'You're just in time to help me get Michael into his wheelchair, and then you can join us in the grounds for his archery lesson. He's really rather good — certainly one of the best amongst the patients. D'you fancy a go? Michael tells me that fighter pilots have excellent eyesight and are always great shots. Would you care to prove it? How about a little contest? You lot against the rest of my patients. I must warn you — they've been practising. Poppa wants to organise matches against other hospitals and include all sort of sports, like some sort of mini-Olympics. Yes, he has grand plans, and our Michael here is one of our stars.' She smiled at him, revealing even white teeth, and placed a hand on his shoulder with obvious affection. She ran it down his bare arm and when their hands met, he gave hers a little squeeze.

Jox glanced over to Fisken, whose eyes twinkled behind his golden spectacles.

In the weeks that followed the Dieppe raid, there was ceaseless speculation, evaluation and discussion over whether the operation could or should be deemed a success. Setting politics aside, what was in no doubt was the bravery displayed during the hard-fought hours on, over and just offshore of the blood-soaked shingle beaches on the 19th August 1942.

Jox heard that the Canadians and Commandos were awarded an impressive haul of medals for valour. Airmen who had flown alongside the Treble Ones were also recognised. Amongst the American Eagles, Squadron Leader Chesley Peterson was awarded the DSO and Flight Lieutenant Don Blakeslee the DFC. Members of No. 111 Squadron were similarly rewarded, with Bars to two existing DFCs and a new DFC awarded to Axel Fisken for his combat victory and then his subsequent daring escape. Young Ralph Campbell was awarded a Distinguished Flying Medal for managing a hard-won victory over a tenacious FW 190, then limping home in his damaged aircraft to crash-land in the barren moors of the New Forest amongst the wild ponies.

The citations in the *London Gazette* regarding Wickham and Jox were:

Awarded a Bar to the Distinguished Flying Cross.

Squadron Leader Peter Reginald Whalley WICKHAM DFC (33403) Royal Air Force No. 111 Squadron. This officer, who has led his squadron in a large number of operational sorties, has displayed outstanding leadership, skill and initiative. During the combined operations at Dieppe on 19th August 1942, Squadron Leader Wickham led his squadron in the first sortie before dawn and in a further four during the same operations. He has personally destroyed 9 enemy aircraft, probably destroyed 5 and damaged several others.

Awarded a Bar to the Distinguished Flying Cross.

Acting Squadron Leader Jeremy Argyll Easton McNABB GC MC DFC (41276) Royal Air Force No. 111 Squadron. This officer has flown on a large number of combat sorties, displaying outstanding leadership, skill and initiative. He has personally destroyed over twenty enemy aircraft. During the combined operations at Dieppe on 19th August 1942, Acting Squadron Leader McNabb flew with his squadron in the first sortie of the day, then led two further missions with partner squadrons, during which he shared a destroyed enemy aircraft. Shot down during his third sortie, he displayed keen spirit and tenacity by evading capture and making his way to friendly lines with a fellow squadron pilot.

On the sunny, windswept afternoon of Tuesday, 25th August, 1942, Kenley aerodrome played host to Their Majesties the King and Queen. The medal ceremony was held outside one of the airfield's great curved hangars with a tea party laid on afterwards in a marquee.

The king looked rather gaunt and tired but was being urged along by his queen. Wickham finally got his moment in the sun, since Jox made a point of not 'monopolising' the conversation, as he'd been accused of doing on the previous occasion. An enthusiastic Ralph Campbell had no such reservations, regaling Her Majesty with tales of his lonely few hours with the moor ponies of the New Forest.

Jox had spotted the Macneal twins and Tony 'Bolshie' Bartley in the crowd earlier. To his immense relief, Moira frostily ignored him, content to hang onto Bartley's arm and admire his film star good looks. Jox had to admit, they made a handsome couple.

After exchanging a few more words with Wickham, the king moved onto Axel Fisken, who came stiffly to attention and saluted.

The king's eyes lingered on his missing fingers. 'I-I see you've been in the wars, Flying Officer…?'

'Axel Fisken from Norway, sir,' he replied. 'My missing fingers are old injuries. I have a new one too.'

'Oh dear, h-how have you been hurt?'

'I injured my arm at Dieppe.'

'Ah, yes, I can see that,' said the king.

Fisken's left sleeve was puffy with a bandage under the sky-blue bands of his rank. The hand protruding from the sleeve was swollen, purple and bruised. 'Flight Lieutenant McNabb and I were injured but managed to make our way back.'

'Ah, yes, our d-dashing escapees. I was told about that. Jolly well done,' said the king. He turned to Jox. 'Ah, McNabb! I might have known. I'm so glad you b-both made it back, more or less in one piece. How were you hurt, McNabb? Nothing too serious, I hope?'

'Nothing that won't mend, sir,' replied Jox. 'I took a rather nasty crack on the ankle when I baled out. I'll be back on my feet soon enough.'

'I'm very g-glad to hear it,' said the king.

Before Jox could answer, one of the king's equerries or perhaps a bodyguard appeared beside him. There were several of them about, clearly all chosen for their bulk. The king frowned as the Coldstream Guards officer whispered urgently into his ear. The king's thin face paled and he stammered, 'G-good Lord. Yes, yes, tell the queen. We must leave immediately.'

The guardsman rushed to her side and again whispered furiously. The queen gave a little cry and was bustled away towards their waiting vehicles. The king looked a little lost.

Jox and Fisken glanced at each other, and Jox asked, 'Is there anything we can do for you, sir? You seem as if you've had quite a shock.'

'No, no,' he replied. 'Some frightful news. It … it appears my younger brother Prince George, the Duke of Kent, has been reported killed in a plane crash in Scotland.' He seemed struck by the finality of his words, then became quite flustered as the Coldstream Guards officer returned to hustle him away. The king's parting words to the pair were, 'We must be leaving. I'm sorry, gentlemen. Thank you for everything you've done.'

CHAPTER TWENTY-ONE

After the royal visit, No. 111 Squadron were swiftly put on active duty again. In the absence of Wing Commander Brian Kingcome, Peter Wickham was tasked with leading the Kenley Wing and Jox was given the responsibility for the Treble Ones for the first time. As yet unofficial, it still felt like the highest point of his aviation career to date.

Ant Glasgow, his faithful wingman and mentor, was the first to congratulate him. He knew better than most what it meant to his protégé. 'Aye, you'll do fine, Jox my lad. Don't go changing everything: just be yourself, stay consistent and the boys will appreciate it.' Jox was grateful for his words, knowing he owed a great deal to the grizzled veteran and his twin brother. He'd had many mentors in the service, but these two were amongst the few that were still around to be thanked.

Today the wing was tasked with escorting a squadron of American Boeing B-17 Flying Fortresses on their first daylight bombing mission over continental Europe. It was expected to be a 'milk run' on some soft targets: textile factories east of Amiens in the Somme *département* of Picardy. The Kenley Wing would rendezvous with the B-17s over the green mosaic of Kent, the dozen or so heavy four-engine bombers dwarfing their escort in the bright blue sky. The hulking Yank airships were painted matt green on their backs and had battleship-grey bellies. Long shiny lines of rivets reflected sunshine at thirty thousand feet, and the fuselage bore the white star, blue roundel and white bar, an as yet unfamiliar sight in European skies. Each aircraft bristled with brutish heavy machine guns, paired up in the tail, nose and belly, and with single .50 calibre weapons poking out from either side through crude cut-out side windows. Jox flew close enough to inspect one and spotted the silhouette of a gunner at his window, gloved hands on his gun and swaddled in bulky clothing against the bitter cold. He seemed barely human, with goggled eyes, a thick furry helmet and the long proboscis of oxygen apparatus reaching down from his face. Jox sensed movement and realised the Yank was waving at him. He waved back and dipped his wings in acknowledgement.

They were flying at the upper ceiling, for the Spits and the Treble Ones were also on their bottles. They would be flying over one of the enemy's airfields situated on a bend in the river Somme, directly between today's target and the sea. That was the reason the beehive was flying so high, keen to avoid their attention. Perfect weather conditions and crystal-clear visibility made that a difficult endeavour. The wisdom of choosing this particular target as a milk run troubled Jox. They could only hope that since it was quite late in the day, the dreaded FW 190s might already have been up a few times and were hopefully refuelling and rearming.

The formation followed the meandering course of the mighty Somme from its mouth to the ocean, high over Abbeville and on towards Amiens. Beyond the city, they were approaching the pulverised terrain that still bore the scars of the last war. Fortunately, they reached the target unmolested. With the Spitfires circling like protective raptors, the B-17s lined up their bombing run. Their vaunted, top-secret Norden bombsights should have aided their precision, but from Jox's vantage point the explosions seemed terribly widespread. It seemed likely that more damage was inflicted on the French landscape, livestock and populace than on the enemy.

Once they were back over Blighty, the squadron turned away from the bombers and made their way back to Kenley. They were in time for a quick sprint down the road to the Wattenden Arms in Kenley village, where they had a few frothy pints of English beer. The evening soon got quite rowdy as the Treble Ones celebrated Jox's first day 'in charge'.

The next day the squadron was rostered for a diversionary sweep over the Belgian seaside town of Ostend. The wing had attacked the harbour facilities here before but were doing so again in the hope of drawing up a fighter response.

A few days later, Jox was again leading No. 111 squadron on a Rodeo 'search and destroy' mission to Hardelot, halfway between Boulogne-sur-Mer and Le Touquet. Peter Wickham was RAGGLE Leader, responsible for the entire Circus of aircraft, bombers and fighters on the mission. As they approached the port city of Boulogne, Morgan Chalmers was on the R/T, joking about pushing on through to Le Touquet to see if they might find Moose Grant's missing toes.

The resulting chuckles had barely settled before black flak began bursting amongst them. The formation manoeuvred through the boiling explosions, as they were thumped about by powerful claps of air. Some of the aircraft were peppered with whirring pieces of shrapnel.

'WAGON Squadron, this is WAGON Leader,' said Jox in the microphone of his mask, hoping he'd be heard over the tumultuous noise. 'Let's get above all this. Things are getting a little uncomfortable.' His pilots confirmed in turn and began complying, when an angry burst detonated at the wing root of the Spitfire three along from Jox. There was a sudden flash, and he turned his head just in time to see the explosion. The pilot stood no chance and was probably dead before the tumbling wingtips, tail and engine hit the earth several miles apart.

'Who was that poor sod?' cried a horrified Jox.

After a brief silence, Pritchard, the pilot's flight leader replied, 'Bubbles Broughton, he's gone.'

'God damn it to hell,' said Jox, picturing the young pilot that he'd first picked up, keen as mustard and precociously talented, from RAF Dyce near Aberdeen. He remembered the more mature, and yet still youthful fighter ace he'd become by the time Jox returned from Malta. Now there was nothing left of him, other than perhaps some broken remains in some French field. Jox felt the loss deep in his stomach and took several gulps of oxygen, trying to master his swelling nausea.

'WAGON Squadron, spread out!' he croaked. 'We need to get above this. Climb to Angels Eighteen. The German gunners certainly have their eyes in today.' He pulled on the stick and heard his ears pop. His breath rasped in the mask as he fought greyout. He glanced across to Ant Glasgow, who was tight on his shoulder and also climbing.

'This is RAGGLE Leader. Disregard that order, WAGON Squadron,' said the clipped voice of Wickham, high-pitched on the oxygen-rich mix. 'The heavies are our focus. Protect the heavies.' On the far starboard side of the formation, there was a sudden flash. It was immediately followed by a trail of fire crawling across the wingtips of another stricken Spitfire. The cockpit was rapidly engulfed, then the flames streamed down the other wing. Within seconds the aircraft was a fiery comet streaking towards the ground. Above them, one of the bombers was also alight, but the attention of all was on the blood-curdling screams that flooded the R/T airwaves. Shrill words were garbled but the voice was unmistakably that of Morgan Chalmers. His canopy was open as he flailed, attempting to get out, hair and clothing on fire. Fanned to crucible heat, the flames finally claimed him, just as they had his closest friend, George Milne, and many more besides.

Their return to the Wattenden Arms that evening was a mournful one. The squadron had lost two stalwarts, long-serving men who'd been lost for no discernible gain or benefit. Jox, Pritchard, Ant, Fisken, Reeves and de Ghellinck silently raised a glass to their fallen comrades. Of the seniors, only Franti Vancl was missing, as he'd received orders to report to No. 312 (Czechoslovak) Squadron at RAF Churchstanton in Somerset, to take over a flight of his countrymen until a squadron leader opening arose with a Czech squadron. At the current rate of attrition, Jox thought it wouldn't take long.

The veterans were joined by Ralph Campbell, whose recent decoration had earned him a place in the circle. He'd also matured over the last few months, exposed to enough of the white heat of battle to know this was no time to chatter, rather to remember and honour.

Peter Wickham entered the low-ceilinged pub, dipping his head through the doorway. He looked flustered. Spotting the group, he signalled to the landlord for another round for his men, then indicated that Jox should join him at the bar.

'I was sorry to hear that Bubbles and Mogs bought it,' he said. 'That bloody mission was supposed to be a milk run, but I haven't seen flak that heavy for a long time. Damned shame. Broughton was an excellent pilot who showed great promise, and Mogs — well, he was just Mogs. A great flight commander, always the life and soul of the party and such a rascal.'

'Yes, he was,' said Jox, a wobble in his throat.

Wickham lit a cigarette and took a deep breath. 'Look, Jox, we're in a bit of a bind. Today's milk run turned out to be anything but. On top of losing our two chaps, No. 401 (RCAF) Squadron lost Jimmy Whitham, Moose's oppo as flight commander, as well as two of the USAAF's brand new Flying Fortresses. Can you believe that's two whole crews of ten men each?'

Jox's mind flashed to the door gunner who'd waved at him during a previous mission.

'Since I was in command, I'm getting a bit of stick,' Wickham continued. 'It's really not my fault — just a lack of photoreconnaissance with the boffins not telling us that Boulogne was crawling with ack-ack guns.' As he puffed on his cigarette, his hand shook. 'I realise now that I shouldn't have told you to bunch up around the bombers. I'm sorry.' There was something else on his mind. 'Look, the Yanks are playing things very much by the book. They're new to the war and don't want to put a foot wrong. Today's fiasco doesn't exactly make for an unblotted public relations copy book.'

'I'm not following you, Pete.'

'Well, you're aware the RAF's Eagle Squadrons are transferring to US control shortly. After today's disaster, they want a "perfect" mission to plaster all over the newspapers, so that back home they can celebrate the transfer. Things have to run smoothly for the reporters. The problem is we don't have enough people to ensure that happens.'

'What do you mean?'

'Well, you see, I'm under a bit of a cloud, so I can't be directly involved. There's a plan afoot to showcase the brand-new Spitfire Mark IXs of No. 133 (Eagle) Squadron at Biggin Hill before they transfer. Another milk run is planned to give them a chance to baptise their Spits with minimum risk, as well as being a final farewell to the RAF. Morlaix aerodrome on the Brest peninsula has been selected as the target, as it's strategically important in providing air defences for the Kriegsmarine facilities at Brest and is the home port for the 1st and 9th U-boat flotillas, which are causing havoc on the Atlantic convoys. It's normally too far south for the Spits' range, so Jerry won't be expecting the raid. The plan is to dogleg to a temporary strip at Bolt Head in Devon, refuelling on the way out and on the way back. The Eagles will fly with No. 64 Squadron from Hornchurch and Moose's No. 401 (RCAF) Squadron at Kenley. The squadrons will fly from their respective bases, meet in Devon, then with the B-17 heavies west of Guernsey. On the way back, the fighters will refuel at Bolt Head before heading their separate ways.'

Jox looked at the CO pointedly. 'Why are you telling me this, Pete?'

Wickham peered at him, then dropped his cigarette and ground the butt into the pub's grimy floor. He lit another immediately and inhaled deeply before speaking. 'I want you to lead the Eagles on this mission,' he said. 'Brian Kingcome is in overall charge of the Circus, with Aussie Tony Gaze, CO of No. 64 Squadron as his second in command. Moose will lead the Canucks, and you'll lead the Yanks.'

'But why me?' asked Jox. 'What about Don Blakeslee? He's a solid chap and showed his mettle at Dieppe. He shot down a couple of Jerries, made ace and even got awarded the DFC from the king. Surely, he's next in line?'

'He was, but like I said, the Yanks are playing everything strictly by the book. Apparently, Don over-celebrated his gong and is in hot water for having a drunken party in their mess, involving unauthorised female visitors and booze pilfered from the stores. The Yanks' commanding general has taken a dim view of that, and so Don has been shipped home. There's a new CO lined up, a tough disciplinarian called "Red" McColpin, but he isn't available to take command just yet. That other chap Darren Beans was also involved, but it seems it was Don who took the fall.'

'That doesn't surprise me one bit. Beans has always been a loose cannon.'

'Well, hopefully he's not too much of a liability,' replied Wickham. 'He's your second in command on the mission. Look, you've got about a week to familiarise yourself with the Mark IX and to chat things through with Beans and the others. They're all rather hacked off about Blakeslee being canned but think highly of you after Dieppe. I know this is a bit unexpected but needs must. Take it as a command opportunity and valuable experience. To be honest, you'd also be doing me a huge favour, getting me out of the doghouse with Yank senior command.'

Jox appreciated being asked but knew he didn't have much choice. 'All right, Pete. I'm your man. Happy to help.'

CHAPTER TWENTY-TWO

The Spitfire Mark IX was a joy to fly. It took Jox's breath away, both figuratively and physically. This new variant had been developed as previous Mark Vs were increasingly being outclassed by the dreaded Focke-Wulf 190, in terms of speed and rate of climb above twenty thousand feet.

The Mark IX was equipped with a two-stage supercharged Merlin 61 engine, which Jox had been told represented a marked leap forward, but he still wasn't ready for what he experienced. From the outside, the aircraft didn't look so different from the Mark V; the airframe had just been modified to accommodate the larger, more powerful engine. During his pre-flight inspection, nothing had seemed out of the ordinary. It was only when he got to altitude that Jox discovered the stunning difference.

He'd expected some increase in power, but reality exceeded all expectations. The automatic second stage boost cut in without warning. As he was climbing at a steady rate to Angels Fifteen, he was suddenly hurled upwards and forwards. He grunted at the G-force, screaming in his face mask with the sheer thrill of it. This was going to be one hell of a surprise for the Germans, and he was already relishing the thought of giving them a damned good fright.

Jox took the Spit through its paces on several occasions over the next few days, trying to get a grip on her foibles and tremendous capabilities. She was performing rather better than the average Spitfire V at lower altitudes, but it was above Angels Twenty that she came into her own. He pulled her into a vertiginous climb right up to Angels Three Eight — thirty-eight thousand feet, and she coped easily, the pressurised cockpit allowing for an unexpected level of comfort. Above that, the aircraft began to wobble and bump a bit, but still within margins that he felt comfortable with and could control. Throughout, she manoeuvred beautifully, pirouetting across the intense blueness of the high-altitude summer skies, but best of all she was fast. Tipping over in a near-stall, she fell in a thundering dive. Jox gradually realised that the Mark IX was travelling at over 360 miles per hour, faster than he ever been before. It was exhilarating and he felt like a master of the air.

On the day of the mission, Jox was up early, meticulously preparing for the task ahead. He'd relocated to the RAF Duxford's satellite field at Great Sampford in Essex a few days earlier and had spent time flying with the Eagles, getting to know their capabilities and foibles.

He already knew the two flight leaders, Darren 'Bayou' Beans and Marion 'Jack' Jackson. Amongst the others, he recognised easy-going Italian American Dominic 'Don' Gentile, known as 'Buckeye-Don' since his two victories during Operation Jubilee. The rest were a collection of exuberant young men, many with English-sounding names like Baker, Smith, Cook and Miller. From a distance, they might well have been Treble Ones, but were in fact all American volunteers who'd come a long way, many risking their US citizenships to join the RCAF and serve alongside the RAF. They had a confidence and informality that Jox found endearing but perhaps a little disconcerting. Their Eagle badges identified them as much as the casual manner in which they greeted a superior officer with 'Hey, buddy' in voices that could be heard from across the room. They were generally loud and rather boisterous, but undeniably friendly.

He quietened them down for the pre-flight briefing from Debden's meteorologist, who explained that the weather should be clear all the way, with perhaps some cloud cover as they approached the target. They'd be flying into a headwind, predicted to be a gentle thirty-five miles per hour as they climbed up to a cruising altitude of Angels Twenty. Intelligence and radar tracking indicated no particular enemy activity, but the outward leg would still be under radio silence to ensure the raid would be unexpected.

After the briefing, Jox caught up with Beans and Jackson. The Louisianan had put on some weight and looked sweaty in his flight gear. His damp ginger-blond hair was on the long side, and he wore his peaked cap perched on the back of his head like a sailor. Chewing gum energetically, he seemed distracted, almost bored. His smile was sincere enough, though, when he spotted Jox. His colleague Jackson was a Texan from Santa Anna, tall and fair-haired with the craggy face of a man who'd spent a lot of time exposed to the elements. Aged thirty-one, he was older than most of his squadron mates and spoke in a slow drawl. In fact, he seemed to be everything that Jox imagined a cowboy might be. Like Beans, he wore stitched black boots with a sloping heel, instead of regulation flight wear.

'Right, chaps, this should be a pretty straightforward operation,' said Jox. 'You're all experienced pilots, and we don't need to make this any more complicated than it needs to be. Flight conditions appear decent, but let's not take any chances. There are fourteen of us rostered for the mission, so please make sure your chaps know what they're up to, where they need to be and what's expected of them. Wheels up in twenty minutes and I expect we'll get some final details at the briefing at Bolt Head field, south of Salcombe. It's about two hundred miles south-west of here, so we should get there easily by midday. The strip is our closest to the target in Brittany, so our second leg should be uneventful too. Everything clear?'

'Piece of cake,' said Beans with a grin, revealing green chewing gum between his teeth.

Jox glanced at Jackson, who clicked his tongue. 'Let's round them up and head them out. Let's get them dogies moving.'

Jox had no idea what dogies were, but the sentiment seemed appropriate enough. They gathered up their equipment and started heading to their assigned aircraft. Approaching the Mark IX he'd been assigned, Jox waved to the British groundcrew fussing about her and began his walk around. Once completed, he inspected the parachute that was laid out on the portside wing like a dissected octopus, all straps and buckles. Since his brolly-hop over Dieppe, Jox had become obsessive about checking his chute before every mission. He fiddled with a buckle and once satisfied, turned his back and shrugged it on, jumping up and down on the spot to get it positioned correctly. He tightened the straps with the help of one of the crewmen, then checked his pockets contained his switchblade and doll's arm. He waddled to the aircraft, raised his right foot to the toe-step by the wing root, and was helped up by the crewman pushing against his back. The metal wing twanged under his weight. Before climbing into the cockpit, he reached for the piece of chalk in his pocket and quickly scrawled *Marguerite IX* on the cockpit edge. He didn't actually know if it was the right number anymore, but it seemed fitting for the new Spitfire Mark IX.

He stepped into the cockpit and then wriggled down into the seat until he was ready for the Sutton harness to be secured. He pulled on his flying helmet and goggles, put on his gloves and plugged in the leads. Finally, he secured the map with the planned route pencilled on it to the space beside the Spit's hinged side door.

In front of him the Mark IX's updated dashboard already looked pleasingly familiar. The rigger leant into the cockpit and secured the harness straps, physically connecting Jox to the aircraft, who now scanned the flight and engine instruments, mostly dormant as the engine was still off. Twin green lights told him the undercarriage was down and locked. He gave the thumbs-up to the fitter standing off to one side of the aircraft, then opened up the throttle, setting the fuel mixture to lean. With the brakes on and ignition switches on, he pressed the starter button. The engine churned and coughed, the spinner starting to turn until it burst to full power, pluming bright flame and blue-white smoke from the exhaust stubs on either side of the aircraft's long nose. There was little doubting why she was called a Spitfire.

The flight down to Devon was uneventful, landing at Bolt Head at 12:30. Lunch had been laid on, and as an unexpected treat they were even offered scones with Devonshire cream and jam. Jox was perplexed to see several of the Eagles covering theirs with meat gravy and calling them 'biscuits'.

After lunch, Squadron Leader Tony Gaze confirmed that he would now be leading off the mission as Wing Commander Kingcome was delayed and would catch up, flying down from Kenley with Moose's squadron. Gaze decided that fourteen No. 133 Squadron Mark IXs was more than required, so stood two Eagles down with instructions to return to Debden.

The briefing was a rather chaotic affair, as several pilots had wandered off after lunch and others hadn't yet arrived. Gaze explained that the three fighter squadrons would provide a Circus escort to three American bomber groups, comprising seventy-five B-17 Flying Fortresses from the 92nd, 97th and

301st Bomber Groups of the USAAF. Some high command genius had decided the public relations opportunity was too significant to miss, so had upped the number of bomber groups involved. There were now almost twice as many heavy bombers as escorts. The fighters were assigned their positions within the formation. Moose and the Canucks of No. 401 Squadron had the overwatch position, No. 64 Squadron were assigned the low position and Jox's Eagles would be in the middle of the bomber formation.

Flight conditions were fine and clear as they took off, but five miles off the English coast a thick blanket of cumulus gradually developed to 10/10 cloud cover at Angels Seven, obscuring the sea and any identifying landmarks. They were reduced to navigating using instruments above the clouds, which continued to thicken as they approached the Continent. The headwind above the clouds was weaker than forecast and they were making good time. Jox ordered the Eagles to climb so as to get a better chance of spotting the bombers at the rendezvous point. They circled in a loose formation, the Eagles searching the mountainous skies for any signs of the errant bomber formations, but also their fellow fighter squadrons.

Jox managed to raise Brian Kingcome on the R/T, who instructed him to continue circling. He wasn't far behind with No. 401 Squadron and would be on station soon. He too was having trouble raising the bombers and hadn't heard anything from ground control for a while. He wanted to keep radio traffic to a minimum as per standing orders but was glad to hear from Jox and his Yanks.

After nearly forty-five minutes of aimless circling and using up precious fuel, the Eagles were starting to feel frustrated and keen for something to happen. It was sharp-eyed Darren Beans who suddenly cried out, 'Hot dog! Friendly bombers below at estimate Angels Fifteen.'

It was early evening as the three fighter squadrons formed up around what turned out to be a solitary bomber group. They created a protective box around the Flying Fortresses, now outnumbering them with No. 64 Squadron positioned on the portside, No. 401 starboard and No. 133 to the rear and higher up. Climbing to take up their assigned configuration, Jox noticed a faint drumming coming from his engine. The oil temperature gauge to the right of the instrument panel indicated the engine was running hot. Reluctantly, he pressed the button on his throat microphone. 'RAGGLE Leader, this is EAGLE Leader. I'm having a spot of bother with my engine temperature. Something's rattling about in there and I seem to have gone through a fair bit of fuel.' There was momentary confusion between Kingcome and Gaze as they decided who was leading the combined formation and should answer.

'No point in taking any chances, Cobber,' said Gaze. 'There's more than enough of us to take care of things. Abort the mission and get back to Bolt Head. We'll see you there, Jox.'

'I concur,' said the measured voice of Kingcome. 'Good luck, Jox. Watch the weather down there — it seems to be getting a touch nasty, over.'

'Roger, RAGGLE Leaders,' replied Jox, scanning his instruments again. 'EAGLE Leader complying.' The engine temperature had moved up a notch. 'EAGLE Yellow One, this is EAGLE Leader. EAGLE Squadron is in your command. Do you read, over?'

The Louisiana drawl of Darren Beans came onto the R/T. 'Yes, sir, I have command. EAGLE Squadron on me. You okay with that, Blue One?'

Through the static, from the other side of the bomber formation came the voice of Jackson. 'Sure thing, partner. You're in the saddle. Let me know what you need from me.'

Jox felt a flash of irritation at them not following proper R/T procedure. He was about to comment when the Aussie accent of Squadron Leader Gaze said, 'RAGGLE Leader here. Let's keep the chatter professional and to a minimum. You never know who's listening.'

'Roger that,' replied the Americans.

'EAGLE Leader returning to base,' said Jox, turning away from the formation. 'See you back in Blighty, chaps.'

He recognised Moose's voice, somewhere amongst the No. 401. 'Take it easy, old chum. See you back on the ground, eh.'

Jox banked his Mark IX on a homeward course, turning a hundred and eighty degrees from the formation's current vector. He was immediately hit by wind resistance from a fierce headwind that began thumping and bumping against him, the aircraft juddering in the unexpected turbulence. His windspeed indicator told him he was flying into a headwind of over a hundred miles an hour. He realised the weak headwind that had been predicted had in fact been opposed by a powerful tailwind. That explained why the formation had reached the rendezvous point in such good time and couldn't find the bombers. The fierce tailwind had blown them far off course.

By his calculations and the pencil trace on his map, he reckoned they were currently some fifty miles beyond Brest, too far south and somewhere over the Bay of Biscay. They had overshot Morlaix, which was further to the north and east of their current position. Both the B-17s and Spitfires had been pushed across Brittany, invisible under the cloud blanket, and were scattered by the tremendous air stream he was now battling against.

Jox tried to raise the Circus to pass on what he'd discovered. If they continued on their current vector they'd be even further off course, all the while using up precious fuel. He could hear them communicating with each other in his earphones but couldn't seem to get through. The voices in the static were growing fainter and ever more distant.

Jox heard Bayou Beans' distinctive voice say, 'There's a gap in the cloud cover ranging from about Angels Three to Angels Seven. I can see some south-facing clifftops, which must be England.' Jox was dumbfounded; there was no way that could be right. Beans continued, 'RAGGLE Leader, EAGLE Leader here. Can I go and check it out? We're getting low on fuel.' Jox didn't hear the reply, but it must have been affirmative since Beans replied, 'Roger, wilco. EAGLE Squadron investigating.' Jox heard several American accents confirming they were following him down.

Why the devil are they all going down to investigate? wondered Jox. He was still battling against the rattling headwind and his engine was making worrying noises. The wind resistance of the prevailing wind was burning fuel reserves at a terrifying rate. He tried to raise the Eagles once again, but realised he had to concentrate on getting his own ailing kite back home in one piece. The contrast between the powerful creature from earlier that week and its fragile state now couldn't have been more marked. He began losing altitude in a long, shallow glide, straining his eyes as he tried to catch a glimpse of a friendly coastline.

Over the R/T there was the faint sound of booming, then a sharp cry, identifiable as Bayou Beans. 'God damn it! Why are those guys shooting at us? Can't they see we're friendlies?' Things appeared to be going from bad to worse for the Eagles. Jox was frustrated he wasn't there to lead them out of trouble but knew they were experienced airmen. There was nothing but static now and Jox refocused on the job at hand.

He tried to raise ground control and was startled when a voice came through, loud and clear. 'Where the devil have you been, EAGLE Leader? We lost track of you almost two hours ago. Your trace was almost off the Fighter Command board. You're still eighty miles south of base. Fly due north on course 020, and for God's sake watch your fuel, over.'

Jox adjusted his vector. He was feeling completely disorientated and growing increasingly anxious as the Mark IX steadily lost altitude. He was enormously relieved when he finally spotted some pale cliffs ringed with the dark, exposed rocks of low tide. He managed his glide very carefully over an expanse of flat sand at the mouth of a river. It was criss-crossed with squares he suspected were oyster cages. On the horizon he recognised Salcombe Castle above the headland. He tilted the aircraft away from the town and followed what his map told him was the Kingsbridge Estuary, with countless small fishing boats beached on the sand. According to the map there was a nature reserve to the north, so there would be less danger to the local population should his pancake go wrong. He reckoned his best bet was to find a flat stretch of beach, clear of obstructions, rocks or oyster cages. In any case he was running out of options.

Jox powered down and applied maximum flaps, then lowered the undercarriage. It whistled eerily, then thundered in his ears on making contact with the wet sand. He was counting his blessings at having managed a successful emergency landing when there was a sudden bang. The starboard wing dropped, the tip gouging into the wet sand. Fortunately, his speed was already low enough to avoid flipping. He cut his engine as the aircraft spun like a dog chasing its own tail. The propeller dug in, churning up a fan of sand that showered down upon the canopy. The aircraft came to a grinding halt, nose down, but Jox was held securely by the straps of his Sutton harness. Exhaling with relief, he pulled back the canopy hood, unclipped his oxygen mask and could instantly smell the sea. Above him was the plaintive cry of the gulls over the ticking of the ruined Spitfire, cooling down in the mud. He undid his straps, stood up on the seat and was about to clamber down. The stink of burnt engine oil, glycol and aviation fuel brutally overpowered the gentle aromas of the coastline.

'Oy, you there, lad,' said a strong Devonian accent. 'Stay right there, son. You've only gone and crashed your blasted Spitfire in a flipping minefield! Now, don't you move an inch. I'll get you out in a jiffy, never you mind.'

CHAPTER TWENTY-THREE

The fisherman wore yellow oilskins despite the warm weather on the Kingsbridge Estuary. He had a tatty sou'wester on his head and lifted a hand to shade his eyes from the glare of the water. His boat was piled high with lobster pots and bobbed midchannel about seventy yards from where Jox's Mark IX Spitfire was nose-down in the wet sand.

'You all right there, matey?' he called, the burr of Devon in his voice. 'I don't dare beach the boat, but if you can make it to the water's edge and swim out a bit, I'll come by and get you.' He gave an encouraging grin, exposing the few teeth he had left. 'Mind how you go, though. Them blasted Navy Tars have riddled that side of the creek with their ammunition. It was a target beach when Jerry was still coming. They never bothered to clear them up, and now the harbour seals get blown up regularly. Mind you, the gulls and lobsters appreciate the free feed, and that's why I put my cages along here. They're rich pickings, I can tell you.'

'How ... how far am I from the water's edge?' asked a bewildered Jox. He was keen to get away from the wreckage that threatened to go up at any moment.

'You got about thirty yards to cover across the sand, then about the same again to wade or swim out to me,' said the fisherman. 'It'll be cold, but I don't suppose you'll be complaining if it gets you out of that tight spot. I'd follow the trace of your tyres as far as you can — they show where the mines ain't. Trouble is, I see you've already run over one and that's what lifted your aircraft's arse in the air. One of your wheels is blown clear off.'

'How far is the gap to the tyre tracks?' Jox asked nervously.

'I'd say about fifteen yards.'

Jox scrambled from the cockpit as delicately as he could manage, then slid along the slippery starboard wing projecting into the air, whilst its twin was embedded in the sand. He perched gingerly in the nook of the wing root, gathering his thoughts. With shaking hands, he reached under his Mae West to his breast pocket and felt the hard lump he'd hoped was still there. He wasn't reaching for his lucky charm this time, but rather the cold metal of his Maltese switchblade. It had saved his life once and perhaps it could do so again.

The knife gave a comforting click and Jox leant earthwards, intending to start probing the wet sand with it. He was too far up to reach it properly, and had no option but to take a leap of faith onto the sand. He took a deep breath, as in the distance the fisherman dropped anchor and made encouraging noises. Jox gently lowered himself off the wing, delicately placing one foot then the other onto the sand. He crouched down onto his knees and began to probe with the steel blade. It was about six inches long and very sharp, slipping easily through the grains of wet sand. He was making steady progress, shuffling along on his hands and knees, getting thoroughly soaked in the process.

He'd covered about ten feet when his blade scraped against something rough and metallic. A bead of cold sweat trickled down his face. There was a thin, three-pointed spike projecting from the sand, and he assumed it was a trigger. It took a while for his thumping heart to calm, and he started probing again, carefully doglegging around the lethal hazard.

After what felt like hours, Jox reached the track left by the aircraft's undercarriage. The tide was coming in now, bringing sanctuary closer but also washing away the grooves he'd planned to follow. By the time he finally reached the water's edge, he was utterly exhausted but encouraged the entire way by the weathered Devonian fisherman.

Things moved quickly after that. The cold water was bracing, as Jox tasted the saltiness on his lips. In a clumsy doggy paddle, he negotiated the shallows, desperately trying not to touch the bottom. Once he was deeper, he inflated his Mae West for greater buoyancy, then began swimming in earnest. He quickly reached the flaking, painted side of the timbered boat, where strong arms reached for him and hauled him easily over the side. His new friend smelt of fish, sweat and tobacco, but Jox wouldn't have swapped that for anything as he hugged him with relief. The fisherman laughed as Jox slumped to the bottom of the boat amongst the pungent lobster pots. He was frozen and exhausted, but he'd made it. He was alive.

'My name's Duncan,' said the fisherman. 'You're one lucky fellow. By my reckoning, if you were a cat, you'd be short of a life or two after that caper.'

'Lost more than a few, Duncan,' said Jox wearily. 'Can't have all that many left. I'm Jox, Jox McNabb, and I'm very grateful to you, I'd have been completely sunk without you.'

'Right you are, lad. Happy to be of service,' Duncan replied. 'Always got time to help our flyboys. Now, tell me, how'd you get yourself into such a pickle?'

'I was coming back from a mission in France when things went a bit awry. I took off from Bolt Head. Is that anywhere near here?'

'Bolt Head? Why, sure, that's just down the estuary a bit, past Salcombe. It's the first headland out to sea. It won't take more than half an hour to get you there. It's just a quick scramble up the chine from the cliff bottom.'

Jox made his way up the winding valley that cut through the sloping cliff-face. He was delighted to find the grassy airfield he'd left earlier that day and was well out of breath by the time he reached the solitary wooden dispersal hut at the clifftop. Beside it was a fuel bowser, a couple of armoury vans and several canvas-covered lorries. About a dozen scattered Spitfires had ground crew crawling all over them. Just beyond the hedge he spotted the wreck of another on the airfield perimeter. When he entered the modest hut, he was surprised to find it remarkably crowded, recognising several familiar faces from the squadrons that had participated in the Morlaix mission.

In the smoky fug, he smelt the familiar post-op odour of damp clothing and the adrenaline sweat of many men in a confined space. An ironic cheer went up when he was spotted, then Moose came wading through the throng.

'Jox, thank God, you made it. I was losing hope.' He wrapped his bulky arms around him in a tight bear hug.

'What on earth's going on, Moose? What's all the fuss about?'

'The operation was a complete disaster. Most of us got home on fumes. It's just been confirmed that one of our new guys has ditched into the sea. I saw him drop in a long flat dive then splash down. We don't know if he baled or stayed with the kite, but either way there's no sign of him. Shame, he was a nice kid and a fine pilot. He came a long way to join in this fight.'

'How many of my Eagles made it back?' asked Jox, searching the hut.

The pained look on Moose's face was chilling. He shook his head and anxiously cracked a meaty knuckle. 'None,' he replied, unusually monosyllabic.

'What do you mean none?' The implication took time to strike home. Moose would never joke about something like this.

'I'm afraid they're all gone, Jox,' said Moose. 'I thought you were with them, but Brian Kingcome remembered you turned back with engine problems. I hoped you'd be all right, but as time ran out I feared you must have gone down somewhere, eh.'

'I did, just north of Salcombe. Got delayed working my way out of a minefield.'

'A minefield? What the hell were you doing in a minefield?'

'It's a long story. I'll tell you some other time,' replied Jox. 'I'd better report to Brian. He's coming over and doesn't look too happy.' Jox had never seen the usually laconic, easy-going wing commander look quite so serious.

'A bad business, Jox,' Wing Commander Kingcome said. 'Looks like the whole squadron is lost. The Yank public relations people and their "Airships" at the Ministry in London are doing their nut.' He chewed at his lip, staring intently at the floor. 'They want full reports by tomorrow and proper write-ups for the Operational Record books for all three squadrons. There'll undoubtedly be an enquiry and they're going to want their pound of flesh from somewhere or someone.'

'Good God,' replied Jox, aghast. 'What on earth happened?'

'A combination of cockups,' replied Kingcome. 'We were all blown off course by the tailwind you reported and didn't realise it, as we couldn't see through the blasted cloud cover. On top of that, ground control failed to warn us we were off-piste. To compound things further, when Darren Beans took over in his usual gung-ho style, he charged off through the gap in the clouds, taking the whole flipping squadron with him. The last we heard they'd run into enemy ground fire and a couple of marauding FW 190s. I guess they were just desperate to land since they were so short of fuel.'

'Are you sure they're all gone?' asked Jox.

'Well, if they're not shot down, they'll have certainly run out of fuel by now. Either way, I fear the best we can hope for is that most have been captured. It rather looks like we've handed the best part of an entire squadron of our newest and best Spits to Jerry on a plate. Any technological advantages we might have hoped for have surely been lost. What should have been a cushy PR exercise has turned into a flipping disaster.' He ran shaky fingers through his hair, then lit a cigarette. 'I'm the one who has to tell 133's CO, Red McColpin, that his new squadron is dead in the water. They were due to transfer to the USAAF in a couple of days. In fact, that's why he wasn't on the raid; he was being officially sworn in at their embassy in London. That's why you were asked to step in, Jox. He's really not going to be happy.'

'If it's any consolation,' said Jox, 'McColpin hasn't lost his entire squadron. Don Gentile and Dusty Miller were sent home before the mission and Darren Beans made it back. They should be back at Great Sampford by now. I expect they'll be facing a long and rather lonely night in the mess.'

Kingcome gave Jox a sad smile and clapped him on the shoulder. 'I'm really glad you made it back, Jox. I couldn't have faced losing you too. I'm sorry, but I expect we're going to face a tough few weeks. Please pull your mission report together as soon as you can.'

CHAPTER TWENTY-FOUR

Jox and Moose met in the elegant library upstairs in the Kenley officers' mess, where they could talk undisturbed.

'It's all in the lap of the gods now,' said Jox. 'The after-action reports are in, and we can only wait to see what fate brings. I can't help feeling we're heading for bad news.'

'They can't hold you responsible, eh,' said Moose. 'You handed over command to Darren Beans and turned back with engine problems well before things went wrong. Also, don't forget it was you who warned the rest of the Circus about the tailwind. Otherwise, we would have simply ploughed on, going further and further off course, and things would have been a hell of a lot worse.'

'Couldn't really be much worse for No. 133 Squadron,' replied Jox. 'They were my responsibility, Moose. There's hardly any of them left, and that happened on my watch.'

'The powers that be can hardly blame you, if you weren't even there.'

'Stranger things have happened,' replied Jox. 'Brian Kingcome and Tony Gaze certainly don't look very happy and the last time I saw Pete Wickham, he couldn't look me in the eye. I thought that was pretty rum considering I only took on the job as a favour to him.'

'He's always been a shifty fellow, that one,' said Moose. 'It's better not to dwell on it. Whatever comes will come. I tell you what: let's get a change of air. How about a little road trip? I've got the loan of a jeep, and I've been meaning to head down to Brookwood in Surrey. Want to come?'

'What about Stephanie? Shouldn't you be spending leave time with your new bride?'

'Chance would be a fine thing,' he replied. 'My good lady wife is off for an interview for a new job at some place called Bletchley Park in the wilds of Buckinghamshire. Won't even tell me what it's about — all pretty hush-hush, it seems. My time is therefore my own, eh. Want to hit the road and get a breath of fresh air?'

'But why Brookwood? There's nothing there but a big cemetery.'

'Yeah, that's right,' replied Moose. 'It's the main cemetery for Canadian soldiers in the United Kingdom. Many of the men who died of wounds from Dieppe have been laid to rest there, but the person I want to visit is a kid from my squadron called Willy Rowthorn. I know him from back home. Actually, I was his coach; I taught him to swim, and he got pretty good. He was Ontario's junior swimming champ, actually. A great kid. I got a hell of a surprise when he turned up here. Apparently, I'd inspired him to become a fighter pilot. A bit like you and that kid Ralph Campbell. It's weird being someone's idol, eh?'

'How old was he?'

'I guess about twenty.' Moose laughed. 'Yeah, I know you're not much older, but somehow you always seem older. In any case, you've been around for as long as I have.'

Jox wasn't quite sure how to take that. It was undeniable that whatever innocence he may once have had was burnt away a long time ago. With everything he'd seen and the pain he'd endured, it was hardly surprising.

'So, what happened to Rowthorn?' asked Jox.

'He got hit on a Circus mission over Belgium, a couple of days before Dieppe. He managed to get the kite back to England but was probably already hurt. Anyhow, his Spit crashed in a hop field in deepest, darkest Kent. The local police and some farm labourers pulled him out of the tangled wreckage, but in bad shape, all cut up by the steel wires they use for the hop plants to grow up. Willy never regained consciousness and died in hospital on the same day as the Dieppe operation. That's what bugs me: he died forgotten because the eyes of the world were elsewhere. He deserved better than that. I just want to pay my respects. I know his parents well, and I want to be able to tell them where he's buried and that his passing was marked, at least by me.'

Brookwood Military Cemetery in Surrey was at the bottom of a long tarmac road that ran between an avenue of red pines leading up to some impressive wrought-iron gates. Once through, Jox and Moose were confronted by the sight of a vast open expanse completely covered in white wooden crosses as far as the eye could see. They parked the jeep and got out to stretch their legs after the drive from Kenley. The graveyard was bisected by wide avenues lined by enormous pine trees separating the distinct plots of massed grave markers. The scent of pine needles filled the air as the trees swayed in the autumn breeze.

'These trees are giant sequoias. Brookwood is famous for them,' said Moose. 'They remind me of the forests back home, where my brother and I used to play as kids. Makes me feel kind of homesick and a little choked up. I'm sorry, Jox. This never happens to me.'

'What are you apologising for? This is a moving place — truly humbling and heartbreaking. There are just so many crosses.'

'I think a lot are from the first war, plus a bunch who died from the influenza just after that.' He sighed. 'By the looks of things, we're having a darned good go at pushing the numbers up too. The newer plots are over there, on the other side of the road. I've got the location of Willy's grave jotted down. Let's see, it says 38 G 12.'

'There are some freshly dug graves over there,' said Jox, pointing towards an area of disturbed ground where the earth was mounded up in front of several wooden crosses. They were painted white with names and numbers inscribed in black lettering. Each row was within a numbered plot, identified by a letter, then with each grave numbered sequentially. Some were grouped by nationality, others by the date of their death.

It didn't take Moose long to find his former pupil and squadron mate, and Jox let him have a little privacy. Earlier, Moose had told him that a number of the casualties from Dieppe had been buried here in a ceremony on the 25th of August 1942. Jox recalled seeing photographs in the newspapers. Since then, a mass of red maple leaves from the trees planted to honour the Canadian dead of the last war had been collected by local school children and placed on the raw sandy mounds of earth in a tribute to the fallen. Only forty-three men lost at Dieppe were actually buried here, but the leaves represented the many comrades they'd left behind.

Jox continued down the forlorn rows, respectfully keeping his hands out of his pockets, clasping them instead behind his back. He found the Dieppe men and scanned the names for those he feared he'd find. He could picture their faces, the pale French-Canadian lad and the burly Royal Marine Commando, last seen waving him and Fisken off from the doorway of the fish shop. He felt overwhelming guilt at having abandoned them to their fate, but perhaps that had already been written and all he'd done was delay the outcome. Eventually, he found where they had been laid to rest.

D.62923 PRIVATE
LOUIS PHILIPPE GRENIER
LES FUSILIERS MONT-ROYAL
LE 19 AOUT 1942 AGE 24
A LA DOUCE MEMOIRE
DE CE BRAVE SOLDAT
HEROS DE DIEPPE

PO/X3497 CORPORAL
W.A. ROBERTSON
NO.40 R.M. COMMANDO
19TH AUGUST 1942
HE WILL NOT AGE, HIS SONG IS SUNG
AND HE REMAINS FOREVER YOUNG

The following morning at Kenley, Jox was sent for and told to report to the CO's office. He knocked and entered to find a grim-faced Pete Wickham, Badger Robertson and unaccountably, Tony Bartley.

'Sit down, sit down,' said Wickham. He looked strained, drawing on a cigarette held between yellowed fingers. 'There's no point beating around the bush, Jox. The results of the inquiry over this Morlaix business are in. The Yanks are calling it a disaster and it's all become a terrible embarrassment, especially after the fiasco of Dieppe. To make things worse, Jerry has been crowing to the international press that they've cobbled together two working Mark IX Spitfires from the wrecks of the seven that went down. Therefore, any technological advantage we may have had is out the window. Frankly, it's a massive cockup. As you might expect, they're trying to apportion blame and I'm afraid none of us escapes the splatter.' He puffed on his cigarette. 'Poor old Tony Gaze,

CO of No. 64 Squadron, has copped the worst of it. Officially the debacle is being attributed to several contributing factors, particularly the incorrect weather forecast, but Tony is being made into something of a scapegoat. He's been demoted back to Flight Lieutenant and transferred to No. 616 Squadron under a bit of a cloud.' Wickham's voice wobbled. 'For my part, I'm being sent on a spell of enforced rest. Apparently "the strain of command" has taken its toll. I'm not sure quite how Brian Kingcome has managed to swerve the bullet, but I suspect there may be a letter of reprimand for him too.' He took a deep breath. 'With me moving on, I know we'd discussed you taking on the Treble Ones. You've done a fine job when put into command roles. The Belgians, and before they copped it, those poor Yanks were full of praise for you.' He lifted his dark eyes to gaze directly at Jox. 'The thing is, this Morlaix business has rather blotted your copybook too. I'm sure it's only temporary, but the powers that be are unwilling to be seen to "reward disaster". The long and short of it, Jox, is that Bartley here will be taking over as the new CO of No. 111 Squadron. I'm sorry to be the bearer of bad news.'

The room swirled about him and Jox felt short of breath. He'd feared something was coming but had never thought they'd take away his squadron, his dearest ambition to lead the Treble Ones. The stars had somehow aligned to make it a possibility, but now it was gone in an instant. He fought to control his disappointment. He swallowed hard, nodded and gave the best impression he could manage of a smile. 'Right.'

'I know it's a rotten blow,' said Tony Bartley. 'If it was happening to me, I'd kick up a stink. How'd you think I got to be known as "Bolshie"? Trust me, Jox, it doesn't help, and things will come good in the end. It's not going to be popular with the squadron. I know you're a long-serving favourite amongst us. I'm going to need your support to make this work. I'll understand if you choose to transfer elsewhere, but I'm asking you to please stay. Losing Mogs Chalmers has opened up a flight leader spot, and you're good friends with Pritch. On top of that, the boys are really going to need you for what's coming next.'

'What *is* coming next?' asked Jox, more petulantly than he'd intended.

Badger Robertson, who had been filling the bowl of his pipe, spoke for the first time. 'The Treble Ones are shipping out. The squadron's bound for North Africa. You've got experience of the region and conditions, experience that the squadron needs. I also hope you'll stay on, if nothing else, as a final favour to me.'

'What do you mean final, Badger?' asked Jox, suddenly alarmed.

'There are some other changes afoot. It's time to bring in some new ideas and new blood,' replied the adjutant. 'It's time for me to hang up my operational wings. I'm getting rather long in the tooth to go gallivanting about the Med and especially the desert. It's not really a place for an old codger like me.'

'But Badger, you're the heart and soul of the squadron, the keeper of our flame. We can't manage without you.'

'Time to pass on the baton, old boy. The keeper of the flame is you now, and old Pritch, of course. The two of you are the longest-serving members of the squadron.'

'No, that would be Ant Glasgow. He and Cam were here well before Pritch and I.'

'I'm afraid Ant's packing it in too,' said Wickham. 'He's still not right on his feet, despite his grim determination to get back to operations. That tough little Scotsman takes my breath away, but even he has come to realise that his time in the camps and the long trek home has taken a lot out of him. There was only so long that we could have a worn-out warrant officer flying in slippers and bright red socks. The desert is no place to be carrying invalids, however stubborn, bloody-minded and utterly determined they might be.'

'Listen, you shouldn't worry about us,' said Badger. 'Training Command is crying out for chaps like Ant and me. We might even see if I can pull a command post together at RAF Montrose. I've such fond memories there, eh, Jox? Maybe Ant will come along. He deserves a posting nearer home, and that way he can still scare the bejesus out of new recruits. His experience is too valuable for the RAF to waste.' He pointed the stem of his pipe at Jox. 'It's you that I want to focus on. You're still young and have got plenty of time for the next step. This squadron needs you as it faces fresh challenges in African skies. Pete, Ant and I send you off with our fondest wishes. Isn't that right, Pete?'

Wickham forced a smile and looked at Bartley for a response. Jox could see Bartley was watching him carefully. He'd always rather liked the man; he was good fun, charismatic and jovial, always with some starlet on his arm. He could trust him in a way that he'd never quite managed with Wickham. Bartley held out his hand and Jox reached out and grasped it.

'All right, come what may, you're still stuck with me, Tony. Let's go scare some Germans.'

CHAPTER TWENTY-FIVE

The weeks before leaving Blighty had been a flurry of dull administration and frustration at the Air Ministry's bureaucracy. On the eve of departure, there were last-minute goodbyes and not a few tears from the bevy of WAAFs and assorted starlets who had associated with Bartley and Pritchard. Stephanie and Moose had volunteered to be Georgie the Border Terrier's foster parents. Taking Jox aside, Moose had said, 'You're actually doing me a favour. Steph is getting kind of broody, and Georgie will be a good distraction, eh.'

No. 111 Squadron flew into Gibraltar on an overnight flight of Douglas C-47 Skytrains, known as Dakotas by the RAF. Landing under the cover of darkness, the lumbering aircraft cut through probing searchlights that silhouetted the black asymmetric profile of the Rock. Circling to make the approach to the notoriously short runway, they were watched by countless twitchy anti-aircraft gunners. Jox and his squadron mates, unused to being passengers, warily watched the light show, silently praying the gunners were up on their aircraft recognition. The aircraft bumped down on the airfield's concrete strip with the familiar squeal of rubber and a rapid deceleration that told them the jovial Canuck pilots were standing on the brakes to get the aircraft to stop. When finally at a halt, they all exhaled in unison, the tension palpable in the stuffy cabin.

Allowed forty-eight hours to acclimatise, the Treble Ones would re-join the Dakota crews for the next leg to Malta. Jox's mind was awhirl at the prospect of getting back to the island and seeing Julianna. He knew he wouldn't have much time, as they were only allowed a few days' stopover before heading on to Alexandria in Egypt. By the time the long-haul journey was done, the squadron would have travelled some three and half thousand miles.

They would be reaching their final destination well before their aircraft would arrive. The Spitfires were being transported by sea in crates to Freetown in Sierra Leone, then overland to Takoradi on the Gold Coast, before being flown over four thousand miles across the continent, with refuelling stops in Nigeria, newly recaptured French Equatorial Africa, Sudan and finally Egypt. The aircraft would be well-worn by then and requiring a major overhaul before being handed back to the Treble Ones.

Until then, the squadron would make do with whatever fighter aircraft were available, most likely outdated Hurricanes or American Curtiss Kittyhawk P-40s, which had a solid reputation for ground attack and were often painted with a fierce shark's mouth and teeth. However, Jox had learned that these were susceptible to the Luftwaffe's Jagdgeschwader 27 Afrika's new BF 109 Gustavs, and losses during the summer of 1942 had been quite appalling. Redeployment of the Treble Ones along with several other UK-based squadrons was an attempt to build up reserves again.

Bartley had been informed that a shipment of forty-two Spitfire Mark Vs, originally bound for Australia, had been rerouted and unloaded at Freetown. They were earmarked for the Treble Ones and other fresh squadrons sent to bolster the war-weary Desert Air Force. The shipment also included eighty Kittyhawk P-40s, enough to equip an entire fighter group, delivered directly by a United Sates Navy aircraft carrier to Takoradi on the Gold Coast.

The drone of the Dakota's engines was soporific, and many of the Treble Ones dozed in the narrow canvas seats running down the ribbed interior of the cabin.

De Ghellinck was talking French in his sleep as Pritchard snored quietly. Bartley was awake, the glow of his cigarette pulsing every time he inhaled. Smoking was probably prohibited in-flight, but no-one was about to reprimand him as the senior man aboard.

Jox couldn't sleep either. He was far too excited about returning to Malta. He was determined to be the first to spot the island and peered anxiously through the rectangular window in the fuselage. The Mediterranean sky was slate-grey, just beginning to lighten from the east, the direction of Egypt and their ultimate destination. The outline of land began to materialise, and before long he recognised the clifftops that lined the southern shore of the kidney-shaped island. Somewhere down there was the narrow sandy beach and ancient ruin of a Hospitaller castle where he and Julianna had got to know each other, swum together in the sea and made love. The Dakota was taking him back to her, and he was almost giddy with anticipation.

The pace of the war had meant that he'd not written as often as he might have. Julianna's letters from the besieged island, going through the worst of times, had also been few and far between. From newspapers and service gossip, he'd picked up that Malta's people had suffered terribly, earning the island the dubious honour of being 'the most bombed place on Earth' and then the greater honour of being awarded the George Cross. It seemed laughable that he'd been awarded the same medal for doing so little. Jox could only pray that Julianna, her family and those he'd left on the island had made it through the storm unharmed.

Malta was about the size of the Isle of Wight, the staging post for so many of those who'd set off for the fateful raid on Dieppe. This morning, the light and sea conditions weren't so different from what had preceded the horror of Operation Jubilee. He could see the whole island now, with Gozo to the west. To the north, he could make out the warren-like neighbourhoods of St Julian's, Floriana and Valletta. Further east was the harbour at St Peter's Pool, where he'd earned his Military Cross during what the Royal Navy insisted on calling the Battle of Marsaxlokk Harbour. A sudden thought occurred to him. Beneath the aircraft's wings, entire sections of the towns and cities were lit up as the island awoke. There were none of the inbound and outbound pyrotechnics of gunfire or explosions that had been routine when he was last here, just the mundane, everyday glow of electric lighting. Neither could he see the harsh searchlights stabbing the darkness like in Gibraltar. It was still too dark to see the undoubted ravages and destruction wreaked upon the island. Appearances could of course be deceiving, but conditions seemed to have improved. Proud and undefeated, Malta had apparently weathered the storm.

On cue, a first ray of sunshine broke over the eastern horizon. The grey sea was turning blue in increments as Jox watched. It was a beautiful sight and he felt moved by a deep sense of homecoming.

The Dakota circled the dusty plain of RAF Luqa airfield. It was pockmarked, streaked and stained by fire, smoke and oil. It had the face of an old friend, aged and weathered by time and events but still familiar. As they disembarked, he was hit by the blast of desert-warm air, loaded with the smell of aviation fuel and the old ash of a thousand fires. It also carried a hint of the sea's iodine and the scent of fragrant herbs and flowers that grew wild on the scrubland beyond the perimeter fence.

Despite the early hour, there was a reception committee waiting for them. News of their arrival must have got around, as Jox spotted the walrus moustache of Wing Commander Tommy Thompson and the bemused pale eyes of Cameron Glasgow standing beside him. Both were already sweating in their tropical uniforms and baggy shorts, the temperature evident in their flushed faces and sunburnt knees.

'The bad penny always turns up,' roared Thompson as he wrapped his burly arms around Jox. The last time he'd seen Tommy, he was Malta's Wing Commander (Flying) but may well have moved on to something more senior by now. He was also Jox's first commanding officer when he'd led the Treble Ones during the battles of France and Britain. The pair of them had a father-son relationship — the nearest approximation that Jox had ever experienced.

'Hello there, sir,' said Jox. 'This is quite the welcome.' He reached out to Cam Glasgow, who saluted smartly and then grasped his hand. The rank tabs on his shoulders indicated he'd been promoted again since taking the step of a commission, the incentive that Thompson had offered for staying on in Malta when Jox had returned to Blighty. The prickly former NCO was the spitting image of his elder twin, lean and wiry, and clearly thriving in his new role.

'Great to see you back on the sunny isle, sir,' said Cam, with a twinkle in his eye.

'There's no sirs with me,' replied Jox. 'Anyhow, we're both the same rank, I see.'

'Yes, Cam's the wing adjutant for me at Luqa,' said Thompson. 'Without old Badger about to keep me straight, I was getting rather unstuck administratively — then providence delivered Cameron Glasgow. Thank heavens for that. You've taken to it like a duck to water, eh, Cam?'

'That's not for me to say, sir,' said the usually dour Scotsmen, with a hint of pride. 'It helps to know how things work, and I've been in the service long enough to know that.'

'As far as I'm concerned, you're heaven-sent, you old rascal,' boomed Thompson. 'Hello there, Pritch. Glad you're still with the Treble Ones.'

Pritchard grinned. 'Yes, sir, for my sins. Just about the last man standing.'

Thompson frowned. 'Yes, I see. Where are Badger, Mogs and Ant? Don't tell me…'

'Where's my brother?' added an anxious Cam.

'No, no. No need to worry, Ant and Badger are fine,' said Jox. 'But I'm afraid we did lose Mogs and Bubbles Broughton over Belgium. That was a bleak day.'

'What about Ant? Why's he not here?' asked Cam.

'He and Badger have transferred to Training Command. Badger was starting to feel his age and somehow convinced Ant to join him. To tell you the truth, Ant's time as a prisoner and his year on the run took a lot out of him. He deserves a rest, but stubborn as he is, it took a while for him to realise it. He wasn't going to listen to anyone telling him so. I'm afraid he's not the man you'll remember, Cam. He's a lot older, thinner and almost worn out. His feet are pretty much ruined. I'm sure he'll get better, but it'll just take time.'

Cam looked upset, then suddenly snorted with laughter. 'Aye, he's a canny one all right, is Ant. He's the oldest and was damned if he was going to come here and have to salute his wee brother. I know his game, I tell you, the canny old so-and-so.' They all laughed, realising there could well be some truth in that.

'Now then, who's this?' asked Thompson, eyeing Tony Bartley. 'I don't believe I've had the pleasure, Squadron Leader.'

'May I present Squadron Leader Bartley, sir,' said Jox. 'The CO of the Treble Ones.' The surprise on Thompson and Cam's faces was marked. This was not what they'd expected.

'Ah … Bartley, is it? Welcome, welcome,' spluttered Thompson, rubbing his finger through his moustache, a sign that he was flustered. 'So how have my Treble Ones been treating you? Fine fellows in my day. How's the new crop behaving?'

'Fine, sir,' replied Bartley warily. 'There are a good number of experienced chaps like Jox, Pritch, Ghillie and Axel, then a smattering of newer ones, but all with operational experience. Most went through Dieppe and have had several Circus operations over occupied Europe.'

'Dieppe, eh? That was a rum job. Poor bloody Canucks got chopped to bits,' replied Thompson. 'The Canadians have been the backbone of our defence of Malta. Couldn't have managed without chaps like Wally Macleod, Butch Barton, Buck McNair, George Beurling and many others. The finest fighting men I've ever led, present company excepted, of course. Come now, you must be parched and getting rather warm in that get-up, Bartley. Bit early for a drink, but we can certainly rustle up some iced tea, if you like.' He bustled Bartley towards the comparative coolness of the terminal building. The rest of the pilots followed them in, grateful for the shade and the promise of a cool drink. Jox walked with Cam Glasgow.

'You seem pretty comfortable in your new role. Still operational, though, aren't you?' asked Jox. 'I can't imagine an old warhorse like you hanging up your spurs.'

'No chance,' growled Cam. 'Me and Tommy like to get up there every now and again. We like to pop up unannounced at the various airfields to keep the boys on their toes. Just following the example of the old Skipper, Air Vice Marshal Park who's now AOC Malta. You remember how during the Battle of Britain he'd pop up all over the place, in that white siren suit of his? He's still at it, and that inspired Tommy to do the same. I just tag along so he doesn't get himself into too much bother.'

'He's lucky to have you,' said Jox. 'I've certainly missed you, especially now that Ant has effectively retired.'

'Aye, it's hard to believe, but if he's as worn out as you say, it's for the best.'

'Well, he's earned a rest. To be honest, we all have.'

'There's no rest for the wicked, and this war is nowhere near done. Things are quietening down a bit here, but are warming up in the desert and you'll be heading straight for the eye of the storm, so I'm told.'

'You know more than me, but all that can wait,' replied Jox. 'I've got important business to deal with — catching up with Julianna.'

The expression on Cam's face hardened. He couldn't look Jox in the eye. 'It's not my place to interfere, laddie, but you need to be having a word with Cocky Cochrane. He's transferred back to the Fleet Air Arm and is now leading a Royal Navy flight out of RAF Hal Far on the eastern end of the island. He's often here and up at the mess at Rabat when he flies into Ta Kali, so you should catch him before you're off. I'm not kidding: you need a word.'

CHAPTER TWENTY-SIX

Jox was dropped off in Rabat by the wheezing shuttle lorry doing the rounds between the RAF airfields across Malta. It had puffed around the twisting corners and rubble-filled streets for the best part of an hour before depositing him on the corner, feeling hot and rather nauseous. At least he'd been able to borrow some shorts and a short-sleeved shirt, far better-suited to the blistering temperature than the woollen garments he'd brought from Blighty.

As he walked up the cobbled street leading to the Point de Vue hotel, where Julianna worked, he felt self-conscious of his fish-belly white knees and the fact that he was sweating so profusely. Perhaps it was just the heat, but he was excited, and a bag of nerves. Hardly the returning lover and dashing war hero he'd hoped to present as. He'd been unable to contact Julianna by telephone, so he hoped she would be at work today. He also hadn't spoken to Cocky Cochrane, who Cam Glasgow remained curiously adamant he should speak to.

Approaching the hotel, Jox noted that the tall palm trees that had once lined the slope were missing. He recalled that some had been knocked down when the Point de Vue was bombed on the day before Jox had first arrived in Malta. A thousand-pounder had collapsed an entire section of the seventeenth-century villa, resulting in a great loss of life amongst the resident officers. He expected that the rest of the trees had been felled when fuel on the island had become so scarce. What a shame, he thought, knowing they were quite ancient, and that he'd always enjoyed the sound of the wind in their feathered fronds. Not that there was any wind today — just a wobbling heat haze rising off the hot limestone surfaces of the buildings. Bomb damage was still evident on the hotel's façade, with angry gouges in the honey-coloured rock.

Jox gazed up at the hotel's terrace and his heart skipped a beat as he recognised a familiar silhouette. There she was, petite, slim, with long dark hair. She was utterly exquisite. It was his Julianna.

He was about to call out when he noticed she wasn't alone. Someone was holding her hand and whispering in her ear. With a sinking feeling, he saw them kiss, then hold one another despite the cloying heat. Jox's mind was swirling, and he felt sick. He'd been holding his breath and now let out a gasp of disbelief and pain. The man wore the blue uniform of the Fleet Air Arm, and Jox knew immediately it could only be Cocky Cochrane.

Cochrane pulled back from their embrace, his eyes on Julianna's face and a smile on his lips. He glanced at Jox, frowning, then his eyes widened.

'Jox?'

Julianna turned. Her face was flushed but beautiful. There was a flash of fear across her dark features.

'Jox, let me explain!' cried Cochrane. He broke away from Julianna's grasp, quickly crossing the terrace, and began struggling with the locked iron gate onto the street.

Jox had seen enough. He had to get away. He began running down the hill, as fast as his legs could carry him.

'Jox, wait!'

He had to escape this betrayal, the ripping sense of loss. Worse than that was the sheer agony and humiliation of being taken for a fool. Heartbroken, he felt hot tears of indignation streak down his cheeks, already reddening from the sun. The sound of footsteps behind him stopped as he ran on.

He didn't know where he was going; he just had to escape the pain of what he'd seen. He only stopped when utterly exhausted, his collar and shirt soaked with sweat and filthy from the road's dust. He found some shade beneath a hunched-over olive tree, the gnarled trunk and branches drooping with age rather than the weight of fruit.

Sitting in the shadow of the ancient tree, Jox clasped his arms around his bare knees and rocked back and forth. From deep within came a howl, which broke into eviscerating sobs. He cried for his abandonment, for the betrayal and once again for the loss of everything he'd hoped for. Finally, feeling utterly drained, he curled up and fell into a deep sleep, shaded by the old olive tree that had doubtless seen it all many times before.

'Did you not at least speak to them?' asked Cam, when Jox explained what had happened. 'You deserve an explanation, surely, laddie.'

'I saw them together and just ran,' replied Jox.

'I'd have punched the fellow right on the nose,' said Pritchard. 'Pinching a chum's girl like that is unforgivable in my book.' The three of them were sitting in a café, nursing some fearsomely strong coffees in tiny porcelain cups, doubtless of contraband origin.

'You should have let them explain,' said the usually uncompromising Cam. 'It was grief that brought them together — they didn't plan to deceive or hurt you.'

'What do you mean, Cam? What grief?' asked Jox.

'When that wee laddie was killed, Cocky was heartbroken. It was like losing a brother to him. Christ, what was his name again?'

'What boy?' asked Jox, fearing he already knew the answer. 'Do you mean Elias, Julianna's brother?'

'Elias, that was it,' said Cam. 'Aye, poor wee boy. He was making his way to school when one of those damned Jerries out on a free fighter sweep found him. They'd been shooting up fishermen on the water, the livestock in the fields and any vehicle out in the open. The lad was unlucky and got caught by a marauding raider. There wasn't much left to bury. Those cannon shells make a hell of a mess.' Cam's face was grim. 'It destroyed that lassie of yours, Jox. Cocky was in a bad way too. I know it's no excuse, but I suppose they found comfort in each other. You were so far away and no one knew when or if you'd make it back. I know this is a damned mess, but surely you can see how it could happen? Will you at least let them try to explain?'

Jox stared back at him. 'Will it make any difference? I don't think I could cope with seeing them together, explanations or not. The sooner I get off Malta and put all this behind me, the better. I'm not hanging about for explanations or excuses.'

'I'm with Jox on that one,' said Pritchard.

'Look, I'm not exactly the forgiving type myself,' said Cam, shaking his head sadly. 'But I think you'll come to regret that, my boy. Life is too short to leave things unsaid, and God knows a fighter pilot's life is short enough. I'm not excusing what they've done, but Julianna meant a great deal to you, and Cocky's still a good pal and comrade of yours. They deserve the chance to have their say, don't you think?'

'Maybe one day, Cam, but I couldn't face them now,' said Jox with icy finality.

It was two weeks later and if Jox thought Malta was hot, it was nothing compared to the desert. The blinding glare, the liquid heat and the teeming flies made it a boiling vision of hell.

Their flight from Malta had been uneventful, but Jox's first glimpse of Egypt, cradle of civilisations, was exhilarating. The dramatic curve of Abu Qir Bay and the verdant Nile Delta lying beyond it was stunning. Alexandria's sand-coloured minarets appeared to be propping up the blue sky, and the Treble Ones knew they were somewhere very far from home.

The Dakota landed at RAF Aboukir, east of Alexandria and in sight of the sea. The men were given twenty-four hours to get used to the heat and their surroundings. They spent the time drinking ice-cold Danish Carlsberg in shadowy bars and getting fleeced by hucksters in the souk.

Leave complete, with some more exhausted than others, the Treble Ones were instructed to collect their well-worn Spitfire Mark Vs, which had survived the Pan-African delivery run from Takoradi, off the Atlantic coast of Western Africa. Jox had never seen such worn-looking aircraft, sand-blasted and weathered by the harsh elements. However, they had at least had a desert paint job, albeit one that could do with a touch up after their long journeys in transit.

Their first pre-flight briefing in the desert was held in a ribbed metal Nissen hut, and it felt like they were sitting in a giant bread oven. The metal sides were scalding to the touch, a new hazard that the Treble Ones had to get used to. So far, in their brief sojourn in the desert, they'd learnt to be wary of the flies tormenting their every moment, the tiny scorpions that regularly took shelter in unguarded flight boots, coiled snakes who hid under the latrine and then the packs of feral dogs running wild on the dusty back streets of Alexandria. Only the

Aussies seemed to thrive in this desert environment, seemingly hardy to the conditions.

Squadron Leader Bartley kept it short, principally providing vector coordinates, a weather update of 'fine and clear' and the name and map references for their destination, an improvised desert airfield southeast of a railway junction called El Alamein. It had been hotly contested earlier in the war but was now the jumping-off point for the next big push expected later that week.

'Today's op is pretty much a shuttle run,' announced Bartley. 'We're getting our kites to a forward position, where we'll be available to provide air support to our advancing troops. There are plenty of ground attack P-40 Kittyhawks and tank-busting Hurricane Mark IIs about to target the enemy on the ground, so our role is to keep Jerry's fighters off their backs. Mark my words, gentlemen, the Germans out here are no slackers. They're desert veterans and have been here for a while. I'm told there's one mob in particular that have been chopping us to pieces. We'll get a fuller briefing on the opposition when we reach our destination. Any questions?' He searched the room of scarlet, perspiring faces. 'Right, let's get out of here before we dissolve into pathetic puddles of sweat on the desert sand. Pritch, I'll join your flight, but you're in charge. Jox, can you leave with your lot ten minutes after us?'

Once outside, in the marginally cooler air, he added, 'Later this afternoon, I want the two of you to join me at a briefing from the 51st Highland Division, who we'll be supporting. They'll be providing details of what they're calling Operation Lightfoot. Apparently, that's pongo humour referring to the sappers making their way through the minefields to clear them under the cover of darkness. Given they're nicknamed the "Devil's Garden", that doesn't bode all that well. Once the way is clear, the armoured thrust is called Operation Supercharge. We'll get all the information later, but for now let's keep what we know under our hats.' His bare head was sweating. 'Eyes open as we head east. We're in Jerry's back yard, and he doesn't appreciate poachers. I fear they're all as canny as their commander, Field Marshal Erwin Rommel, the Desert Fox.'

Jox knew the 51st Highland Division well. Dollar Academy, where he went to school, had strong links with the local regiment, the Argyll & Sutherland Highlanders, a key part of the division. He'd spent happy days shooting at Bisley and romping about in their uniform on exercises in the Ochils, the verdant round-shouldered hills that dominated the school.

The regiment and division had already had a tough war. Over ten thousand serving in the division had been taken prisoner at St Valery at the fall of France. Jox and the Treble Ones had flown in support of an attempted evacuation, 'a second Dunkirk', but the Argyll's 7th Battalion had borne the brunt of the enemy's thrust, suffering the worst losses in the regiment's lauded history. Many Argylls were now languishing in POW camps and Ant Glasgow had met several during his time in there and during his escape to freedom.

The briefing was held in an enclosed space with bare brick walls but no roof. Instead, a large camouflage net, the type used to disguise artillery emplacements, was spread over wooden tentpoles. The sunlight shone through, casting a criss-cross pattern onto the large sand table map of the planned operation.

Crouching on his knees in the middle of the map was a tall, gangly colonel with a bushy moustache, sand-coloured shirt and shorts, and a Tam o' Shanter worn at a jaunty angle. He was using a long wooden pointer to indicate the different phases of the forthcoming battle and was careful where he placed his big feet to avoid treading on objectives, labelled with little panels stuck at different points in the sand. Around the map were gathered an assortment of uniformed officers, several unexpectedly wearing green tartan kilts with mahogany-coloured tasselled sporrans. Amongst them, Jox recognised the faces of Manuel Powell and Mark Schofield. They were older than him but had been in the same boarding house at school. They smiled and nodded their recognition. There were others who wore the red-trimmed peaked caps of General Staff, including another chap from Jox's school. He was a good deal older, but still rather young to be a brigadier. Jox struggled to remember his name but thought it might be Gavin Robertson. His face was etched with deep lines of anxiety, which were presumably also responsible for his prematurely greying hair. Robertson had undoubtedly been involved with planning the op, and that responsibility weighed heavily. Amongst the smattering of berets and Glengarries from other regiments were attendees from the Desert Air Force, conspicuous in slate-blue forage caps with wings pinned upon their chests. Jox couldn't help wondering how many amongst this gathering of the clans would survive the next few days and weeks.

The colonel spoke in a deep Scottish brogue that reminded Jox of his old school rector. He was sitting on his haunches, pointing a bony finger at a point on the sand table labelled START. 'Right, laddies, our forces will provide the Northern thrust for Operation Lightfoot. We will advance between the 9th Australian Division to our north and the 2nd New Zealand Division to the south. You can see our starting line, and facing west there are four progression paths marked out in Green, Red, Black and Blue. These will help us control and phase the creeping artillery barrage as we progress forward.' He looked up at the assembled men. 'The attack begins on the night of the twenty-third of October. Every phase of our advance is detailed, as are our objectives, and all enemy positions on areas of high ground have been named after towns that you should find familiar, and more importantly that your Highlanders will too.'

Jox scanned the sand table, spotting the coloured lines the colonel had described. A panel saying '9th AUS DIV' was placed by a position called VICTORIA. Following the green and red lines, he saw others labelled ABROATH, then FORFAR and MONTROSE north of it. Beside the colonel's big desert boot was DOLLAR itself — the name of Jox's school. These would be the objectives for the Black Watch and Gordon Highlanders. The southern portion was allocated to the Argylls, the Cameron Highlanders and the tanks and mechanised vehicles of Recce units.

'We will be facing the German 21st Panzer Division, desert war veterans supported by extensive Italian units who have also been here far longer. They are perhaps less well equipped and a good deal windier, but we cannot depend on that.' He gave a nervous smile and waved his pointer across the table. 'The entire enemy front will be pulverised by enough artillery fire to put the barrages of the last war to shame. You will need to insist that your men protect their hearing, as it will be ear-splitting.' The colonel stood up, dusting sand off his bony knees. 'In summary, gentlemen, XXX Corps' infantry regiments will advance in the north onto the German positions near the rail junction at El Alamein, while XIII Corps will attack from the south. Our first task is to seize all allocated ground objectives, clear the enemy's minefields and then create a path for the tanks of X Corps.' He added grimly, 'As ever, we do the hard graft and the glory boys punch on through, but to be honest, they're very welcome to it. I can't imagine anything more uncomfortable than charging forward in a metal box in this blazing sunshine. At the very least, our operation kicks off at night.' He paused and seemed to cheer up. 'General Montgomery and his staff have devised a surprise which will aid our task. Batteries of Royal Artillery searchlights will provide artificial light called "Monty's Moonlight". Apparently, it's designed to illuminate the Highland Division's path to glory, or some such rot! For my part, I much prefer the words of the immortal bard — ours, mind you, not that imposter from England.' He began to recite:

'Scots, wha hae wi' Wallace bled,
Scots, wham Bruce has aften led;
Welcome to your gory bed,
Or to victory!'

CHAPTER TWENTY-SEVEN

The Scots officers began to disperse as Jox tried to make his way through the throng to say hello to his old school mates. His progress was arrested by a hand on his arm, sending a painful twinge through his shoulder, an old wound that occasionally bothered him. Irritated by the pain, Jox turned to find it was Bartley holding him back.

'Hold on a sec, Jox,' he said with a disarming grin. 'We've got the RAF briefing now on our part in the show. It's in a tent just alongside. Come on, we don't want to be late.'

Jox reluctantly followed.

'Yah, so men, you are very welcome,' said a tall, bulky and well-tanned group captain in a gravelly Afrikaans accent. 'My name is Menneer, Scottie Menneer, and I am responsible for the air operation supporting our brave Jocks as they embark upon this exciting new adventure on the native soil of my Africa. God speed to them and we promise to be the vengeful angels at their shoulders, protecting them with our air shield from those who would do them harm. Let's be clear: that is our mission.' He held up a fleshy hand. 'Before we begin, come now and help yourselves to some tea or water. I know some of you *rooinek Engelsman* suffer terribly from the heat. Please refresh yourselves before taking your seats.' He smiled benignly, indicating some tea urns set up on a table, next to glass barrels filled with water and floating sliced lemons. 'I expect some of you may be Jocks like our pongo friends, and I don't want to see you falling over with heat exhaustion or sunstroke. You are far too important to this operation.' He grinned at his audience as he removed his forage cap to reveal receding dark hair that glistened with sweat and the large cauliflower ears of someone who had played a lot of rugby in his youth. 'Come now, chaps, we have a lot to cover.' His blue eyes sparkled with humour as he stood hands on hips, waiting for them to settle down.

He pointed at the large map pinned up behind him. 'Right then, on this map is the area we are responsible for. It is nothing as fancy or detailed as the sand table our ground-based friends are so very proud of, but we only need to know the broad strokes of what they'll be attempting. With the exception of our night-time bombers, we will be flying during daylight hours when there should be good visibility, weather permitting, but the prognosis is favourable. During the army's nocturnal ground operation, we will be stood down, meaning that in the days before, it will be absolutely crucial that we take out all enemy reconnaissance flights and interdict all positions that pose a threat to our troops as they first advance.' He pointed at various points in the enemy's lines. 'We will be specifically targeting any of Rommel's Deutsche Afrika Korps rapid response capabilities, laagered-up armour and the first line of artillery positions endangering the opening phases.'

He flexed his broad back like a pugilist preparing for the ring, swinging his chin from side to side as the bones of his bull neck cracked audibly. 'It goes without saying that the enemy won't stand idly by. We are facing Jagdgeschwader 27 "Afrika", a very experienced desert fighter wing. Mark my words, they are redoubtable opponents, their ranks stuffed with the Luftwaffe's finest experts. I know some of you are veterans too, aces from the Battle of Britain, Malta and elsewhere, but consider this: many of these chaps have vast experience from the slaughter on the Eastern Front, and now here in North Africa they have become absolutely deadly.'

Menneer pulled a face and reached for a magazine on the table behind him. He held up the front cover, which featured a handsome young aviator in a peaked cap and a black leather jacket. At his throat was the distinctive shape of the Knight's Cross. 'This is the best of them, Hauptmann Hans-Joachim Marseille. The Germans call him "The Star of Africa" and he has over a hundred and fifty confirmed kills to his name. That's a hundred and fifty of our people. This pretty boy is a ruthless bloody killer. This German magazine, *Signal*, claims his record is seventeen kills in a single day. His preferred prey are our ground-attack P-40s, but he's not fussy. It's our job to stop him and his rather too numerous friends. Here, I have several copies. Pass them around and take a good look at your enemy. There are a dozen others featured in the article, but Marseille is the best of them. Yah, I suppose, he is their star.'

He scanned the room, nodding to faces he recognised. 'I know there's a lot of experience amongst you, some aces with multiple double figures, but out here we're outclassed. Not because of the skill of our fighter pilots, but because of our equipment. Our only hope is that if we work together, we can use the Luftwaffe's overconfidence against it. When JG 27 arrived in North Africa, they were equipped with Bf 109 Emils, more or less a match against our Hurricanes. Since then, with the Fritz and Gustav variants, from a technical standpoint they've got us beaten. Our Kittyhawk P-40s are solid ground attack performers but aren't cutting it in air combat.' Menneer gave an embarrassed laugh. 'If I'm honest, the only thing keeping Jerry off our backs at the moment are the Long-Range Desert Group and Special Air Service knocking out more of their fighters on the ground than our glorious Desert Air Force is in the skies. Frankly, it's getting embarrassing and well past time we got ourselves back in the game. By the way, if you do ever come across any of those "secret squirrels", make sure you buy them a drink.'

He smiled disarmingly. 'Thankfully, we've been joined by the newly restructured No. 324 Wing, and I think now we stand a chance. Please give a warm welcome to the "Basutoland" boys of No. 72 Squadron, No. 93 Squadron, the Treble Ones, the "Black Panthers" of No. 152 Squadron and the "Seahorses" of No. 243 Squadron. You are very welcome to the ranks of the Desert Air Force, and your Spitfires even more welcome.' He laughed and the room was soon laughing with him.

'So, for our new boys and maybe not so new boys, the task is to keep Marseille and his comrades off our Hurribombers, P-40s and twin-engine fighter bombers, so they can take care of ground targets. You are their only hope, so no pressure,' he said with a wink.

Menneer turned to the map and pointed to several desert airfields marked in the middle of nowhere. 'From these positions, your squadrons will be allocated sectors to patrol and protect across the forty-mile front running from the Med to the Qattara Depression. Once the advance is underway, we will hop forward to new positions, depending on the success of operations on the ground. Your squadron officers will brief your respective aircrew. Right, men, that's it.' He suddenly raised his hand in salute. The airmen in the room got to their feet and came to attention, saluting back. Menneer's pale eyes glistened. 'That means a lot to me, boys. Thank you. Good luck, and I wish you good hunting.'

Later that afternoon, Bartley, Pritchard and Jox briefed the rest of the squadron on what was planned, the scale of the operation and the objectives for the next few days. They'd gathered the men in the shadow of a hulking, blunt-nosed

Vickers Wellington B Mark III bomber of No. 150 Squadron, with whom the Treble Ones were sharing their temporary airfield.

A line of delicate-looking Spitfires Mark Vs were parked under camouflaged tarpaulins down one side of the sand-covered runway, dwarfed by the giant twin-engine heavy bombers being prepared for their night missions. RAF armourers, stripped to the waist, were working on the next bomber along, marked 'JN-L' on its side in giant white letters. Another gang of ground crew were wheeling a trolley-load of 500-lb General Purpose bombs for loading. It felt like a rather precarious place to hold a briefing, but no one seemed unduly perturbed. Several more fitters were up ladders and on top of the massive wings wielding outsized spanners and finalising an engine inspection. 'JN-R', which was currently providing the Treble Ones with welcome shade, was already ready for action.

The CO addressed the gathering of airmen as Jox listened distractedly, fascinated by the antics of some tiny jerboa — the ubiquitous kangaroo-like hopping rodents, after whom the Eighth Army were named the 'Desert Rats', scurrying about between the massive black rubber wheels of the bomber.

'This Friday, the twenty-third of October at 21.40 precisely, the Eighth Army will launch Operation Lightfoot with the biggest artillery bombardment since the Great War,' said Bartley. 'In two days' time, Axis positions from the sea to the Qattara Depression will be decimated along a forty-mile front. Every known Deutsche Afrika Korps and Regio Esercito position, every concentration of Panzerarmee armour, every fuel or ammunition dump, headquarters, airfield, trench complex, artillery or observation post will be hit. Desert crossroads, waterholes and wadis will also be targeted. Our engineers will then clear safe corridors through the enemy's minefields, to allow further troops and armour to push through behind a creeping barrage. It will be a hard, dusty and bloody business, and our job is to make it less so.' He looked at Jox and Pritchard, who nodded. 'Your flight commanders will brief you on the threats, but know this: Jerry is a shrewd and wily operator out here in the desert. It'll be no piece of cake.'

He glanced skywards. 'Out here there's nowhere to hide, so keep watch for the Hun in the sun, for he is surely there or coming down at you from high altitude.' He pointed. 'Look, there's someone copping it right now.' To the west, the infinite blue of the desert sky was marred by angry white streaks like the claw marks of a cat. These vapour trails betrayed a high-altitude battle, too far away to be a threat but a timely reminder of what to expect.

The men separated, Pritchard heading off with A Flight and Jox with B Flight, comprising Yellow and Green Sections. The squadron had been up-manned to seventeen aircraft, eight in each section, with Squadron Leader Bartley flying supernumerary. Jox took a moment to register the eagerness on the younger faces and the calmer, more detached confidence of the veterans like de Ghellinck, Fisken and even young Ralph Campbell now, who'd seen enough combat to no longer be a novice.

Yellow Section was led by Jimmy Baraldi, a veteran of No. 609 'West Riding' Squadron during the Battle of Britain. He was Scottish but of Sicilian extraction, and his family owned a chain of ice cream parlours across western Scotland. Baraldi was one of the pilots Bartley had brought to his new command. Others included William 'Mack' Gilmour, a fellow Scot, and Brummie Tommy Tinsey. Baraldi's section was made up of Antipodeans, including veteran Shane 'Kanga' Reeves and the equally experienced Barry 'Gusty' Gale. The Aussie pair flew with James Waring, a Kiwi, the trio always horsing around, perhaps more comfortable in the heat and dust than their Canuck and British counterparts.

In Jox's section, he had Ralph Campbell, Ernest Mouland and twenty-year-old Sergeant Nigel Steevenson from Lancashire, so a combination of youth and experience. Mouland was a French-Canadian Warrant Officer, newly promoted and now the squadron's senior NCO since Ant Glasgow's departure.

After the briefing, Jox approached de Ghellinck and Fisken, who were chatting in the shade of the Wellington's broad tail assembly.

'What are you pair of reprobates up to?' asked Jox. They were looking skywards, in the direction of the vapour trails from earlier.

'I think someone is in trouble,' replied Fisken.

'Yes, he has fire on board, the poor man,' said de Ghellinck.

Jox peered where they indicated. A tiny dark speck grew larger as it got closer, becoming more distinct and trailing a thin line of smoke, like a stroke of black ink across azure paper. Closer still, it materialised into a sand-coloured, tiger-striped Kittyhawk P-40 fighter-bomber with a bright red spinner, shark eyes and a mouth bristling with white teeth. There were puncture wounds down the side of the aircraft's fuselage and smoke was pouring from the exhaust stubs, flowing over the stubby wings and the trio of cannon barrels that protruded from each wing.

The Kittyhawk had its flaps fully depressed to maximise drag, decelerating as the pilot eased the revs off his ailing engine. He was desperately trying to get down as by the look of things, the cockpit was getting uncomfortably warm. The undercarriage and small, retractable rear wheel dropped into position as the pilot angled for what promised to be a bumpy landing. To Jox, the aircraft's unfamiliar wheel struts looked too long and flimsy for what was expected of them.

There was a sudden snarling roar, then the bark of rapid cannon fire. The aggressive-looking but clearly badly damaged Kittyhawk appeared to fold, collapsing on itself like a shutting clamshell. In an instant, it was reduced to component parts, scraping and bouncing along the dusty runway followed by the boiling roar of aviation fuel catastrophically set alight. Viscous smoke rose from the carcass of the Kittyhawk as a second aircraft punched through the haze, accelerating skywards into the great blue yonder. Once at a safe distance, it banked, then slowly and deliberately executed a victory roll for all to see. The upper surfaces of the aircraft were leopard-spotted in desert camouflage, a mustard colour with darker spots. There were Teutonic crosses on the upper side of each wing, blending into the camo background, but on the light grey undersides they were stark against the cobalt-blue sky. This was unmistakably a Messerschmitt Bf 109 Gustav, the most modern variant of the lauded German fighter. It barrel-rolled once more, then accelerated away as the airfield's Bofors gunners woke up and began banging AA shells into the sky. Too little, too late for the Kittyhawk jockey spread across the desert floor.

It was also too late to help him, but several Treble Ones still ran over to the crash site, now burning in earnest, the entire cockpit and fuselage engulfed in flames. Despite the open cockpit, the stricken aviator was still strapped to his highbacked chair in the heart of the flames. The top of his head was covered by his flight helmet, eyes hidden behind goggles, but the lower half of the face was already reduced to bones. His jaw had dropped in a silent scream, small, white teeth visible through the licking flames.

'*Oh, mon Dieu*,' said Olivier de Ghellinck, as Jox turned away. Anger surged through him at the callous execution of the hapless Kittyhawk pilot.

'He was a sitting duck,' said Jox. 'He was already out of the fight and there was no need for that. It was sheer bloody murder.' He reached into his pocket and found the cool porcelain of the doll's arm. He rubbed it with the pad of his thumb, the only way he knew of calming himself when his blood was up.

'Take it easy, *mon ami*,' said de Ghellinck. 'We'll have our chance for revenge soon enough.'

Fisken eyed them both through his little round spectacles. 'Take the anger and channel it into fighting spirit for what is to come,' he said. 'It is what gives us the edge. Forget about our machines, our technology, or if it's better or worse than theirs. It is with the heart and righteous anger that we carry through to victory.' He had a hard look on his face. 'We Vikings talk of berserkers who can channel the fierceness of the bear to overcome all manner of weapons, injury and opponents. Maybe this horror is what we need to prepare for the fight to come. That way, we show no weakness, no mercy and no quarter. It is a good thing, the night before battle.' He turned abruptly and walked away from them.

Jox and de Ghellinck exchanged glances. The Belgian aristocrat shook his head. 'I love that man like a brother, but he absolutely terrifies me. There's a darkness within him that I find utterly chilling. I'm glad he's on our side, but sometimes I do wonder what this war has done to him. What has it done to us all?'

CHAPTER TWENTY-EIGHT

Jox's shirt was sticking to his back, and the undersides of his legs were damp against the brown vinyl of the pilot's seat. The squadron were sitting in readiness for the second sortie of the day but were being made to wait in open cockpits, the perfect suntrap to slowly roast airmen. The moisture from the sweat and the accompanying smell attracted the usual swarm of desert flies, which Jox swatted at impatiently.

Earlier that day, the Treble Ones had escorted a dozen rocket-armed Bristol Beaufighters from No. 325 Wing, targeting a rail junction halfway between the train station at El Alamein and the coastal town of Sidi Abdel Rahman. They'd met no opposition and during the raid Jox had been struck by the towering plumes of sand drifting high into the atmosphere. If these conflagrations were created by just a few precision rocket attacks, surely these were a good omen for Operation Lightfoot kicking off that night with a vastly larger scale of artillery barrages and bombing raids planned.

The pilots received their long-awaited go-signal via an arching green flare, followed by confirmation on the R/T. Jox was immediately grateful for the fresh airflow into his cramped cockpit, flushing out most of the blasted flies. For this mission, Jox was leading B Flight to a rendezvous with Kittyhawk P-40s of No. 112 Squadron. It was an amusing coincidence that they were numbered directly after the Treble Ones. Nicknamed 'The Shark Squadron', they were the first Allied air force unit to adopt the shark mouth design on their aircraft. It was one of their number that had been spectacularly destroyed before the eyes of the entire squadron the other day.

The combined formation was ordered to come to the aid of a reconnaissance unit that had been probing for weak points in the enemy's defences. They'd run into trouble just north of the Qara oasis in the middle of the open desert. Equipped with light Crusader tanks, they were being chopped to mincemeat by a well-hidden screen of anti-tank guns. The ground-attack P-40s were tasked with seeking and destroying the guns, whilst Jox's flight would keep any enemy fighters off their backs. It was a straightforward enough plan, just made complex by having to find the damned guns.

Viewed from above, the advancing Crusaders reminded Jox of the scarab beetles he'd seen crawling across the sun-blasted stones of the ancient Egyptian temples he'd visited outside Alexandria. Their dust trails made them conspicuous on the flat open desert, overlooked by an escarpment of crimpled rock. Even more obvious, but no longer advancing were several of their companions burning brightly in the sun, thick smoke billowing to the heavens. Jox counted at least three of the buff-coloured armoured vehicles immolated by the accurate fire from hidden gun positions.

The Kittyhawks swung aggressively over suspected lairs, spraying rocket and cannon fire with seemingly reckless abandon. Enemy trench lines, wire entanglements and reinforced blockhouses were ravaged by steely projectiles screaming down from little more than head height. The guns remained elusive and continued to take a deadly toll on the hapless recce armour. Yet another Crusader exploded spectacularly as the R/T traffic from the Kittyhawk pilots grew angry with mounting frustration.

'Blue Leader here,' said an Aussie accent. 'Those tankies are really copping it. Blue Section, form up on me. I think I saw some movement in the ravine below the escarpment. If we swing low, we should catch the rotter before he reloads.'

'Yah, man, but I'm getting a bit low on ammo, Skipper,' replied a South African accent. 'I'm totally out of rockets, as well.'

'Strewth,' replied the Kittyhawk leader. 'Let's do what we can. Those cobbers are getting creamed and really need our help. Top cover escort, Blue Leader here. We're going in; keep your eyes open for any bandits.'

'Roger that,' replied Jox into the mic of his oxygen mask. 'Escort Green Leader here. We have got eyes on you and are keeping watch on the heavens.'

'Appreciate that, Escort Leader. You're our eyes in the skies.'

'Yellow One, this is Green Leader,' said Jox, addressing Baraldi. 'Jimmy, take your mob up for top cover. I'll take Green down to provide close overwatch to "the sharks" as they hit the terrain again.'

'Roger wilco,' replied Baraldi, leading his section into a steep climb. In the meantime, Jox led his flight to a lower altitude, where they could better see No. 112 Squadron in action. He watched them drop onto their targets one after the next and was reminded of blacktip reef sharks he'd seen off the beaches in Malta. They'd skitter frantically after baitfish, occasionally stranding themselves on the sand.

The lead P-40 swooped, firing only with guns as its rocket racks were depleted. It was still packing a hefty punch with four .50 calibre Browning M2 heavy machine guns fitted as standard, plus an additional pair of .30 guns, as these were up-gunned British variants. The P-40 seemed to stagger in the sky as it fired and then glided smoothly through a crack in the rocky defile. Subsequent shark-faced aircraft followed their leader down and through, until the third or fourth was suddenly targeted by AA guns hidden amongst the nooks and crannies beneath them.

From the rattling rate of fire that clawed up towards it, it was clearly a multiple barrelled gun of some sort firing. The terrain was swiftly obscured by heavy smoke from the gun, which fired in a steady pulse of fours. Once the smoke had cleared partially, Jox identified it as a Flakpanzer IV 'Wirbelwind' or Whirlwind, a self-propelled ack-ack gun on the tracked chassis of a Panzer IV tank. It was open-topped but had a heavily armoured nine-sided turret, housing a deadly set of quadruple mounted 20mm cannons. The enemy gunners were more or less protected from the P-40s' fire, launching a series of heavy projectiles at the distinctly less well-armoured Kittyhawks. After a sudden cataclysmic tumble, one of the 'sharks' cartwheeled straight into the rocks. Another climbed, trailing smoke and with both wings looking rather ragged, as if chewed on by some giant rodent.

'Disperse, disperse!' cried the Kittyhawk leader, as another of his men was struck by the deadly ground fire. The stricken aircraft veered away almost elegantly, horizontal to the ground until it simply dropped and ploughed straight in, dashed to pieces on the rocky terrain. No evasive action was taken, as the pilot was probably killed outright by the Wirbelwind's devastating firepower. The surviving Kittyhawks regrouped, as Jox and his flight continued circling out of harm's way.

'We've had it,' said the Aussie. 'We've done what we can to help those tankies and I've lost some good blokes in the process. Escort Leader, Blue Leader here: we're returning to base. Sharks, let's go home and see what the damage is. I'm not liking the look of our numbers.'

There was movement on the ground. As smoke cleared, Jox spotted the long, sinister barrel of another gun. From his vantage point it looked like a horizontal telegraph pole attached to a chassis of splayed legs, sort of like a starfish. It was an 88mm Flak gun, developed originally as an anti-aircraft gun, but in the desert landscape it was more often used in an anti-tank role, firing massive armour-piercing shells in a low, flat trajectory. It was the most feared weapon in Field Marshal Erwin Rommel's armoury, with two flak battalions of these guns having reputedly destroyed over two hundred and fifty British tanks during the desert battles of 1941. As if on cue, the long-barrelled gun jerked, and another Crusader exploded on the horizon, hit by a high-velocity projectile that was almost two feet long. It cut through the tank's thin armour like a knife through cream cheese.

'We've got to do something,' said Jox.

'That's not our fight,' replied Jimmy Baraldi, still up high with Yellow Section. 'Our mission is to protect the sharks. We've done that, and what's left of them are heading home. We should do the same.'

'He's right, Jox,' said Ralph Campbell, now Green Two and Jox's wingman. Ralph wasn't usually the voice of reason, always tending to be rather impulsive, but war had changed him. He had become more cautious and measured.

Jox was about to agree, when the 88 fired again. This time it missed but sent up a plume of soil just a few feet away from a pinned-down tank.

'I'm not having this,' said Jox, hot anger surging through his body. 'I'm going on my own. I've got an idea; you lot keep circling and keep that quad-gun's attention off of me.'

He pulled on his stick and banked into a climbing loop. The Mark V's Merlin engine complained as he gained altitude. All the while, he kept a close eye on the rotating turret of the open-topped Wirbelwind. He could see its gunners tracking Campbell and the rest of the section, tantalisingly grouped together but just out of range. As he'd hoped, the flak gun had lost track of him. He was now directly above the eggcup-shaped turret. Jox dove at an almost vertical angle and at an eye-watering speed, well over three hundred miles an hour. Falling towards the ground, the accumulated dust and debris from the cockpit's footwell flew up, coating the surface of his dashboard. He noticed several dead flies as he rotated the gun button to FIRE with his gloved hand.

Still vertical, Jox opened fire straight into the open turret. He caught a momentary glimpse of a sleeved arm pointing in his direction. His concentrated burst of fire hit the gun, the extended arm vaporising into red mist from the elbow up. He pulled the Mark V from its precipitous dive, feeling several hard thuds on the fuselage as he corkscrewed out of harm's way. The 88 boomed again and Jox was dimly aware of Jimmy Baraldi shouting, 'Bandits at twelve o'clock! Huns in the sun, defend yourselves, Treble Ones.'

Focused on his task, Jox banked the Spit for another pass, now that the 88 was unprotected. Oblivious to what was happening overhead, he lined up the targeting rings projected on the canopy and fired with his guns down the entire length of the monstrously long gun barrel. Dust and debris rose up from the position, setting off a secondary explosion. Jox pulled on his stick, straining for altitude as he searched for his comrades. He could see several condensation trails high above him, evidence of air combat overhead. He stared into the sun for rather too long, until black blobs danced before his eyes as he manoeuvred by instinct, hoping to provide as small a silhouette as possible.

It didn't do him much good. He was distracted by Ralph Campbell screaming on the R/T, 'Bank, bank left, Jox! Jerry on your tail.'

Jox's eyes flicked to the mirror above his head, where he caught a glimpse of a white-nosed spinner, a sand-coloured body and white wingtips. The enemy pilot had him and Jox felt a cold frisson of fear run through his body. He could almost hear the calm Scottish brogue of Ant Glasgow saying, 'Most pilots are right-handed. When shot at, most instinctively pull left. A good pilot uses that knowledge to kill you, but doing the opposite might just save your bacon.'

Jox jinked to the right, then dropped, hoping to lift his nose as his opponent overshot, passing over him. He'd used the manoeuvre once before to miraculously escape an aggressive Me 110 that he'd managed to best off the beach of Dunkirk during the Battle of Britain. It worked again, but not perfectly, his opponent managing to fire a few solid hits into the Spit before scraping just over the top of him. Jox fired a desperate burst at the fleeting shadow that loomed above for the briefest instant. He doubted he'd registered any successful hits, but he heard, then felt several rattling impacts along his own starboard wing. They weren't exactly bangs, more like hailstones against a car. He was tumbling now and saw several fist-sized holes in his wing. Glancing over his right shoulder, he was horrified to glimpse some blue liquid spouting out under pressure and frothing up into his wake. His 33-gallon rear fuel tank was breached, and it was only a matter of time before it caught fire. He had to get out and get out now.

His cockpit canopy was already back because of the earlier heat. He tightened his parachute straps, then unclipped the Sutton harness to detach physically from the aircraft. He pushed with his feet against the foot wells then climbed up onto the seat. The hot blast of rushing air plucked him from the cockpit, sending him tumbling away in the slipstream of his dying aircraft. He was splashed by leaking aviation fuel but miraculously avoided striking the rear tail assembly.

He was dangerously low, so he pulled the cord of the parachute almost immediately. It deployed with a gut-twisting wrench, and he found himself hanging beneath the canopy in the bright glare of the sun with the wide expanse of the desert stretched out before him. He heard the boom of an explosion somewhere below, realising that the latest iteration of *Marguerite* had met a fiery end in the desert wasteland. He looked for signs of her but was distracted by the sound of an approaching engine, rougher and more burbling than the smooth tone of the Merlin that he was used to. This was no Treble One approaching. He twisted in his straps, alarmed that his opponent might be coming to finish him off. He'd heard stories of fanatical Nazis attacking airmen hanging helpless in their parachutes.

Jox was surprised when the approaching, white-nosed Bf 109 waggled its square-cut wings. The pilot bowed in the cockpit and raised a hand to wave chivalrously towards his fallen rival. He continued to circle as Jox drifted through thermals rising from the hot sands. The aircraft bore the number 14 and had a swastika on its tail. The multiple kill tallies on its rear aileron spoke of an experienced ace. Jox was too far away to see exactly how many, but there were certainly enough to prove he'd been bested by someone very skilled.

Jox watched the enemy pilot orbit. The aircraft was one of the new Bf 109 G high-altitude fighters known as a Gustav, equipped with a powerful Daimler-Benz DB 605 engine, nitrous oxide fuel injection and a pressurised cockpit. The engine seemed to be struggling, though. Jox wondered if his rounds might have found their mark after all. The automatic hood of the Gustav slid back, releasing a dark trail of smoke from the cockpit. The pilot waved his arms, apparently blinded and disorientated. The fighter slowly rotated until the cockpit was facing groundward, its downward trajectory promising imminent disaster. Jox saw his erstwhile opponent launch himself from the cockpit and get immediately caught in the slipstream. His body struck the tail of the aircraft very hard. For a brief instant, he was wrapped around it before being violently flung away. The pilot tumbled through the air, but Jox lost sight of the falling man and saw no parachute deploy.

Horrified by what he'd witnessed, Jox had not noticed the scrubby ground approaching very fast. Distracted, he was unprepared for the brutality of the rough landing. Thumping down heavily, he was dragged along by his canopy through bushes of spiky camelthorn and boulders, jarring his old shoulder wound in the process. When he finally came to a stop, he lay panting until the growing heat of the sun on his body made him sit up. Getting groggily to his feet, he unclipped the parachute harness, releasing the silk canopy that threatened to pull him further along in the hot desert wind.

Jox raised his goggles and scanned his surroundings. He didn't know where he'd landed but estimated he was some miles south of Sidi Abdel Rahman. In every direction he looked, the terrain appeared the same, the sole exception being some wreckage on the horizon, maybe a mile or two away. It offered the only shelter from the sun that he could see, so he began trudging wearily in that direction. He didn't know if it was his aircraft or his opponent's, or maybe one of the Kittyhawks they'd been tasked with protecting. Either way, it was searingly hot and uncomfortable getting to it, and the whole experience was starting to feel rather like the infamous French Foreign Legion edict of 'march or die'.

'March or die,' he mumbled to himself. 'That sounds about right.'

CHAPTER TWENTY-NINE

The crumpled wreckage of the Bf 109 lay nose-deep in the ground. It had gouged a vivid scar across some dunes, a surprisingly straight line in the endlessly shifting peaks and troughs of the sand.

Black propellers were peeled back from the white nose like petals on a dead daisy. On the tattered side of the fuselage was a stark black and white-edged cross, alongside the number fourteen picked out in canary yellow. Most of the aircraft's rear assembly was missing, as were the engine block and cockpit canopy, such had been the violence of its impact with the ground. Miraculously, there was no fire and the wreckage had become a magnet for the nocturnal creatures of the desert. Jox was no exception.

After the heat of the day, he was sitting in the lee of the wreck, sheltering from the chilly breeze that nightfall had brought on. He had a raging thirst and felt chafing sand in every orifice. Seriously dehydrated, he was chapped and sunburnt, stinging salt around his red-rimmed nostrils. The day's exertions had taken their toll, and he faced a long, thirsty night.

Earlier, overheated and sweating, his perspiration had drawn the flies, desperate to get at the moisture in his eyes, nostrils and mouth. Once he'd reached the wreck, his only option was to sit out the daylight hours in its poor shade, enduring the shimmering heat and his aching shoulder with his flying helmet and goggles on. Every time he flailed, a buzzing murmuration of the ravenous insects would rise above him. He also had to be careful not to touch the metalled fuselage of the wreck.

Remarkably quickly, the strength of the sun had got it so hot that he could have fried an egg on the wings.

Despite the ache in his shoulder and the weeping scratches on his face, the result of his poor landing, Jox thought physical activity might keep his mind off his predicament. He collected up some rocks, boulders, and bits of debris from the wreckage, and spelt out HELP in the sand, hoping perhaps over-optimistically that some Allied flyer might pass overhead. Inspecting the wreckage for anything useful, he found only a discarded white silk scarf crumpled in the footwell. It was monogrammed with the letters HJM in blocky Gothic script, telling him that whoever the pilot might have been, he was certainly something of a dandy. Jox wrapped the scarf over his nose and ears to protect them from the sun and could smell expensive cologne in the soft silk.

The Gustav's nose was buried in the sand. Jox noted the 'Leopard over Africa' emblem of JG 27 painted on it, with a crude representation of an African native confronted by the growling head of a big cat. Silhouetted behind it was the African continent. The drawing seemed rather childish and derogatory to Jox, but he still decided to hack it out as a souvenir. He reasoned it might be worth a beer in the mess, if he made it out of here, and anyway, it gave him something to do.

As dusk fell, the trophy was safely tucked away in his tunic pocket, and the flies had mercifully disappeared. A pair of yellow lizards began wrestling nearby and he watched them chase one another across the wind-ridged dunes beyond the wreckage. They kicked up spurts of sand with their clawed feet in the fading light, flinging it into the air. From various nooks and crannies, tiny translucent scorpions began to emerge, bristling angrily at Jox but then squaring up to each other like miniature knights in armour. Conflict, it appeared, was everywhere in the desert tonight.

Earlier, Jox had seen carrion birds circling, but they had also disappeared. They'd reminded him of the Stukas in France, waiting their turn to strike at the huddled lines of terrified refugees. Perhaps these scavengers had also spotted the cream-coloured parachute billowing on the horizon. Whoever lay at the end of it no doubt offered a better prospect of a meal than he did. Perhaps it was the pilot of Yellow 14, whom he'd seen strike the tail assembly when baling out. Jox hadn't seen the parachute deploy, but perhaps it had burst open on impact with the desert floor.

Jox would have liked to have gone to investigate, but just beyond the wrecked Gustav a single line of barbed wire was hung with a rusty sign warning 'ACHTUNG MINEN.' He surely wasn't going to blunder into another minefield if he could help it, especially the 'Devil's Garden' as night approached. He'd heard terrible things about Jerry's S-mines or 'Bouncing Bettys', which popped up three feet in the air when triggered, then detonated at groin height. Jox decided to sit tight until someone came along. It was just a matter of luck which side would come first.

It was already quite dark when he heard high-pitched snickering and the sound of squabbling. The noises weren't particularly threatening, but he was still glad of the switchblade in his pocket and the reassurance of his lucky doll's arm. He peered into the gloom when the eastern horizon suddenly lit up with silvery beams of diffused light. They seemed to bounce off the harsh landscape, softening everything but also revealing every shrub and feature. In the ghostly glow, a pair of Fennec foxes with huge batlike ears and dark eyes were squabbling over the desiccated carcass of a baby camel he hadn't noticed earlier. It had probably been separated from its mother and was too young to survive. Now, it provided Jox with a chilling presentiment of his fate if rescue didn't materialise.

It was getting colder under the starlit sky, but Jox was reluctant to light a fire that might attract attention to his poor shelter, especially given what was about to begin. He glanced at his wristwatch and was grateful for the radium on the dials. It was seven-thirty, just an hour before the diversionary barrage in front of the 24th Australian Brigade was due to begin. Then at precisely 21:40, Operation Lightfoot's thousand-gun barrage was set to follow. Coordinated fire would land right across the battle front and then would switch to precision targets in direct support to the advancing infantry.

Jox looked expectantly up at the sky, lit by both artificial light and now the full moon. It was coming up to 20:30 hours. It wouldn't be long now. He didn't know how loud the opening barrage would be or whether he was sitting on a spot marked on some Royal Artillery gunner's target map.

The barrage opened with a few sharp cracks of high-altitude airbursts to test the accuracy of the weathermen's predictions and to allow the plotters to calculate the trajectories of subsequent volleys. After the briefest of pauses, the eastern horizon lit up as the massed batteries of medium and heavy guns opened up. Flashing pulses of light blinked before the rumbling sound came to him. It was accompanied by a deep baseline, presumably from the big naval guns of the fleet that were gathered offshore. There was a shrieking overhead, like the call of Valkyries crying for souls they'd been sent to collect. Moments later the western horizon erupted in flashes of scarlet and gold, burning out Jox's night vision and brutalising his ears. The ground beneath him rumbled and the carcass of the Bf 109 Gustav rattled like an old train carriage.

His watch told him the opening salvo had lasted fifteen minutes. To the east, men, materiel, vehicles, tanks and trucks would be moving west. He checked his watch again; when the dials reached 22:00, the rolling barrage was set to begin once more. The question was where it would roll to, and whether he was in its path.

The sky suddenly burst apart, turning night into day. He'd been told a thousand guns would be firing across the front. Explosions began to mingle with secondary bangs as mines were detonated by the advancing fire. Engineers were no doubt also cutting through wire entanglements and detonating ordinance to open clear tracts in the enemy's minefields. These narrow, cleared paths through fields of death were simply marked by flimsy white tape that bowed and flapped in the sandstorm of blasted soil that was being projected skywards.

Above him, Jox could now hear the dull throb of formations of medium and light bombers making their way across the night sky, as yet unopposed as they targeted strategic points behind the enemy's frontline. In the maelstrom of fire, Jox knew men and machines were being shredded and minced, mangled and burned, blown to fragments, decapitated and disembowelled. Humanity was being reduced to mere flecks of flesh, pools of blood, oily residue on the sand or the delicate ash that was floating across the desert.

For five long hours the barrage continued without pause. Then just as suddenly at 03:00, the darkest hour in the desert, it stopped. Cordite, choking dust and acrid fumes hung over the dunes, shrublands and rocky outcrops. From the east came the sounds of gunning engines, the clanking of armoured tracks and then quite unexpectedly the haunting swirl of distant bagpipes. Two powerful beams of light crossed high in the heavens to form the Scottish saltire, the flag of St Andrew in the desert sky.

The Jocks were on the move: the glorious Argylls, the Black Watch, the Gordons and the Cameron Highlanders were on their way. The whole bloodthirsty lot of them were coming to avenge St Valery, and Jox's heart soared with pride. He'd have given anything to be with them, rather than cowering here beside the mangled wreckage of his enemy's aircraft.

The barrage was due to resume at first light, but Jox couldn't remember exactly when that was. Was it 06:00 or 07:00? His brain was fuzzy, his eyes hazy and his ears still ringing. Perhaps it was the repeated violent changes in air pressure during the barrage that had concussed him, or maybe his raging thirst was taking its toll. His shoulder still ached, and his left arm felt numb, but he forced himself to his feet. He staggered up to the fence line of the minefield and peered at the horizon, lit by the early rays of the pre-dawn. Over the brow of the high ground to the east, he thought he'd spotted the dust trails of approaching vehicles. Unseen but heard came the sound of small arms fire, followed by a hollow detonation. He wanted to go and investigate, and it took every bit of his self-discipline not to go blundering into the minefield.

Reluctantly, Jox returned to the shelter of the wreckage. He pulled off his now not so new moleskin desert boots, realising they'd really been lifesavers. He poured a fine trickle of sand from each, before shaking out his socks and putting everything back on again. These small tasks seemed to clear some of the fog in his head and gave him something to think about other than his thirst.

He looked up at the sound of another explosion. This one felt closer and was followed by a sharp report, then some keening cries. He got to his feet and staggered back to the fence. Thirty yards into the minefield was a drab-coloured two-seater half-track with an enclosed rear cab for carrying equipment. Stencilled on the passenger side door was what looked like the Luftwaffe eagle, but it was facing the wrong way and was red rather than the usual white. It was the emblem of the Red Eagles, the 4th Indian Infantry Division. In grim confirmation and hanging from the driver's doorway was a portly havildar with a full beard and a khaki turban that had come undone from the blast of the mine the halftrack had evidently run over. The sergeant was quite dead, his shoulder-length hair hanging like a curtain over his face. There was blood dripping from his hanging arm, pooling in the sand below his fingertips. A steel bangle glittered on his wrist.

Closer to Jox was the source of the keening: a young Sikh soldier, little more than a boy. He didn't have his sergeant's full beard, just a fuzzy down. He was writhing in agony, his left leg missing from the knee with bleeding in his groin and abdomen. Tears streamed down his handsome face from large, dark eyes. From the brass laurelled stars on their shoulder badges, the men appeared to be combat engineers, but that hadn't stopped them from blundering into one of the Devil's Garden's minefields.

'Water, please, sahib,' croaked the wounded sapper, his lips ringed with blood. Jox wasn't sure if water was a good idea with a gut wound, and he had none to give anyway. The boy's hand scrambled at his own belt.

'Let me help you,' said Jox, stepping over the wire. There was twenty yards to cross, and he did so at pace, putting his safety in the hands of fate to get to the wounded man. He knelt beside him. 'There, there.' The boy's lips had a blueish tinge and he'd evidently lost a lot of blood. He'd been trying to get at a canteen attached to his webbing. Jox unclipped it, and in spite of his reservations, carefully lifted the boy's turbaned head so he might drink. It took every ounce of willpower not to help himself to some too.

'What's your name, my lad?' he asked, gently removing the sapper's webbing belt and strapping it around the stump of his leg as a tourniquet.

'Ravinder, sahib,' he replied, wincing as Jox pulled the webbing tight. 'Sapper Ravinder Punjabi at your service. I am Ravi.' He fell silent for a while. 'Am I going to die, sahib?'

'Not if I can help it,' said Jox. 'We need to get out of this minefield. I'm going to carry you out, but before that may I have a drink from your canteen? Would that be all right? I haven't had any water for over twenty-four hours.'

'Please,' replied the sapper weakly. 'Drink, you are most welcome. There is more water in the back of the truck. Medicine and bandages too.' Jox looked over to the mangled remains of the half-track.

'We'll get to that,' he replied. 'First, I need to get you to safety and out of the sun before it gets too hot.' It was still quite early, but dawn had broken, and the sun would soon be blazing, if yesterday was anything to go by. 'All right, Ravi. My name is Jox. This is going to hurt, but the only way I can be sure of sticking to my footprints is by carrying you on my back. You don't look too heavy, but it'll be important you don't struggle. I can't risk stumbling or losing my footing. I'm going to use a fireman's lift. Can you just hang like a deadweight, Ravi?'

'Yes, surely, sir,' said Sapper Punjabi. 'I will do as you order.'

'No need to call me sir. Just Jox will do.'

'No, sir, I cannot,' replied Ravi. 'You are an officer-sahib. This would not be correct.'

'In that case, I order you to stand at ease, Sapper Punjabi. It's the only way we can get out of this predicament.' Jox hitched the water bottle to his own belt. 'Right, I'm going to lift you now. Please focus on not flinching when I do so. I'm sorry if I hurt you.'

'I will not cry out, sahib. I will not move. This I promise you.'

Jox took a deep breath. He was still feeling a bit giddy, but the few mouthfuls of tepid water had already had some restorative effect. He lifted the maimed sapper over his shoulder, face down with Ravi bent at the waist, the stump of his leg against Jox's chest. He was heavier than he looked, or maybe it was just that Jox was weaker. The pair staggered dangerously, with Ravi quietly moaning. Jox gritted his teeth and began placing his feet in his spread-out footsteps, made when he'd run out to the sapper. The length of his stride was proving problematic, especially with Ravi's weight on his back.

Jox's view of the world narrowed to just the square yard of desert sand directly in front of his feet. He could see the finishing line in his peripheral vision, the single strand of rusty barbed wire that marked the limit of the minefield. Holding his breath, he shifted the weight on his shoulder and gingerly stepped over it. As he did, there was a scraping metallic sound, and his blood ran cold.

CHAPTER THIRTY

Jox teetered with one foot on either side of the strand of rusty barbed wire stretching across the barren landscape. He held his breath, expecting the worst, but nothing happened. The sound of metal against metal turned out to be the canteen on his hip tapping against the jagged barbs of the wire.

He gingerly lifted his back foot over, staggering under the weight of the sapper. Shifting the load, he made a final effort to reach the shelter of Yellow 14, moving painfully slowly. When he got there, Jox lay Ravi down as gently as he could manage, but the young sapper still groaned.

'It hurts, sahib, so much,' whispered Ravi. 'Please help me. There is medicine in the truck: morphine, needles and pipettes that can help.' He panted with the effort of speaking. 'I know it is dangerous and a lot to ask, but I cannot stand this pain.' His voice trailed off as he sank mercifully into unconsciousness.

Jox glanced back at the devastated half-track in the minefield. It didn't really look so far, but there was plenty of danger around it. He stood up, trying to catch his breath after the exertion of carrying Ravi. He took a final deep breath, building up his resolve.

'All right, I'll try,' he said to himself. 'Let me just have another sip of water.' He swallowed greedily from the canteen, and it was an effort not to drain it all at once.

Ravi awoke and began to writhe, his head rocking back and forth, dusting his sweat-covered face with fine sand. His evident suffering made up Jox's mind. He trudged back to the fence line, shoulders slumped with exhaustion, but his mind was racing, and his heart in his mouth.

It was mid-morning now, and there was smoke on the horizon with a constant rumble of small arms and artillery fire in the distance. Occasionally, there was the snarl of aircraft passing overhead, but never close enough for Jox to identify or signal to. He returned his focus to what lay directly in front of him. He thought back to how he'd made his way out of the minefield in Devon. Here in the desert, though, the sand was bone-dry, very fine and interspersed with rocks and boulders. The beach at the Kingsbridge Estuary was gloopy and wet, so there was very little comparison to be made.

Jox pressed the button of his Maltese switchblade, and it gave a reassuring click. He dropped onto his knees, gazing across the expanse of sand between him, where Ravi had been hurt and then onwards to the halftrack. He felt reasonably confident he could make it back to where the young sapper had lain, as it was unlikely another S-mine would have been placed within a yard or two of the one that had taken Ravi's foot.

The top of the anti-personnel mines had three-inch-long wire prongs that projected upwards like the forefingers and thumb of a cupped hand. They were usually attached to a tilt-trigger but sometimes also had a tripwire that extended out for several metres, most effective in long grass or shrubland where vegetation might hide the wire. Here, he expected the simpler triggers and hoped the shifting sands blown about by the Saharan wind might work in his favour. Perhaps, if he looked carefully enough, he might see where the covering of sand around the S-mines might have been blown away, enough to leave the triggers standing proud of the ground. Conversely, blown sand might accumulate around anything protruding from the ground: rocks, vegetation or the triggers themselves, thereby hiding them from view.

The risk from Teller mines was less of a concern, since they required the weight of a vehicle to set them off. It seemed unlikely that the halftrack was sitting on a second mine, since the driver's side of the cab had already been destroyed by one, the blast of that explosion having killed Ravi's havildar.

He carefully followed his footsteps for the second time that day. Sweat trickled down his back and dripped from the tip of his nose as he reached the blood-splattered spot where Ravi had been hurt. Remains of his pulped foot lay in the sand like a dog-chewed joint. It made Jox feel slightly queasy when he noticed it was crawling with countless, blue-bellied flies. Averting his eyes, he dropped back to ground level, his eyeline just inches above the sand rising away at a slight incline. As a fighter pilot, he had better than average eyesight. His keen vision had kept him alive many times, and he hoped that today would be no exception.

Jox realised that between his position and the vehicle there were about half a dozen regularly spaced-out grouped spikes standing clear of the ground. At this distance, they looked like the stalked eyes of the little hermit crabs he'd seen crawling across the Devonian mudflats. These, however, were static and malevolent, promising only agony and death if disturbed. He stepped delicately between them, growing in confidence as he got closer to the stranded vehicle. So far, the shifting sands and wind had helped him, but as he approached the rear of the vehicle, he saw there was a new challenge to overcome.

The jolt of the initial explosion under the driver-side wheel had pushed the rear of the vehicle backwards into the ground. The sand behind it was ruched up, exposing another bristling S-mine just inches from the back door. There would be no way of opening it without setting off the mine. Frustrated, Jox crept down the side of the half-track and climbed into the cab for some precious shade and thinking time. He checked over the body of the bulky havildar hanging from the driver's door, but he was clearly already dead. He searched the cab for anything useful and found another full canteen, some dry biscuits, a bolt-action wooden-stocked SMLE rifle on a rack and a flattop helmet, of little use to the turban-wearing Sikh engineers. Jox munched on the biscuits and washed them down with some tepid water. He considered his predicament, knowing that he had to act swiftly to be of any use to Ravi, out there suffering on the sand. An idea suddenly came to him, an unpalatable one, but an idea nonetheless.

Carefully checking that there were no further mines where he'd land, Jox pushed the bulky Sikh sergeant out of the cab door using both his feet. The body landed with a sickening thud. Jox put on the helmet, shouldered the rifle and delicately made his way around the front of the vehicle, checking his path was clear of any visible triggers. Jox then grabbed the havildar by his webbing and began to drag his imposing bulk across the sand, leaving a red trail that quickly attracted legions of flies.

Once far enough away from the vehicle to have a decent view of its rear, Jox propped the sergeant's body up with his broad back and buttocks facing towards the halftrack. Jox lay flat behind him, the helmet on his head and the rifle propped up on the sergeant's fleshy hip. He was a good shot; had represented the school at Bisley and was a keen game and clay pigeon shooter. It was hot, though, sweat was streaming into his eyes, and he was aiming through a heat haze at a very small target.

His first shot missed, as did his second. The third pinged metallically, a small sound followed by a mighty woosh and a sharp crack of an explosion. The prostrate body he was cowering behind shuddered as it was struck by several ball bearings from the S-mine. Jox was stunned by the violence and peeked cautiously over his makeshift fleshy shield. The doors of the truck were peppered with fresh holes, ringed in raw metal where ball bearings had punched through the dun-coloured panels. He got unsteadily to his feet, laying his hand on the sergeant's shoulder in a brief prayer of thanks. He removed one of the havildar's identity tags and pocketed it. He couldn't give him a proper burial, but at least the man wouldn't simply disappear into the desert sands, unknown and lost.

Jox made his way cautiously to the back doors and found that they opened easily. Inside, the S-mine's deadly halo of ball bearings hadn't wreaked as much damage as he'd feared. Scrabbling through the contents of the cab, he was struck by the withering temperature in the enclosed space and worried that the medical supplies might be affected by the extreme heat. He found a large canvas bag with a white circle and red cross on it and rummaged until he located needles, vials of clear liquid, bandages and disinfectant. He also found a large water barrel in the back. It was holed and leaking, but Jox managed to refill his canteen and find a battered bucket to capture more. The water would be gritty but was wet and would sustain them for a few vital hours, perhaps even days. He also found some compo rations, which he stuffed into a tatty duffel bag along with the medical supplies.

Loaded like a mule, he made his way back along the trail that he'd taken into the minefield. He didn't know how long the expedition took and was already dreading the state he might find Ravi in. When he got to him, the sapper was still unconscious, but came around when Jox wet his lips, trickling water from the German aviator's silk scarf that he still had around his neck.

'Am … am I going to die?' asked the frightened sapper in a hoarse whisper.

Jox took a deep breath before answering. 'Yes, I'm afraid you are dying. I'm sorry, Ravi, but I can promise you, there will be no more pain.'

The young Sikh nodded weakly. 'It is my fate, sahib,' he croaked. 'I am ready.'

Jox squeezed a pipette of morphine into his arm, then another, and kept going until Ravi calmed. His breathing eased and he was still, no longer thrashing about. Instead, he had settled into a mumbling sleep. As Jox watched over him, he opened a few cans of compo rations with his switchblade. The first was tinned peaches that tasted like the heavenly ambrosia of the Gods to Jox. The next was labelled 'M & V' and contained a dubious combination of unidentified meat and vegetables. To finish off the ad hoc meal, he ate a small tin of cheddar cheese. Almost immediately, his stomach began to burble in response to the rushed compo feast after his prolonged period of fasting. Rubbing his abdomen with discomfort, Jox noticed Ravi watching him.

'Do you feel unwell, sahib?' he asked, but didn't wait for an answer. 'I feel my time is near. I must prepare my *Pañj Kakār*, the five symbols of my faith. My hair is *kesh*, uncut, and I have my *kangha* comb, and I am wearing my *kara* bracelet and *kachera* garment. I have no sword, though, sahib. I must have a *kirpan* to die as a Sikh warrior.'

Jox wiped the processed cheese off the blade of his Maltese switchblade. It was precious to him, reminding him of what he'd had and lost in Malta. Julianna was no longer his, so what did the blade now signify? Perhaps it could mean something again. Without hesitation, he offered it to the dying sapper, hoping it might ease his passing.

'I don't know if this would do,' said Jox. 'It means a lot to me, but it's yours.'

'Thank you, sahib,' whispered Ravi. 'It is not a curved blade, but it must do, thank you. Please let me hold it.' Jox placed the knife handle in the sapper's hands. He gripped it tightly. 'Tell my brothers that I died a proud Sikh warrior. I am the youngest, you see, and they always teased me, calling me a sissy. I volunteered for the Indian Army to prove them wrong. Please, sahib, tell them I died bravely.'

Jox nodded, then hung his head as Ravi's breathing grew shallower and shallower. He held the sapper's hand until a final rattle escaped his throat. The brave Sikh warrior was gone, and Jox was struck by a powerful wave of grief. Perhaps it was delayed shock or simply that the night was falling after a long and arduous day. Exhausted, Jox slept beside his fallen comrade. Side by side, they lay oblivious to the bitter fighting that was going on all around them.

In the morning, Jox awoke refreshed but still feeling queasy. He boiled some gritty water in a compo tin over a fire of camelthorn twigs, hoping some tea might see him right. He was determined to bury Ravi properly and used a combination of the Tommy helmet and an aileron from Yellow 14 to scrape out a shallow grave for the sapper. He laid him on his back, straightening out his uniform and doing up his buttons. Jox wondered whether he should go and fetch Ravi's leg but dismissed the idea as pushing his luck too far in the minefield. He placed the Maltese blade in Ravi's hand and took one of his identity tags. He covered the young sapper's face with the helmet and filled the grave with dry sand and gravel. It was laborious and physical work, especially in his weakened state.

To Jox it felt important to do it right, with Ravi representing the many he'd lost. He then sat hollow-eyed and mournful until his guts told him he urgently had to relieve himself. Lurching away from the wreckage and the grave, he found a secluded spot. Whilst focused on answering the call of nature, he was startled by the familiar sound of a Merlin engine passing directly overhead. Quickly pulling up his trousers, he searched the sky, spotted the silhouette and rushed over to the word HELP that he'd lettered out in debris and rocks. Waving frantically, he was gladdened to see the Spitfire Mark V pitch over, change course and begin to circle. As it got closer, he shaded his eyes from the bright sun and his heart leapt as he recognised the lettering on the fuselage: JU-G. It was a Treble One.

The aircraft dropped with full flaps, decelerating rapidly as it lost altitude. For a horrifying moment, Jox feared he would land in the minefield, so he ran towards it, gesticulating and shouting at the top of his lungs. The pilot must have spotted the devastated 4th Indian Infantry Division halftrack and the splayed body of the havildar and adjusted his trajectory accordingly. Within moments, he'd bumped down and was taxiing towards Jox. With his engine still running, he waved and indicated that Jox should approach. Buffeted by dust and sand thrown up by the spinning propellor, he struggled to get close. Jox suddenly turned away and ran back to the wreckage of Yellow 14, where he grabbed his abandoned flight goggles and helmet. He checked that his doll's arm was still in his blouse pocket, then searched for his switchblade. He remembered with a start that it was buried with Ravi. He picked up his trophy emblem from the downed Bf 109 Gustav and wrapped the German aviator's silk scarf over his nose and mouth, before heading back to the stationary Spit, spinner turning but with the engine at low revs.

The noise and backdraught from the engine had lessened enough for Jox to scramble up onto the portside wing, where the pilot had lowered the Spit's side hatch. In white cursive letters below the windscreen was the name 'Véronique' — the name of *Chevalier* Olivier de Ghellinck's sister, a brave resistance fighter in his native Belgium. The slim-faced aristocrat raised his goggles and beamed at Jox.

'Ah, *mon vieux*, Ghillie has found you!' he shouted over the strobing propeller. 'We've been out looking for days.' He unclipped his straps and stood up on his seat, then pulled his parachute out of its nook and threw it out of the cockpit. 'Get in, Jox. We are in the middle of a big battle.'

'Get in? Where?' said Jox incredulously.

'There is room,' de Ghellinck answered. 'I am skinny, and you are not so big. Come on, we must hurry. Get on my lap. You lean left and keep your foot on the left rudder pedal, and I'll control the right. You handle the throttle and I'll take care of the control column with my right hand. It can be done, if we work together.'

Jox didn't hesitate. He reached into the cockpit with his leg and settled on de Ghellinck's lap. There wasn't much room, but they would manage. He raised the revs and with de Ghellinck steering, the Spitfire rumbled forward over the uneven terrain. After what felt like a long time, the overloaded aircraft lifted off the ground.

'Close the hood, so we can talk!' de Ghellinck shouted into Jox's ear.

Jox struggled with it and the Spitfire jinked about clumsily, but he got there in the end. The sudden silence in the cockpit was unsettling.

'Flying like this is very dangerous,' said Jox. 'You're going to catch hell from the CO.'

'No,' replied de Ghellinck. 'It was Bolshie's idea in the first place that we go and look for you. If we found you, he said we must return by "piggyback". He said he has done it before during the Battle of Britain, to get to a party. But you stink, *mon ami*. I have a sensitive nose, you know.'

'I'm sorry, but it gets pretty hot in the desert, and a man sweats.'

Jox looked down at the desert that had been his open prison for the last few days. Spread across the bleak open landscape were countless wrecks, burning equipment and smashed gun emplacements. The carnage was widespread, and he spotted the crumpled forms of several bodies amongst the debris and charred spoil. Between it, there was armour moving forward with various supporting vehicles advancing in their wake, leaving long trails of rising dust. Together they were like successive waves breaking on a beach, one line chasing the next.

'What's going on down there?'

'That is the enemy in full retreat. Monty says the Deutsch Afrika Korps and their Italian allies are "crumbling" before the Eighth Army. We've penetrated three lines of heavy fortifications, and our tanks are chasing after theirs to reach Objective Skinflint, deep within their defensive system at the Rahman Track. There will no doubt be a German counterattack, as the fight's far from over, but things for now are looking good. We are finally winning, *mon vieux*.'

'Winning?' replied Jox wearily. 'If that's what winning looks like, God help us if we ever lose again.'

EPILOGUE

London, 1990

David 'Pritch' Pritchard's funeral reception was held in a vast hall known as the King's Room at the Royal Star & Garter Home. The hall was festooned with memorials with shiny brass plaques, military portraits and paintings of various battles, soldiers and martial scenes. The fading colours of long-defunct battalions were hanging from the ceiling, a stark contrast to the latest examples of wheelchair technology propelling chairbound residents between the more ambulatory guests. They moved with such speed and dexterity they were known as the 'Flying Squad' by the staff, despite having an average age of eighty-six.

Melanie entered the room on Nancy's arm, filled with unexpected trepidation. She was nervous at the prospect of seeing the mysterious Belgian again and intrigued about the identity of the American politician. She was also apprehensive about the prospect of entering a roomful of strangers. She needn't have worried on that account: as Pritchard's adoptive niece, Nancy Wake's new ward and the granddaughter of the famous fighter ace Jox McNabb, she was already amongst dear and doting friends.

She chatted with Derek, a cheerful older man in a wheelchair. He told her that he'd missed the fighting in the war as he was too young, but he had served in the Royal Army Medical Corps, completing six return trips by ship to Hiroshima in Japan to collect and care for severely malnourished and mistreated prisoners of war. His repeated exposure to the radiation had got into his bones, and he was now confined to his chair with a degenerative bone disorder. It didn't stop him from being utterly charming and making Melanie feel welcome.

Nancy crossed the parquet floor from where she'd collected some drinks and pointed discreetly towards the doorway. Standing in a well-cut navy-blue suit was the Belgian officer from this afternoon. He and Melanie locked eyes. Nancy observed them expectantly and watched the young man negotiate his way across the crowded room.

'Good evening, Mademoiselle McNabb,' he said. 'We didn't get much of a chance to speak this afternoon. I was sorry about that.'

'Please, no need to be so formal. You should call me Melanie.'

'All right, but only if you call me Luc. My name is Luc de Ghellinck.' Nancy silently materialised beside them and Luc came smartly to attention.

'It is a privilege to see you again, Madame Andrée,' he said.

Nancy smiled sweetly and flashed her steely eyes at him. 'Ah yes, *mon capitaine*, good to see you again. Melanie tells me your parents were friends with her grandfather and my dear Pritchy. Well, do tell.'

Luc was unused to being questioned so directly. He cleared his throat before replying. 'Yes, that's right, my father *Chevalier* Olivier de Ghellinck served with both of them during the war. My father was especially proud of being a Treble One and was so fond of them both. He told me many times that David Pritchard was always the life and soul of any squadron party and made the hard days of war more bearable for all his comrades. Your grandfather, the famous Jox McNabb, was like a brother to him.' He smiled as he remembered something.

'My father once told me the story of how he saved Jox from the desert during the Battle of El Alamein. In the middle of the vast desert and raging battle, he found him and picked him up in his Spitfire. They flew back together to their airbase, both in the same tiny cockpit. It sounds impossible, but he assured me it was true, even saying that Jox was rather fragrant in that enclosed space after several days in the hot desert. He has many stories of their war years together. It was Jox who introduced him to my mother later in the war and also saved my father's life in Italy. Without your grandfather, I wouldn't even exist, and I suppose without my father you wouldn't either. There's a bond between those two men that is hard to fathom. It is something my father is eternally grateful for. My father sends his apologies for not attending in person, but he is very frail. He does not travel well, and it has been many years since he visited with Jox at our family's estate in Scotland. He used to go regularly to see your grandfather and to drink too much whisky together, according to my mother.'

It came to Melanie in an instant. That was why Luc's surname was so familiar. Her grandfather's lodge on the Dundonald Estate in the Highlands of Perthshire was owned by a family of foreign aristocrats. She recalled the estate factor, Angus Dundonald, once telling her his employer owed a 'great debt of honour' to her grandfather and that the hunting lodge had been gifted to Jox and his descendants as a mark of eternal gratitude. *Chevalier* Olivier de Ghellinck, Luc's elderly father, she now realised, was that aristocrat. Angus had spoken of 'His Lordship' visiting half a dozen times over the years, usually during the salmon season. They would fish the Isla bordering the estate and then lustily bay at the moon during whisky-fuelled nights.

Luc smiled shyly. 'I believe we may even have met once, when we were young children,' he said. 'It was the one time my mother insisted we should accompany Papa to Dundonald, but she was so horrified by the loutish behaviour of the two old fighter pilots that she cut our holiday short. Unfortunately, I have no memory of it.' He shook his head. 'The thing is she always blamed my father for the excesses, never her dear Jox. For her, Jox was a hero, and she would forgive him anything. She was very sad to hear of his passing, and now of course that of Squadron Leader Pritchard. "All my heroes are dying," she told me, before I set off for the UK to attend the ceremony.'

'I don't remember that,' said Melanie. 'How strange to think we met all those years ago.'

'Well, I'm very glad we've met now. It's a pity it's under such sad circumstances. I know it may seem a little inappropriate, but since I am a stranger in London, I wondered if you might consider showing me the sights and perhaps having dinner with me? We can swap stories about our illustrious forefathers, if you like.'

Melanie smiled, but not as broadly as Nancy Wake, who was watching them like a hawk.

'Ooh, this is getting good,' the elderly lady whispered to herself. 'My darling Pritchy would love this,' she went on in a louder voice. 'Go on, *mes enfants*, you go and live. Leave all this dull dying business to us old fossils. We've had our time, and such fine times they were too. If either of those old fellows were here, they'd say look forward, not back!'

There was a loud clatter in the background as one of the 'Flying Squad' collided with a large burly man wearing sunglasses.

'Why don't you bloody watch where you're going!' yelled Admiral Sir Stephen Ronson-Pidgeon, the notoriously hot-tempered former First Sea Lord and Chief of the Naval Staff. He was not one with a lot of patience for clumsy landlubbers walking into his chair.

The secret serviceman was clearly flustered, his colleagues grouping defensively around their principal before the irritated Royal Navy octogenarian.

'Cool it, boys,' said a voice from behind the cluster of bodyguards. It had the twang of the American South. 'My sincere apologies, sir. From one old soldier to another, I do hope you'll forgive the clumsiness of my men. You know how it is: they're so full of zeal that they don't — how would you Limeys put it? — "look before they leap."'

The phalanx of dark suits parted to reveal the bulky shape of the eye-patched VIP who'd been helicoptered down to the crematorium that morning.

'I know you,' blustered Admiral Sir Stephen. 'You're the United States Secretary of Defense. I've seen you on television and I've come across you earlier in your military career.'

'Yes, sir, I do have that honour,' replied the southerner, his solitary eye glinting with humour. 'I had the pleasure of attending several of your lectures during my service. It is a great pleasure to see you again, Sir Stephen, in spite of the sad occasion. You will forgive me if I make my excuses. I must express my condolences to those closest to my dear old friend Pritch, a fine comrade from the good old, bad old days.'

He strode purposefully towards Nancy and Melanie. He stopped smartly before them, bowed his head and offered his hand.

'My sincere condolences for your loss, ladies. My name is Beans, Darren Beans the Third. I had the honour of serving with Squadron Leader Pritchard during the war. He was one hell of a guy. My dear, might you be his daughter?'

Melanie shook his meaty hand but found it surprisingly soft. He may once have been a soldier but had obviously been a politician for quite a while. 'No, Uncle Pritch was my godfather. He was one of my grandfather's best friends and a big part of my childhood. They served together during the war.'

'And who might your grandfather be, my dear?' asked the white-haired politician.

'Group Captain Jeremy McNabb.'

'McNabb! Hot dog, Jox McNabb. Well, I'll be a son of gun. He knew me as "Bayou" Beans back then, and I damned near killed him twice. That good old boy still forgave me and helped get me home after I got this.' He indicated his hidden eye behind the patch. 'I owe him a lot. Young lady, I sure could tell you some war stories about your granddaddy. He helped me become the soldier I am, after what wasn't the most encouraging of starts. I ain't done so bad since then, for being just a fellow born on the bayou. A lot of that is down to Jox, and I'd surely love to see him again.'

'I'm afraid he passed away last year,' replied Melanie, biting her lip. 'Now with Pritch gone too, the Few just keep getting fewer.'

'Aw hell, I'm real sorry to hear that.' Beans's face was genuinely pained. He wiped his pale blue eye and shook his head. 'You know, we escaped with our lives so many times that sometimes we felt invincible. But then we lost many friends and comrades along the way. I never thought that I, or Jox, or Pritch for that matter would ever die as old men. Hell, I still remember that lame old gag that Pritch always cracked. Now, what was it? "Old pilots never die; they just go to a higher plane." Well, I sure hope that's true and pray that one day, I might catch up with them again.' He grinned. 'Amen to that and God bless them all, every one.'

A NOTE TO THE READER

Jox McNabb is a fictional character, an amalgam of real historical figures I've come across, of people I've met and known, and then perhaps with a touch of author's conceit, a bit of me is in there too. During the course of his very long war, he meets a host of characters, some real, others from my imagination, and I hope you find them authentic, compelling, believable and moving.

To make Jox's story flow, before and during the Dieppe raid and then on to North Africa, I have on occasion been a little creative with timelines. I do hope my readers will be forgiving of that. In no particular order, here are some historical points that I touch upon during the telling of this story.

Wing Commanders Halden and Walker who 'attended' Squadron Leader David Pritchard's funeral were actually in joint charge of No. 111 Squadron when it was part of the Quick Reaction Alert force in 1990, transitioning from Phantom FG.1 jets to the new Panavia Tornado F3. They were based at RAF Leuchars, near St Andrews in Fife, a town I know very well from my youth. It is less than thirty miles southwest of RAF Montrose, which played such a significant part in Jox McNabb's and the Treble Ones' history during World War Two.

Pritch's particular friend at the Royal Star & Garter Home for Disabled Ex-Servicemen and Women on Richmond Hill, Captain Nancy Wake AC GM, codenamed the 'White Mouse' by the Gestapo was also very real. She lived out her days at the home until her death on the 7th of August 2011, at the age of ninety-eight. She is reported to have been a fearsome, outspoken and steely character right to the end.

The Treble Ones did lose their Commanding Officer George 'Wee Brotch' Brotchie in a tragic flying accident on the 14th of March 1942, involving several other squadron pilots. His successor, Peter Reginald Whalley Wickham, was born in Nairobi, Kenya just before the end of the First World War. His was variously described as an ambitious man, sometimes dark and brooding, somewhat ill at ease, prone to being erratic and issuing eccentric orders, but also to occasionally drinking to excess. These behaviours might well be explained today as symptoms of Post-Traumatic Stress Disorder, as there is no doubt that Wickham had a tough war. Even before joining the Treble Ones, he'd been shot down three times serving on the Mediterranean front, involving long treks in the blistering desert. He also participated in the RAF's traumatising and disastrous reaction to the Kriegsmarine's 'Channel Dash' when the battleships *Scharnhorst* and *Gneisenau*, the heavy cruiser *Prinz Eugen* and their escorts escaped Brest sailing for the safety of German ports.

As mentioned, many of the characters that Jox meets are real. I have done my best to represent them as accurately as I can. Naming just a few, in this story they include the glamourous playboy Tony 'Bolshie' Bartley, the experienced Czech fighter pilot Frantisek Vancl, the youthful American Chesley 'Pete' Peterson and the urbane Brian Kingcome. Similarly, Moira and Sheila Macneal, the 'Belles of Biggin Hill' are real too. In actual fact, Peter Wickham would go on to marry Sheila in 1944; sadly, the marriage only lasted a year. Brian Kingcome, on the other hand, married Sheila's daughter, Lesley, in 1957, to the surprise of many of his fellow aces given their age difference. They remained happily married until his death in 1994. Perhaps expectedly, urbane and handsome Tony 'Bolshie' Bartley would go on to marry the glamourous film star Deborah Kerr in 1945 but would live through some tough war before then. We will catch up with him again.

The White Hart public house in Brasted, Kent still exists but in a much-renovated form. It was a legendary Battle of Britain pub with a famous blackboard covered with the names of many legendary aces including Sailor Malan, Al Deere, Colin Gray, Bob Stanford Tuck, Johnny Kent and Johnnie Johnson. I have taken the liberty of adding a few of my own. The White Hart's landlady, Kath Preston, is reported to have said, 'If the Luftwaffe had ever chosen to drop a bomb on the pub on any Saturday night during the summer of 1940, the outcome of the Battle of Britain might well have been very different!'

Several photographs exist of various reunions held at the pub after the war between legendary aces, including one of Bob Stanford Tuck showing the board to Adolf Galland, *General der Jagdflieger* of JG 26 fighter group, the infamous 'Abbeville Boys'. It may well have been taken during the filming of the iconic film, *The Battle of Britain*, during which both men served as technical advisors.

The headquarters for Combined Operations HQ at 1a Richmond Terrace on Victoria Embankment is as described. It was here that Operation Rutter targeting Dieppe was conceived and planned, and ultimately would be executed as Operation Jubilee, with Canadian ground troops still playing the primary role. During air operations over the French seaside town, Pete Wickham did lead four sorties, an exploit for which he was ultimately awarded a Bar to his DFC.

The National Spinal Injuries Centre at Stoke Mandeville Hospital where Michael Longstaffe was sent for treatment and rehabilitation after his injury was founded by German expatriate spinal injuries specialist Professor Sir Ludwig Guttmann. It actually opened on 1st February 1944, a bit later than I have suggested, but did become the UK's first specialist unit for treating spinal injuries. Sport was seen as an important therapeutic method for injured military personnel to build up their compensatory physical strength, but importantly also their self-respect. This programme was the precursor to what would become the Paralympic Games and 'Poppa' Guttman is considered to be the father of the Paralympic movement.

Prince George, the Duke of Kent, King George VI's younger brother was one of fifteen fatalities in a military air-crash in Scotland on 25th August 1942; only the Sunderland's rear gunner, Andrew Jack, survived. The king and queen were already at Balmoral when news of the crash reached them.

The events of 26th September 1942 were as described, when a fighter escort force of three Spitfire squadrons, No. 133 (Eagle) Squadron, No. 401 (RCAF) Squadron from Kenley, and No. 64 Squadron from Hornchurch, were tasked with escorting USAAF B-17s on a daylight bombing raid on Morlaix airfield, in Brittany, France. What came to be known as the Morlaix disaster virtually wiped out No. 133 Squadron, after they encountered heavy cloud cover and a 100mph tailwind which blew the formation off course. Eleven out of twelve of the Eagle Squadron's brand-new Mk IX Spitfires were lost, with the twelfth crash-landing on the south coast of England, having run out of fuel after turning back earlier with an engine problem. This is the aircraft I have attributed to Jox.

In the North African desert, Hauptmann Hans-Joachim Marseille was known as 'The Star of Africa', the top-scoring ace of this theatre of operations with a reputed 151 aerial victories. He is said to have bested seventeen Allied opponents in a single day, 1st September 1942, and seven in just eleven minutes fourteen days later. Marseille was reportedly killed in a flying accident when he was forced to abandon his fighter due to engine failure. Baling out from his smoke-filled cockpit, his chest is believed to have struck the vertical stabiliser of his aircraft, the blow either killing him outright or else incapacitating him so he was unable to deploy his parachute. He was buried in a grave with the single-word epitaph: *Undefeated*, but perhaps readers of Jox's story know something more about that.

The Second Battle of El Alamein was the culmination of the torrid campaign in the Western Desert, finally eliminating the Axis threat to Egypt, the Suez Canal and the oil fields of the Middle East and Iran. It was so profound a victory that in November 1942, Prime Minister Winston Churchill authorised the ringing of church bells across the United Kingdom, something unheard of for the last two years of bloody war. Churchill was famously recorded as saying, 'Now this is not the end. It is not even the beginning of the end. But it is, perhaps, the end of the beginning.' Later, he would reflect, 'Before Alamein we never had a victory. After Alamein we never had a defeat.'

The Allies had gone from the tragedy of Dieppe to the triumph of El Alamein. Jox has survived to fight another day, but there's still a lot of war left, and he will no doubt see more than his fair share of it, for better or for worse. He sets off on new adventures in *The Vulcan and the Straits*, where we see him and his beloved Treble Ones participate in the invasion of North Africa and then move onto Sicily, the first of the enemy's home territories.

I hope you've enjoyed reading my third instalment of Jox McNabb's war. Reviews and ratings are always important to authors, so if you've enjoyed *The Maple and the Blue*, I hope you would be willing to post a review on **Amazon** or **Goodreads**. Readers can also connect with me on **Twitter (@P33ddy)** or **via my website**. Also, for anyone who may be interested, I have loaded some images on **Instagram (jox mcnabb)** that inspired me to write the story of Jox's remarkable war.

Per Ardua Ad Astra.

Best regards,

Patrick Larsimont

patricklarsimont.com

Sapere Books is an exciting new publisher of brilliant fiction and popular history.

To find out more about our latest releases and our monthly bargain books visit our website:
saperebooks.com